Give feedback on the book at:
lorhainneeckhart@hotmail.com

Twitter: @LEckhart
Facebook: AuthorLorhainneEckhart

Printed in the U.S.A

LOST AND FOUND

WALK THE RIGHT ROAD

BOOK 2

LORHAINNE ECKHART

'A 2013 Readers Favorite Award Winner'

—Touching story of how love wins in the end. Loved the suspense, went through a lot of emotions in this book, I was an emotional wreck. I got into the story line so deep I couldn't put the book down.

DEBI

—"LOST AND FOUND is one of the best romantic suspense books I have read this year! I will forewarn you, you will need a box of tissues and a punching bag while reading this dynamic tale."

ROMANCE JUNKIES

—"A heart-rending tragedy of grand magnitude, faced by one innocent family against whom it seemed the whole world had rallied. It will pull you into the thick of the action, and not let you go until the final page."

LEE ASHFORD FOR READERS' FAVORITE

—"It starts with a heartrending description of every parents' worst nightmare, and keeps the suspense and drama level high all the way through."

LOVES READING

—*"If you want to read a book that will make you think about the depth of relationships, this is the book. What would you do for the person you love?"*

KITKAT

—*"Growing up I have always been a fan of books that contain messages and stories that can relate to real life situations. This definitely covered both of those and more. There were parts where I wanted to curl up with a box of tissues and keep reading and then others I was too caught up in the book I just couldn't put it down."*

REVIEWER NICOLE

—*"This is one of the best books that I've read in a long time. It was a page turner, a thriller from page one until the very end."*

WALK THE RIGHT ROAD

"There was not a human emotion I did not go through while reading this book. I will forewarn you, you will need a box of tissues and a punching bag while reading this dynamic tale."

ROMANCE JUNKIES

"I loved every single book in this collection. I loved Eckhart's writing style and her ability to develop a cohesive story line around strong characters is refreshing! I am looking forward to reading more of her books."

REVIEWER CHERYL

"Lorhainne Eckhart is a master storyteller and this collection is a steal. It includes all of the books in Walk the Right Road Series."

JRA

The Choice: One Woman. Two Men. And A choice that could kill her.

Lost and Found: 'A 2013 Reader's Favorite Award Winner': A hit and run. A deserted country road. A parents worst nightmare.

Merkaba, A Novella: Everyone thought he was dead and that's exactly how he needs it to stay. Until one day he stumbles across a mysterious dark haired beauty. Only, there is nothing average or ordinary about this secretive woman, and she knows exactly what and who he is.

Bounty: *Some pasts are best forgotten.* Most cops have a past. A past, they can speak of. A past, they can share, but not for Diane.

Blown Away: The Final Chapter: Imagine that the man who's been the source of all your misery shows up on your doorstep. Imagine this man wants your forgiveness for every bad thing he's done to you and your friends. Would you believe him?

He Came Back: One woman's haunting journey when her husband returns home and everything she thought she knew about their life together has suddenly changed.

A hit and run
A deserted country road.
A parents worst nightmare.

On a warm fall morning in Gardiner, Washington, Richard and Maggie celebrate happy couple Sam and Marcie's return. What happens next changes their lives forever. A hit and run driver on a deserted country road, and Richard and Maggie suffer a parents worst nightmare.

Now a year later Maggie McCafferty struggles to put her life back together...hiding her pain with outrageous behavior and her own secret she's unwilling to share. Until her friends step in and her strong willed soon to be ex-husband sets out to bring Maggie home— the only way he knows. Just as Maggie begins to trust again, Dan McKenzie calls after disappearing for over a year. But now he's back. And instead of Richard coming clean with the truth of their involvement, Richard digs himself in deeper, with mounting debts, a partner who refuses to buy him out—secrets shared only with Dan. Until one night a mysterious 911 caller witnesses a fight and Richard shooting Dan. But when the police arrive at the deserted construction site the only evidence of a crime is a pool of blood, and a surveillance video.

Under mounting pressure from the police Richard's arrested and interrogated—except fiery secretive Richard is adamant he was home all night. In this bizarre twist of fate, Sam, Marcie and Diane work against the clock and wonder how well they really know their evasive friend. With Maggie by his side, Richard stands by his innocence. Trouble is, if Richard didn't do it, where is Dan? And who is the mysterious 911 caller?

Each choice we make causes a ripple effect in our lives. When things happen to us, it is the reaction we choose that creates the difference between the sorrows of our past and the joy in our future.

—CHELLE THOMPSON, EDITOR OF
INSPIRATION LINE

PROLOGUE

"Hey, you two look great." Richard McCafferty propped his axe against the woodshed and strode away from the large stack of chopped firewood, wiping beads of sweat from his forehead with the back of his heavy work glove.

Marcie shivered underneath her purple down vest, her fingers linked with those of Sam, the love of her life. She leaned against him, into him, and couldn't erase the smile she'd swear was now etched permanently into her face. She couldn't explain the joyful sense of lightness that filled every part of her. Maybe that was why she needed to touch Sam and be with him, near him.

Richard gripped Sam's hand the way good friends do. He winked at Marcie as if he could read her every secret. She dropped her eyes; after all, when had she ever been successful at keeping something from Richard?

"Your cast is gone, Marcie; you're all tanned and healed. Those beaches down in Mexico look like they agreed with you. So when did you guys get back?"

Sam wrapped his arm around Marcie's shoulders and rested his chin on the crown of her head. "Last night. Rented a car in Seattle and drove around the peninsula. Thought we'd stop in, check on you and Maggie before heading over to Marcie's granny's place."

The screen door squeaked.

"Hey, you two! Didn't know you were back." Maggie dashed down the stairs, yanking on a thick green sweater. She skidded around the pile of leaves, nearly tripping over a garden rake before she hugged Marcie and then kissed Sam on the cheek. "You've got quite the glow happening there, Marcie." Maggie shoved in between the couple. "The way you two are glued together, you'd think you hadn't seen each other in, like, forever."

Sam smiled broadly and leaned against the black SUV he'd rented. His blue eyes, brighter than before he had left for Mexico, watching Marcie in a way that let her know how much he loved her. His look would have told her even if he hadn't said the words a few hours ago and every day since she'd told him the big news. Maggie was watching Marcie, and her toffee-colored eyes lit up as if she'd guessed her secret.

"Should we tell them, Sam?" Marcie said. She was teasing, and Richard stared first at Sam and then her.

"Okay, guys, what gives?" he asked.

Sam blurted out, "Marcie's pregnant."

Richard grinned and high-fived Sam. "Congrats, guys."

Maggie squealed and hugged Marcie, patting her still flat stomach. "So, how far along?" Maggie was almost bouncing with excitement as she tucked her shoulder-length, dark curly hair behind her ears. Her pale cheeks glowed a natural rosy pink from the chill in the late fall air.

"Not far, just a few weeks." Marcie could swear her joy shimmered in the air between her friends.

"Mom!" Ryley called from the door.

"Oops. Come on in, guys," Maggie said, hurrying to the steps. Ryley burst out the door, his sneakers undone, wearing only a dark long-sleeved T-shirt hanging outside jeans with patched-up knees. "Put your coat on, young man," Maggie said with a laugh, "and go finish raking those leaves before I kill myself. And this time, put the rake away when you're done."

"Hey, Ryley. No school today?" Sam bent down and retrieved the rake while Ryley pulled on his red jacket.

"Nah, it's a conference day, and Mom won't let me play on the computer. She's making me work," Ryley said, skulking down the steps. Marcie couldn't hear what Sam said when Ryley took the rake, but he laughed so hard he wiped what she assumed were tears from his eyes.

"Sam looks pretty happy, Marcie," said Richard. "He wants kids. See how he is with Ryley?"

Marcie looked up. Richard was so tall, and his dark hair was a little on the shaggy side. "Yes, he does." Marcie swallowed. Her head felt a little thick this morning, but she'd heard that was normal.

"How are you feeling? Maggie was sick the first few months with Ryley. With Lily, she was just tired all the time," Richard said. The lines around his eyes made him appear older, wiser and damn handsome. He knew darn well he still had every woman taking a second look when he entered a room.

"Tired. Feeling like I'm coming down with something. But it's good."

He shook his head; a grim line stretched taut across his lips. "You know, Marcie, I'm glad you and Sam had time to get away. Does Sam regret leaving the DEA?"

"He hasn't said. But being with him in Mexico, just us and nothing hanging over our heads … I've got to tell you, Richard, I didn't want to come back. It was magical, as if I was inserted into my fairytale ending where everything was perfect and nothing could touch us. I worried coming back on the plane if maybe there would be some repercussions when setting foot back here. I can't say this to Sam, but I can't shake this feeling there's something brewing in the wind with Dan and his crew. You know … payback."

Richard pulled off his work gloves and stuffed them into his back pocket. He stared up at the house for a moment before turning and looking at her in a meaningful way. She was sure he knew more than he was telling. "Marcie, this game, this business … even the people who aren't involved but know about what Dan, Lance and that whole underworld do, they don't talk."

"Richard, are we in danger?" Marcie shivered as a light breeze swirled her hair. She swept her fingers through the strands, distracted for a minute by how silky, wavy, and long her hair had recently become.

"You need to know something—and I haven't told Maggie this. I found out one of the disabled kids Sandra Carter had at her home the night you and Maggie delivered all the marijuana … well, he died last week. Whoever his full-time aide was had a way of communicating with the boy, and she said the kid was scared of Sandra. Before he died, he told her … Sandra hurt him."

"Are you sure? I thought those kids couldn't talk. Why does Sandra still have a contract to care for them?"

Richard just shrugged his shoulders. "I don't know everything, just what Diane told me. But they've suspended Sandra's contract pending an internal review."

"Well, how did the kid die, and how's Sandra responsible?"

"I don't know that, either, except they're presuming a mix-up in his meds. Both kids were on so many. Look, Marcie, the reason I'm telling you this is that Sandra's out for blood. She's made drunken threats to some friends against Maggie, and you too. Both of you broke the cardinal rule and ratted them out, her and Dan, and that's her quote. But you understand that world. You knew this was going to happen— we all did when we set them up. This underworld has a way of looking after things in its own way. We all need to be careful. Lance Silver is one dangerous and powerful bastard, and Sandra and her family are unscrupulous. Remember, Dan won't cross Sandra. Not once during that whole mess did he ever point the finger at her."

Marcie glanced over just as Sam dumped a handful of leaves over Ryley's head and then tossed him on the pile. "Why would he protect her, Richard?"

"You still don't get him. He and Sandra go way back. He's cagey, and he knows who he can screw over and who he can't. She encouraged his behavior, and he controls her to a point. If he crosses her, he knows he'll be dead. Have no doubt he'll protect Sandra, because that will protect him, too.

"He casts illusions, even with me, keeping me off guard. He was scared I'd kill him for involving Maggie. What goes through his mind after he screws people is … what he can say to keep from getting the shit pounded out of him. Lance Silver, Sandra, that whole underworld Dan slithered his way into, it's … let's just say that Dan doesn't play by their rules. He's not part of them; he's an outsider who slithered in. Sandra's a part of that world because she grew up in it. I still can't figure out Lance and Dan's connection, or why's Dan's still walking around. I know he's screwed one too many of them."

Marcie frowned, looking back at him, and tried to read past the sudden hardness encasing Richard. "How do you know this, Richard?"

He didn't look at her; instead, he watched his son. "Marcie, you're a big girl. If you're going to live out here, you need to be aware of what's going on around you. There's some ugly stuff, and the people involved lead outwardly picture-perfect lives. You and my wife got dragged into something.…" Richard yanked his gloves from his back pocket and swatted the leather across his jean-clad thigh. He lowered his voice and said, "What you *see* and what is real are two different things."

Marcie looked away, toward the bare towering willow that would shade the front lawn nicely all summer. "Have you spoken with Dan?"

"Nope. I'm just saying you need to constantly watch your back. Retribution doesn't always come in ways we expect."

"Richard, Sam said he took care of everything so we'd be safe.…"

His jaw stiffened, and he scratched his head as he watched Sam and Ryley turn a big pile of leaves into a spread-out mess as Ryley dove in over and over. "There comes a time when you need to look after home first. Sam did that for you. He did what he needed to. For me, that's Maggie and the kids. But make no mistake, whatever Sam and I do, anything can still come out of left field. We all need to be aware and not just trust that we're safe, because that's when mistakes happen … and someone gets hurt." He continued to watch Ryley.

Marcie hadn't noticed before, but tinges of gray now threaded through the strands of hair by his ear. It was thicker than before. Richard turned and smiled at her, but the light didn't reach those steely blue eyes. "Come on, O Pregnant One. Let's go on in and have some coffee."

"Tea for me, please," Marcie said.

This time, Richard laughed, and it wasn't so forced.

MARCIE LEANED AGAINST SAM IN THE WARM, CLUTTERED KITCHEN. Richard shoved a log into the wood stove while Maggie picked up the spoon Lily had tossed under the table—for the second time since they'd walked in. Five-year-old Lily, severely autistic, swayed in her booster seat at the table, lining up Cheerios instead of eating.

"Maggie, leave her. I'll take over," Richard offered.

Maggie handed Richard a clean spoon. "Good luck. She's driving me nuts this morning; she's already dumped her first bowl on the floor."

Richard gently squeezed Maggie's shoulder and then moved to the messy table, kissing the top of Lily's curly dark bed hair. "Come on, my girl. What's this about giving your mama a hard time?"

Marcie would swear Lily smiled in amusement. She was definitely a daddy's girl. Marcie needed to speak with Maggie about adding some natural remedies to aid in Lily's therapy. Focused on diet and vitamins, the holistic approach was controversial, with no track record or data, but it was an approach Marcie was convinced would help Lily be more responsive. Maybe before they left today, she'd broach the subject.

Richard spoon-fed Lily, who leaned in for her daddy and took each bite.

"You know, Marcie," Maggie said, "I remember the first few months with Ryley, just the smell of coffee would send me racing to the nearest bathroom."

Marcie clutched her warm mug of green tea. She could feel how relaxed Sam was behind her. He hadn't worried, like she had, about coming home. Marcie had asked him twice what he meant by "taking care of things" so they would be protected from Lance and Dan, but he wouldn't elaborate. And, try as she might, she couldn't figure out what he'd done.

"Thanks for the coffee, Maggie." Sam's southern charm whispered like honey when he spoke. Marcie would never tire of listening to him talk, because he meant what he said, and he spoke from his heart—always. She knew by the way Maggie smiled at him that her friend, too, loved listening to his smooth southern accent.

"All done, my girl." Richard helped Lily down from her chair. She still wore her fuzzy pink pajamas and fluffy elephant slippers, and she bolted straight for the screen door and pushed it open. Richard grabbed her before she went any farther.

She screamed "Sa, sa!" and reached for the door.

"Let's put your coat on. It's cold outside, silly girl," Richard said. He had just zipped up her purple down jacket when she dashed out the door that he held open. Ryley was raking leaves as Lily dashed past him. "Ryley! Watch your sister. Take her over to the swing and keep an eye on her. I'm going to grab a coffee, and I'll be right out."

"Aw, Dad, why do *I* have to watch her again? You wanted me to rake the *leaves*. Why do I have to do both?" he whined, like any young boy tired of being responsible for his sister.

"Go … now," Richard said. His voice was direct while he pointed toward Lily, now running in circles on the grass. Ryley dropped the rake and stomped after her.

"Richard, did you put her shoes on, or is she still in her slippers?" Maggie asked.

Richard leaned past her and poured himself a coffee. "She's fine, Maggie. Stop fussing so much about what she's wearing. At least she's got something on her feet."

Bile suddenly, burned the back of Marcie's throat and rose up like a sharp wind. She grabbed Sam's arm and nearly dropped her tea as she was flooded by a wave of dizziness. A harsh chill rushed through her. "Oh no," she mumbled.

"Marcie, are you okay, babe?" Sam grabbed her mug and set it on the counter.

Marcie pulled away from Sam just as she heard Ryley's irritated yell: "Lily, come back. Lily, stop!" Richard and Maggie pushed past Marcie and bolted out the door, and Sam and Marcie followed.

"Marcie, what's going on?" Sam asked.

"Something's wrong, Sam."

"You're scaring me. Is something wrong with the baby?"

"No. I don't *know* … something …" She stared off toward the road as Sam's hands fell away from her shoulders.

Time slowed. Sam started running and raced past Maggie, yelling something that stretched out long and loud, waving frantically at Lily, who stood in the middle of the desolate gravel road. Ryley stood only a few feet from her. Marcie blinked through the blur as a black car sped around the bend and hit Lily. A sleek sports car with dark tinted windows, it skidded on the gravel but didn't stop or even slow, speeding away.

Marcie's head ached, and she struggled to breathe, feeling as if her chest had been ripped open by a sorrow she couldn't put into words. Screaming pierced her dreamlike state. A sharp wind rustled the trees as Sam, Richard, and Maggie huddled around Lily, and Marcie moved down the steps, across the grass, and reached Ryley, who hovered frozen behind Sam.

"Marcie, call 911. Now, Marcie, now!" Sam shouted as he crouched over Lily.

Marcie grabbed Ryley's arm and ran. Her ankle, not quite healed from her recent break, throbbed. Ryley said nothing as she all but dragged him back to the house. She grabbed the kitchen phone and dialed. Ryley leaned against the wall, his face white, his big eyes nothing but empty pools. She knew he couldn't grasp what had just happened.

"Oh, God. Please let her be all right," she begged as she closed her eyes.

"Nine one one. What's your emergency?"

"Lily's been hit by a car," Marcie said. "She's five years old. She's lying on the road."

"Is she still breathing?"

"I—I don't know. Her parents are with her. She's covered in blood."

"We've got paramedics and police on their way. I need you to stay on the line with me."

Marcie gripped the cordless phone and glanced back at Ryley, who didn't move. "Ryley, I need you to stay here."

He didn't move—he didn't even look at her. She dashed out the door and could see Maggie on her knees, sobbing. Sam appeared to be giving Lily CPR. Richard was beside him. Marcie relayed everything to the 911 operator until she heard sirens wailing in the distance. She hung up when she saw the first red flashing lights.

She hurried back to the road, limping as she held the disconnected phone. Emergency vehicles arrived—an ambulance, the sheriff, and volunteers from the Gardiner and Sequim fire departments blocked the narrow gravel road. Two paramedics raced over and dropped down beside Sam and Richard as emergency personnel crowded around, leaning in. Lily was still alive, but barely. Marcie pressed her hand against her chest. "Hurry," she whispered.

"We need a medevac here now!" one of the men shouted.

"They're en route. They have to land at the fire hall. Let's move it!" another replied.

Richard pushed past Maggie, ignoring her as if she were of no importance. "Is she going to make it?" he cried desperately.

Sam glanced at the female paramedic, who shook her head. Sam stepped in front of Richard as Lily was loaded on the stretcher.

"I'm going with her!" Maggie screamed.

"There's no room!" someone yelled as three paramedics climbed into the ambulance beside Lily. She appeared so tiny, hooked up to an IV, with splints and a neck collar, strapped to the gurney. A state trooper grabbed Maggie by the waist and held her back when she tried to jump in the ambulance. Richard stalked over to the sheriff and state troopers, who leaned against their cars at the side of the road, lights still flashing.

"What the hell are you still doing here? Get your asses out there and find that murdering coward who hit my little girl!" he yelled.

Sam stepped in and took Maggie from the trooper. She collapsed in his arms, clutching his shirt. "Marcie," Sam yelled, "come here!"

So many people hurried around as the ambulance sped away, lights flashing and siren blaring, just as an SUV raced in and slammed its brakes, sending dust flying. Whoever was driving, Marcie couldn't see, but an angry deputy stormed toward the person who jumped out.

"Sam, Richard!" Diane called, flashing her badge. She pushed past the deputy. Marcie took a step—but then stopped, as Richard abruptly punched one of the deputies before being tackled by the sheriff and another officer. One pinned his knee in

Richard's back, laying him face down on the car's trunk as the other cuffed him.

Marcie touched her head. She didn't know what to do as Diane and Sam hurried over. Everyone was yelling, but the sheriff didn't care. He shook his head and stuffed Richard in the back of his car.

Marcie watched Maggie standing alone, sobbing. The spot she stared at was coated in blood. One fuzzy slipper lay there—alone. She needed to go to her but was stopped when a hand touched her sleeve.

"Ma'am, you need to sit down. Are you family?" It was one of the local firemen, his kind hazel eyes appearing through a film of her tears.

"Ryley. I left Ryley at the house," Marcie said.

"Who's Ryley?"

Her vision blurred even more when she looked up at him, unable to make out any of his features. Her nose was plugged, and she swiped her hands over her eyes and wiped her nose with a sleeve.

"He's their son, Lily's older brother. He watched this. He saw Lily get hit. Oh, God." She couldn't hear him reply as he led her over to the fire truck and helped her sit on the back bumper.

"We asked him his name, but he won't talk. One of the volunteers found him on the road, over there, watching the ambulance leave."

Marcie nodded. "Please keep him away. How bad is it?" she asked. She knew by the way he grimaced that he didn't want to say. "You … you don't think…"

The volunteer had an honest face. "Miss? You'd best be getting the parents to the hospital. Prepare them for the worst."

"What hospital?"

"She's being airlifted to Seattle."

Marcie didn't know how she did it, but she stood up and hurried to

Maggie, pulling her into her arms as crime scene technicians arrived and taped off the area. "Maggie, we need to go."

Maggie pushed her away and swept her trembling hands through her hair as tears fell. "Where are they taking her? Is she all right? She was still breathing, Marcie."

"Marcie!" Sam approached at a jog. The lines around his eyes had deepened, and his face was pale. Marcie wanted to fall into his arms, but Maggie was there first, her arms around Sam. He stared at Marcie and rubbed Maggie's back. "They're airlifting her from the fire hall to Harborview Trauma. She's still alive, but it's touch and go. Diane arranged for another chopper, waiting for us in Sequim." Sam hurried Maggie along, and Marcie fell in step beside them but stopped after a few strides.

"Ryley. I forgot about Ryley. We can't leave him," she said. "And Richard, where is he?"

As the sheriff pulled away with Richard in the back, Diane jogged over. The sheriff could be a hard-ass and didn't take kindly to his officers being hit—even by a distraught parent.

"Diane, please bring Marcie and Ryley with you," Sam said as he hustled Maggie to his SUV and helped her in. Marcie stood at the side of the road, alone, and watched as Sam drove away while Diane hurried off to find Ryley.

CHAPTER 1

Words no parent should ever hear, "Your daughter didn't make it," played over and over in Maggie's head as a cold drizzle deepened the sorrow in her bones. Gray sky battled for space between the puffy clouds.

Black. Everyone conformed. All were shrouded in this drab dress code, which, of course, only emphasized the emptiness infiltrating every pore of the day. For the moment, Maggie had no tears left; but nothing could wipe away the searing pain churning inside her, knotting her stomach one moment, twisting the muscles in her neck and back—then turning them into blocks of ice the next.

Maggie sighed and tilted her head. The white and gold etched coffin her daughter lay in really was beautiful. Pink roses cascaded over the sides like a shrine. A moment of clarity swooped in and intensified the agony. Lily would have loved pink.

Five. She was only five years old, a baby still. That number was engraved into Maggie's every waking thought. The unseen cruelty of God. The hand of fate. How Maggie hated God at that moment. *What did I do to you?* She'd screamed those words over and over with her fist raised in damning condemnation. She hated everyone. Even the damn minister, who went on and on, preaching his sanctimonious bullshit; but no more than she loathed herself.

"We must trust in God. It's God's will."

Screw you, you self-righteous prick. Her mind was disconnected. Even the strong squeeze on her left arm didn't process right away. She looked down, her heavy head swimming from the tranquilizer the emergency room doctor had prescribed. Who was touching her? Ah, yes, her brother John, the one she rarely saw and had nothing in common with; but here he stood, concern for her carved into his face and his stare. Or maybe it was malevolence. After all, what kind of mother allowed her child to wander out into the road? She looked away, unable to take any more blame. She'd heard enough from Richard.

Every motion she made was reactive, numb, drugged. Her mind felt plugged, each one of her senses grating like a rusty piston, catching and then starting again. Her nerves were all over the map, shaking her thin grip on reality. Did she say something? She couldn't remember. John was blocking her view. She couldn't see Lily and was rocked by a lofty wave, igniting her panic. She couldn't remember how to breathe, so she fought for air. *What was that sound?*

Grief was screaming—but who was making that sound? People crowded around her. She couldn't see Lily, only Richard on the ground, weeping beside the coffin. John put his face in front of her, and his mouth moved like that of a marionette, but no sound came forth. Then, in the blink of an eye, she swayed as the darkness surrounded her. *Did someone turn out the lights?*

CHAPTER 2

One Year Later

Maggie stood in the hallway of Westwood Elementary School behind Mrs. Johnson, the special education teacher. She listened as the woman reprimanded two mothers, Angie and Jean, on their choice of therapy for their special needs children. Maggie scrunched her nose and gazed upward.

Give us a break, she thought. How dare this woman publicly humiliate Maggie's friends, fellow parents? Angie was slim, with curves in all the right places, and could be quite the knockout when she put some effort into it, but she chose to play it down. She tied her long hair back, and threw on a pair of glasses instead of wearing contacts over her big blue eyes. Jean was older, plump, short and always stood as if she had a hunch in her back. Both women remained silent as Mrs. Johnson continued to criticize.

Angie glanced at Maggie, her lips twitched as if struggling to hide her smile. Maggie couldn't help herself. She needed to lighten the moment, so she tossed her head side to side, mimicking the woman's tirade. It was so unlike her to pull these childish pranks, but Mrs. Johnson had pushed Maggie's buttons one too many times.

They stood ten feet from the open door of Ryley's fifth-grade classroom. Jean's brown eyes widened, and her mouth opened, but nothing came out. When Angie's eyes went from amazement to horror, Maggie stopped and slowly turned until she was face to face with Jacob Peterman, the tall, hunky principal. His gray-blue eyes narrowed, and Maggie felt her face burn. How long had he been there, and how much of the entertaining display had he seen? Maggie cleared her throat and swallowed hard. She tried to say something but closed her mouth when no reasonable words came to mind. She was aware of an awkward, old feeling, one she'd last felt in high school, the kind of moment you never wanted to relive again.

"Oops, caught red handed," she said, giggling. *Where in the hell did that come from?*

Even Jacob Peterman couldn't keep a straight face; his stern lips twitched.

Maggie realized that she had changed. Not overnight, but gradually … to the point that everyone around her commented on it. She used to be quiet and reserved, pausing first before speaking careless words. Now she felt as if all she ever said was

"I'm sorry" over and over. She wondered if that was what happened when life dumped all its crap on your plate and said, "Deal, baby." Maybe that was what gave her the courage to grin brightly now. *Well, what's the worst that can happen? I can get banned from the school.* Jacob's eyes appeared to soften as he took in everyone with a steadfast glance, and that was when Maggie realized no one was talking.

Mrs. Johnson filled more space than a lot of women. Tall and wide, her self-righteous expression spurred anger inside Maggie. She silently prayed Jacob had heard Mrs. Johnson's tirade. She blinked as her mind fogged again.

What started this? Ah, yes… The school didn't have the funding needed to support all these kids with neurological disorders. Children could no longer be tagged "learning disabled." Mrs. Johnson's tirade had begun: "If I give to you, I have to take away from another child."

From her talks with him, Maggie knew Jacob believed the public education system needed a serious overhaul. Credible therapy with trained aides who understood each child's individual needs were needed. Instead, they had the present "cookie-cutter" therapy thinking

—one size fits all. But sadly, politics, unions and reporting lines came before the best interest of the child. As the commander and chief of this elementary school, Jacob was over everybody … except Mrs. Johnson. The Special Needs Department reported to the district head office, and there was little Jacob could do about her attitude other than continue to override her decisions.

Maggie wasn't sure what to do as she gazed into his dark eyes. Gray tinged the sides of his dark brown hair, which actually made him sexier. The lines around his eyes and his slightly tanned complexion linked him to his Mediterranean ancestry. He was tall, at six-feet two, and was wearing a short-sleeved baby blue dress shirt with a red silk tie.

Maggie opened her mouth to break the silence. "Ah…" That was it, the sum of any intelligent response she could muster. Maggie glanced at Jean and Angie, standing behind Mrs. Johnson who, with her arms crossed, squinted down at Maggie, her rosy lips a tight thin line. But all Maggie could see was the woman's heavy eyebrows, which appeared to be one thick caterpillar.

"Am I interrupting something?" Jacob's tone was quiet but firm, more a statement than a question. Maggie jumped and again faced Jacob just as he swept his flattened hand past Jean, Angie and her, looking at each of them in turn. He then directed what appeared to be his stern principal gaze at Mrs. Johnson. "I presume

you're ensuring these ladies receive the assistance they need?" One of his dark eyebrows rose, giving a look that demanded an answer.

A telltale pink colored Mrs. Johnson's round cheeks. Her curt nod was awkward as she crossed her arms over her large chest. Tension nipped the cool, sterile air. Maggie's underarms were damp as she waited for panicked outbursts from Jean and Angie. This had been Maggie's idea: "Let's have a meeting, power in numbers. We'll confront her with our issues and the lack of support for the kids." As she stood there, waiting, she imagined their confessions.

Each of their kids needed support at school. Jean's son, Adam, had been diagnosed with Asperger's, ADHD and Mild Intellectual Disability. He fell just above the acceptable limits for the school, so he did not qualify for full child support. Angie's adopted daughter,

Sammy, had Fetal Alcohol Syndrome. Ryley, however, was just a typical boy; unable to grasp auditory teaching in the large class. If Maggie asked him what the teacher said, what he had learned on any day, his response was always the same: "I don't know."

She imagined the cruel accusation forming in Mrs. Johnson's eyes: *Why are you here? You have no right to be here with these parents. Ryley doesn't qualify for services. Lily would have—she was autistic. So, again, why are you wasting my time?*

A desperate fight had been stoked deep inside Maggie. She understood now what was at stake for these parents. Early intervention was key. Why hadn't she seen that with Lily? This obsession with helping others was what kept her sane now. Every day, she fixated on what she could have done differently. If she had done something, would Lily be here in this school today?

Her mind drifted a lot these days, but when she looked back at Jacob, he crossed his arms and turned that stern principal gaze on her. She didn't know how long he'd watched her. Then, as if she were a recalcitrant child, he ordered, not asked, "Maggie, I'll speak with you in my office now."

Maggie glanced at Jean and Angie before following Jacob. When they rounded the corner, he slowed his pace and stepped beside her into his office, closing the door behind them.

"Take a seat." He gestured to one of two chairs in front of his desk.

Maggie's insides withered. She tried to swallow past the golf ball–sized lump wedged in her throat. Her hands trembled, so she clasped them together and wedged them between her knees.

Jacob smiled warmly, kindly, as he rested his forearms on the desk. "Do you want to explain to me what that was all about?"

CHAPTER 3

Her breath fogged on this cold and unusually clear day in early December, but the icy chill barely penetrated the ache that shredded her insides. Maggie squeezed her eyes shut as a single tear fell. *Breathe in and out.* She really tried, but nothing would ease the hurt. With her shoulders pulled inward, she hurried to her rusted blue Topaz. Her eyes hurt, swollen from the tears she thought had long since passed. All that unreconciled agony she'd shoved and locked away had flooded her senses—all because of Jacob's kind words.

Maggie slammed her door. "No, no!" She hit the steering wheel with the palm of her hand to change the hurt to a physical one—a real one she could deal with. Then she fought to battle back the agony. Today was not the day she'd face it.

Jacob was a kind man. His gentle eyes never left hers, and she'd be a fool to miss how her feelings mattered to him. The meeting was swift, and even Maggie was aware Jacob could see through the charade and her new motto—"Just do it."

In the end, she had listened quietly as he reminded her to watch her Ps and Qs, especially when dealing with district personnel. Then he had done it, given her the reminder she hadn't wanted. "So how are you really doing, Maggie?"

A jagged knife had ripped open her tender wound. With Jacob, there was no pity and no avoidance. She knew he genuinely cared. On the first day of this school year for Ryley, and in the days following, Jacob had simply touched her shoulder, saying, "If you need anything, I'm just a phone call away." He was a passionate school principal, her friend, and a children's advocate—and he'd been there the day they buried Lily.

Holding on to the wheel of the car, she slumped as the overwhelming grief tore with viscous claws through her chest. She struggled and gasped for breath while hammering those walls back up, pushing the pain back where it needed to go. How, in one single genuine moment, had he managed to knock those barriers down?

"How could he?" she asked. *I am stronger than this,* she chanted to herself as she quickly shoved her dark sunglasses on, hiding her tear-stained eyes. "Suck it up, come on, come on, come on. You can do it." Her determined pep talk helped her refocus her thoughts. Maybe, one day soon, she'd relive the day her heart broke just a little bit less.

CHAPTER 4

The old Topaz spurted and shuttered as Maggie drove home. The rusted muffler, holding on by a wire, vibrated and shook the floor inside the car. Her ears were buzzing from the loud rumbling, which she supposed announced her arrival from blocks away. "Sorry!" she called, wincing as she waved to her elderly neighbors, who frowned as she passed before pulling in to her driveway. The necessary repairs were fast approaching critical, but on Maggie's budget, not even an oil change would happen right now.

She blinked as she stood outside her average box-style house and stared at the front door. She turned and looked back at the faded blue car, realizing she couldn't remember the route she'd taken to drive home. How many times over this past year had she done this?

A familiar scratch and whine yanked Maggie from her funk. She fumbled in her bag for keys while Daisy barked and scratched at the door. Maggie's best friend and companion, who shared her deepest pain without judgment, unconditionally, was always there. She was a black and white dog with golden highlights—a sheepdog, lab, retriever, and a few other unmentionable mixes thrown in. The all-American mutt. Not much of a watchdog, but what she lacked, she made up for in spades with comfort, trust and loyalty. Ten months ago,

Maggie had driven to the SPCA. At the time, she didn't know why she'd stopped. Then she saw Daisy. She Was lying quiet, rejected and unresponsive in that tiny cage. Maggie knew she couldn't leave without her. Even the girl at the counter was shocked when Maggie specifically asked for the old dog. The lady asked her three times if she was sure she wanted a geriatric dog—one slated to be put down at the end of the week. Maggie was convinced the dog had been sent to her. From the first day of her depression, when she couldn't get out of bed, Daisy had stayed with her.

Maggie opened the door. "You need to go outside?" she asked.

Daisy barked and pranced in front of Maggie then raced to the back door, which opened into a small, fenced yard. Daisy was quick in her old age, with the way she darted out into the cold and then rushed back in.

"Is it too cold for you, sweetheart?" she asked. The dog yipped in agreement, and she patted her head and wandered into the open kitchen to brew a hot coffee. The message light flashed on her cordless phone.

She didn't plan on returning anyone's call, but she replayed the messages.

"Just checking to see how you're doing, Maggie. Call me." Her mom, at times, was irritating with how she kept calling and, when she was in town, dropping by unannounced. But that had been in the beginning, after Lily died. Thankfully, over the last few months, this behavior was decreasing.

The second message was from Richard, her soon-to-be ex. "I'm picking up Ryley from school today and keeping him through the weekend," he said. Maggie shut her eyes and pressed her fingers to her forehead when a heavy fog of confusion muddled her thoughts. Finally, her memory clicked: Today was Tuesday. She blinked again. Or had she lost another week? She shuffled through the stack of papers, bills, overdue notices, looking for her calendar.

"No, no, no. I don't think so, Richard," she muttered. Fury pushed the blood through her veins while she looked at the date on the coffee-stained Day-Timer. She punched in the numbers to his cell phone, knowing he'd be somewhere on the forty-acre property and not in the beautiful two-story cedar home he had built after Ryley was born.

"This is Richard. Leave one."

"Voicemail, you jerk? You're screening your calls. You knew I'd call back." Maggie didn't think as she threw the phone down on the counter. She grabbed her purse and keys and tore out the front door, slamming it so hard the front window shook. She gunned the engine and backed out of her narrow, paved driveway. A horn blasted behind her, but she didn't stop to look. Somehow, she made the twenty-minute drive out of town to the Gardiner acreage in just under ten minutes.

Traces of snow scattered the sides of the long driveway, and a big pile had been dumped close to the barn. She jammed on her brakes and, for a second, doubt cut through her anger. Before thinking it to death, she hit the gas and drove past the double-paddock barn, parking outside the West Coast cedar home—her home, their home, the home she had once loved.

Maggie stared at the brown grass where her babies had played, the half-acre she'd dug and seeded alongside Richard. Old growth trees surrounded the perimeter, with a crop of Douglas fir hiding a small tree house—the one Richard had built for Ryley Across the front yard, past the whispering willow, was the road that had killed her Lily.

Her cheeks were wet from the tears that wouldn't leave. She roughly wiped her chapped cheeks and shut her eyes as she leaned back, wishing she could fall into sleep and oblivion. The only place she could forget for a while. But she didn't. Instead, Maggie crawled out of her car as if she'd aged twenty years. And there stood Richard.

The gray blue of his all-seeing eyes now held an edge of hardness. His dark hair had lightened to a sandy gray, and he wore it longer; the unruly waves whipping around in the wind. Maggie couldn't put her finger on it, but there was something different about him, something solid, like a survivor, that wasn't there before. He was tall and broad shouldered, and even wearing his old, torn barn jacket, she knew he could still turn every lady's head.

How long had it been since she was here? With effort, she

remembered: She hadn't been back since the day she loaded Ryley up with their suitcases and drove away.

Watching Richard stare at her in his frigid, unforgiving way, all she could remember was how much she missed the strength of his arms when he enfolded her in them. There was a time when he could have protected her from anything. But not that. Blame had been passed around, the agony—grief. At thirty-seven, the weather-etched lines around his eyes had deepened. His solid jaw now held a bitter edge, and the tiny scar down his left cheek had been her parting gift.

She was rocked by all of it, the regrets. Why was she here? She closed her eyes to blank out his image, but it was too late. She felt the link, the connection to him, and no matter how she tried, she couldn't sever it. However, she'd made her choice—or maybe it had been made for her?

"Richard, I…"

He said nothing. He left her standing there as he climbed the steps and went inside. The door clattered when it smacked the wood frame, dragging Maggie out of her hypnotic stupor and shocking the fury back into her. She marched after him filled with passion or hate, she didn't know which, that drove her until she stood in the center of the open kitchen, facing the brickwork of the stovetop island in the center of this once inviting room.

"Maggie, what do you want? I left you a message." Richard stood at the kitchen sink. He kept his back to her and, from what she could tell, stared out the window at the old-growth forest dotting the perimeter of their property.

"It's Tuesday. You can't pick up Ryley and keep him through the weekend. We have an arrangement. You get him on the weekends, not before. He has school and a routine, and it's important—"

"I don't give a crap about your perception of routine. The boy belongs here. He's my son, and it's time he came home for good."

He cut her off in a way that was unbending, and she knew it was meant to overpower her, but she wouldn't cave, not this time, because she felt something vital being yanked away. "You can't do that! You agreed—we both agreed that Ryley would be better off with me in town. I'm his mother. You can't take him away from me."

Richard pushed away from the sink and stalked toward her. As he moved closer, his face softened. Panic expanded in her chest. There was something different about this man she'd once loved so deeply. It was as if he had peace, or was it resolve? Whatever it was changed her scattered focus—her determination. Her belly ached because she realized he'd healed and left her behind. How could he? His strong hands surrounded her shoulders. Tears clouded her clear vision when she looked up and tried to speak. But nothing would come.

"Oh, Maggie, you have to get past it." His words were soft, but she sensed they were merely his shield.

"I can't. I still see her running around. If I could have just gotten there sooner… Why did you let her go out? I should have gone with her."

He didn't push her away this time. He pulled her against him, surrounding her with his arms—strong arms. She breathed in the piney spice of the trees. He'd been chopping wood. She pressed her cheek against his chest; her head didn't top his shoulders. She gazed up at him, and her fingers traced over each weather-worn line on his face. Her breath mixed with the warmth of his, and his head came down hard. The kiss was brutal, needy, as he backed her to the wall. He unzipped her coat, pulled open her shirt, scattering the buttons on the floor and lifted her bra, skimming his rough hands over both breasts.

Maggie unzipped his jeans, aroused and ready. Her own jeans loosened, and Richard pushed them down, but the pant legs stuck— her shoes, dammit. She struggled to kick them off, freeing one leg from her jeans. Richard lifted her and stepped between her legs, thrusting hard. She closed her eyes and wrapped her legs around his waist, caught up in the frenzy of need, life, and desperation to feel something, anything, again. He filled her over and over, her mouth on his, fast and hurried. There were no passionate or frilly words, just a physical need followed by Richard's muffled curse, and he was done.

Reality was a bitch. Her jeans dangled from one leg, and there he was, still buried inside her. Both of them panted as if they'd just run a marathon, and the dark intruder of truth smashed through the illusion.

His eyes closed, and he rested his forehead against hers before gradually pulling out and setting her down.

Richard moved back and zipped up his pants. Awkwardness rushed in. Her jeans were inside out on one leg, her underwear bunched and twisted. It took her a minute, like a clumsy first-timer, to right her jeans and pull down her bra. The blue buttons on her cotton shirt were spread on the cream-colored floor along with her jacket. Maggie pulled her shirt together and glanced away, an unbearable sense of strangeness lingering between them. She shut her eyes and took a breath. What was the big deal? He'd been her husband for eleven years.

"Um … sorry about the blouse." He gestured to the lost buttons. "Some of your clothes are still upstairs."

Avoiding his eyes, she held the tattered cloth closed over her breasts and hurried through the living room. The open wood beams gleamed as she looked up at the pitch of the high ceiling. The post and beam theme continued up the L-shape staircase. The solid planks had once seemed to vibrate with their love and passion. Nine years ago, side by side, Richard had built her this beautiful house. Eleven months and seven days of sweat, sore muscles, love, tears, joy, short tempers and fierce lovemaking had created this house.

She froze at the top of the stairs. Clasping her hands in front of herself, she fought to hold back the ache that pitched from some place deep within. Her ribs, stomach, throat ached. Whoever said time healed all wounds had lied. The solid wood door was a banishment. She turned the knob and pressed open the door, stepping in.

The twin bed with a pink Cinderella bedspread nearly brought her to her knees, as if someone had rammed a fist into her stomach. The dolls and stuffed animals were assembled neatly on her pillow. The six-drawer dresser with hand-painted rosebuds on the drawer fronts hadn't moved.

When Lily was six months old, Maggie had painted each pink flower as a token of her love. She picked up the silver framed picture of Lily in her arms moments after she was born, tracing the outline of her baby's head, her eyes wide open and filled with a spark of light. But even then, she had gazed into shadows, as if not entirely seeing.

Maggie shut her eyes, pressed the picture frame against her chest, and tried to resurrect some remnant of her precious girl, some piece of her now lost from that horrible, fateful day.

"Oh, God, how could you take her?" Her voice trembled. She ached just being here in this room, except something was different. It was as if Lily was here with her now.

Maggie didn't know how long she lay on Lily's bed, her back pressed into the soft plush mattress, remembering all the nights she had lain cuddled next to her tiny daughter, holding her through one of many night terrors.

How many nights after the accident had she lain here, never leaving this room, while the rift between her and Richard grew wider than the Great Divide? With the blame they had heaped on each other, Richard had spent weeks drunk, disappearing during the day. At night, he'd come and go until the memories and pain of this place became too much to bear.

The furnished house in Gardiner had appeared for rent in the local paper, and Maggie believed it was meant to be. She had phoned, met with the property management company, and signed the lease all in one day. Then she had packed up her and Ryley's belonging in two suitcases and pulled away in their SUV while Richard was gone. She hadn't left a note. Ryley, at nine years old, had screamed and cried as far as the main road before sulking in the backseat.

"It's going to be better, I promise," Maggie had told him. She believed that by leaving, she'd finally be able to breathe without the burning ache ripping her apart.

The eruption from Richard when he tracked her down through the school, and the ensuing fight, had been ugly. She had clawed his cheek with her nails. He seized her SUV and canceled her credit cards. She had obtained a lawyer and filed for legal separation, and he had gotten his own lawyer, too. Hers, as she looked back, had been good. He hadn't been in it for the money, and he had warned her from the beginning to play fair. She and Richard had both been grieving from a terrible loss, but his lawyer had been dirty, only in it for the money.

Her local lawyer, Peter Sullivan, older and balding, had counseled her briefly on their first meeting. If she lashed out in anger and tried to lie or cheat Richard, she'd have to find another lawyer. Maybe some lawyers played that game, but he believed in fair play. That had gotten her attention, but not her SUV back. It was pointed out that the house, the vehicles, and the credit cards were, after all, in Richard's name. The joint bank account had ten dollars left in it. Smart man, he had stashed his money somewhere else.

She had a savings account with a few thousand in it—one her mother had set up for her years before. She had bought her older junkyard Topaz for a few hundred dollars, and it ran and got her from point A to point B. Richard had agreed to child support and minimal spousal, and although not generous, it had been enough for her to buy food and pay rent. Ryley would go back to his dad's on weekends, and weekdays he would live in Gardiner with her. The agreement had been created by lawyers and signed in a cold, sterile legal office on a bleak day filled with torment, blame, and a fine line between anger and love. How had it turned so ugly?

She wiped her face with her ripped shirt and left Lily's room, only this time, she didn't shut the door. She hurried to the master bedroom next to Lily's, the one she'd shared with Richard. Nothing had changed. The same light green floral duvet covered the large bed, flanked by the same oak night tables. The wide dresser was still flush against the wall, where she'd shoved it five years ago. She was drawn to the large bare windows, no curtains, just the way she'd once preferred. Now, her rented house came complete with blinds and heavy drapes to shut out the world.

She glimpsed her red, tear-stained eyes in the dresser's large mirror, her limp, tangled, dark hair, and her now ruined blouse— thanks to Richard. She rested her forehead against the mirror and squeezed her eyelids shut. "We're as good as divorced. What were you thinking, Maggie?" She pushed away, gazed at the disheveled stranger in the mirror, and was shaken from her confusion by the soft murmur of voices downstairs. She dropped her torn shirt on the floor, opened the closet door, and reached for a bright red sweatshirt stacked on the shelf. Richard was right; she'd left many clothes behind.

Maggie pulled the warm sweatshirt over her head and dashed down the stairs into the dim living room. How late was it? She stumbled and grabbed the railing when she heard Ryley laugh. Pots banged and clattered, utensils rustling as she watched from the shadows. Father and son were illuminated in the kitchen. Richard hovered beside Ryley. They were chatting, laughing, and Ryley was chopping what? This wasn't her quiet, shy boy. He was relaxed and joking with his dad. Ryley never joked with her. He hadn't laughed since … well, since she couldn't rightly remember.

Ryley didn't help in the kitchen with her; Maggie did all the cooking for him. They had a routine: eat, homework, watch TV and then bed. Whatever this was with Richard, there was no place for her.

"Hey, are you making dinner?" She tried to sound happy. They both looked up. Richard blinked, and she wondered for a moment if he'd forgotten she was here. Unease filled the room. "Umm, I should go," she said, pointing to the back door. Her hand shook. Where had she put her coat?

"Maggie." His voice was soft and low when he touched her shoulder and rubbed his hand down her arm. "Stay for dinner. Please."

She looked up. Awkwardness lingered. He dropped his hand and stepped back. A fork clattered on the counter, and Maggie blinked. "Richard, I should go." She dropped her gaze to the floor. She couldn't look at him. She stepped around Richard and attempted a smile for Ryley—something that felt more like it had been painted on.

"Are you staying, Mom? We're making tacos." He held a wooden spoon, hovering over the fry pan, and looked almost hopeful for a second. Then something flashed in his eyes that had him stepping back. That carefree easiness he'd had moments ago with his dad, before she walked in, was gone. He appeared nervous and uneasy.

Was it just her? A knot tightened in her stomach, and she felt the dark basement swooping up to drag her back to the pits of despair. She couldn't bear to lose another child. She reached out and hugged Ryley. He was stiff and pulled away. She looked down before she spilled any more tears. She forced a fixed smile again for Ryley. "No, not tonight. I've got to go. But you have fun with your dad." Maggie turned and froze. Richard held her coat and helped her into it. This time, his hand didn't linger.

"Ryley, I'm going to walk your mom to her car. Turn off the burner till I get back."

"Okay, Dad," he said. She heard a relaxed, carefree tone ease back into his voice, as if everything was all right. Of course, she wondered if this was because she was leaving.

Richard's hand touched the small of her back when she walked out into the dark night. The porch light glowed softly, lighting her way as Richard walked her out. He didn't say a word as he opened her door and rested his hand on the roof of the rusty car. "Maggie, about earlier—"

She couldn't bear to hear regrets. "Please, Richard, I just need to go. Please let me go." She climbed in and pulled the door closed. Starting the car, she watched him step back before he turned, hesitating a second, and walked back into the house. Maggie drove away and glanced in the rearview mirror just as the porch light went out, feeling a dreadful loss. Except this time, the loss was different, and she didn't know why.

CHAPTER 5

A pop similar to a gunshot vibrated underneath her car just as
Maggie pulled in to her driveway. She pressed the brakes and
stopped as the passenger front end tilted down. Maggie clutched her
keys and pushed open her door but could do little more than glance at
the dilapidated Topaz in the shadows and see how it didn't seem to sit
quite right. Daisy barked and scratched from inside the house. "Just a
minute, girl. I'm coming. Don't panic." She unlocked the door and was
welcomed by a licking, tail-wagging Daisy, who pranced against her
legs.

She stumbled and pushed Daisy with her knee as she flicked on the
outside light. Daisy continued to step in front of her, her tail still
wagging, her muted brown eyes attempting to pour guilt into
Maggie's heart. "Sorry, girl. I know I left you too long." With both
hands, she rubbed Daisy until she purred like a cat. "Now let me get
the flashlight and check out this mess."

This time, Daisy dogged Maggie's heels when she went outside.
She wondered if maybe she'd driven over a big inflatable toy. That
would explain the pop, but she couldn't remember if Ryley had any.

She shone the flashlight on the front of the car and then

underneath. "Well, crap." The front end on the passenger side leaned heavily, so far it nearly touched the ground.

"Everything all right, Maggie?" June, her eighty-eight-year-old neighbor, walked her poof-ball of a mutt up the street. She was a kind gray-haired woman who knew all the dogs and their owners on this secluded cul-de-sac. She was always stopping to chat and offer home-baked dog cookies to Daisy. She loved animals and was known as the "cookie lady" to all the dogs' owners on the street. Three times a day, she set out for a walk with a Ziploc bag full of fresh-baked dog cookies. Daisy had an innate sense of knowing exactly when June was coming. She'd bark and jump up and down to be let out. Then she'd race out the front door, skidding to a halt in front of June to wait for her well-earned treat. On more than one occasion, June had remarked, "Don't you feed this dog, hon?" But Maggie thought to herself, *I'd do the same thing if someone took the time to bake fresh treats for me.*

Only now, in the dimness of this cold December night, June was not her warm, friendly self. She could tell by the way she approached and absently reached a shaky hand into her pouch for Daisy's cookie. Daisy leaped around excitedly, gobbling down the cookie, and then sat and waited for more.

"You doing okay, June?" Maggie found it helped to focus on someone else. June shook her head and glanced up the street. Maggie shut off the flashlight and touched June's shoulder. "June, what's going on?"

"Oh, Chester's under the house again."

Maggie remembered hearing June call out for the cat last night. "How long's he been down there?" She dropped her hand when the older woman's shoulder appeared to stoop. The lines on her creased face appeared to have deepened.

"Two nights. I call him, but he won't come. I'm getting so worried. He hasn't eaten, and it's getting pretty cold at night."

She bit inside her cheek so she couldn't say anything about the cat and his spoiled, childlike behavior. Although she had nothing against cats, Maggie preferred dogs. They were unselfish by nature and rarely caused the same worry. Chester weighed at least twenty pounds from lazy days and overeating and, in her mind, could stand to go a few days without a meal. Maggie sighed. June's health wasn't great, and another night of worry … well, she hated to think what it would do to her.

"I'll get the cat out," she said with a sarcastic edge to her voice, but June's face brightened, so she apparently hadn't pick up on it.

"Are you sure, dear? I mean, he's all the way under the house."

She nodded. She didn't trust her voice or what might slip out. Side by side, with both dogs following, she and June walked to the old woman's home, two houses down. This time, June's stride was light and peppy as if that little bit of hope had been all she needed.

"Oh, thank you *so* much. You know, I called the fire department, but they said they don't come out for cats under houses. They said not to worry, it'll come out when it's hungry. That's terribly rude, don't you think, Maggie, dear?"

Maggie jammed her teeth together to hold back what she really thought. Truth be told, it was along the same lines as the fire department, except now she had to get the cat. "You're right. That's not very nice of them."

CHAPTER 6

The foundation of June's bungalow was made of old fir posts and beams. Maggie's stomach flip-flopped, and her hand trembled when she accepted the flashlight June handed her. She dropped to her knees and slid away the lattice board covering the opening to the crawlspace. She peeked into the pitch black but saw nothing. Her heart pounded, and for a minute, she found it hard to breathe, her imagination conjuring a preview of what else might be under the house. "Shit, don't go there," Maggie muttered, tapping the flashlight to her forehead. "Get those thoughts out of your head. Fucking cat." For a woman who never swore, she was surprised at how easy it slipped out.

She shut her eyes for a second and then pulled off her coat and tossed it aside. She flicked on the flashlight and tried to hold the beam steady, but her trembling hand wouldn't cooperate. Maggie dropped down on her stomach and scooted under the house. Crawling on her knees was impossible in this enclosed space, so she pushed with her foot and slid across the gravel and dirt while holding the narrow light in front of her. She paused a few feet in and scanned the area around her, but no cat, just shadows and darkness. "Here, kitty, kitty … Chester, where are you?"

She knew she sounded angry, but how did one manage to sound happy or caring at a time like this? She never could pretend. The damn cat, if he was smart, would never answer, not to her. Then she heard a meow. Of course the mewing was way over at the far end of the crawl space. Maggie waved the flashlight and changed directions, pushing hard until the light danced over the orange calico huddled in the corner. Then she slowed and approached cautiously. The last thing she needed was for the cat to bolt deeper into the shadows. One dual goal —get the cat, and get the hell out.

"Chester, baby, I'm coming." This time she really did sound happy. She swapped hands with the flashlight, and the cat rose as if to bolt. "Oh, no you don't." Maggie reached out and grabbed a handful of hair at the cat's neck, and it went ballistic. She dropped the flashlight as Chester screeched and clawed. Maggie locked both her arms around the cat, holding it against her chest. Then, somehow, she grabbed hold of the flashlight and moved, keeping her face tilted away from the wild, razor-sharp claws as Chester struck out again and again. At least it was easier going back, as the outside light illuminated the opening where June crouched.

"Is everything all right, dear?"

"Fine!" she yelled while holding on to the squirming demonic beast, who was clawing and biting, trying to break free. Maggie tried to hold his paws and spit out the cat's fur swirling in clumps into her face, lips, and mouth. The cat continued to hiss, spit, and claw.

Maggie slid out from under the house and dropped the flashlight. She got up on her knees, holding the cat away from her as it sliced at her arms.

"Oh no, Chester, it's all right." June reached for her cat and cuddled him to her chest, transforming the furry monster into a sweet, angelic kitty, purring in the old woman's arms. "Oh, Chester, you're bleeding." June's voice had an edge of worry.

Maggie stood up and held her arms out in front of her. Sleeves rolled up, she glanced down at the tiny slits where blood oozed in several spots up her arm and then over to the orange tabby, with spots of blood dotting the orange, furry strands.

"Oh, don't worry, June. That's my blood." She glared at the cat, who turned his head toward her. She stumbled, and she'd swear the cat smiled and winked. She had nothing against cats but knew with an absolute certainty she'd never in this lifetime own one.

"Oh, thank goodness. My, but he really did claw you good." June's concern for her animals was touching. She had a small dog, a cat, and a budgie in the house.

Maggie picked up her coat and carried it. She shivered as the tiny cuts began to burn. "June, if that cat goes under the house again, I'll shoot it," she said.

June giggled as Maggie hobbled away. "Oh, stop teasing! Thank you so much for getting my baby out."

June's humble appreciation took some of the edge from Maggie's anger until she glanced back and met the cocky gleam in the cat's eyes. *You go under that house again, you'll stay there till hell freezes over.* This time, she winked at the cat and then forced a smile on her face for June. "You're welcome," she said, cutting across the front grass with a forgotten Daisy nudging her leg.

"Maggie, do you want me to take a look at those cuts for you?" June called out.

She didn't stop or look back. "No thanks, June. It's just a few scrapes; nothing to worry about. I'll take care of them myself."

"Call me if you need anything, dear."

She gave a passing wave over her shoulder as she hurried home. Never breaking stride, she snarled at her broken car and popped open her front door, and the gray weather stripping peeled off the doorframe and smacked her on the side of the head just as she crossed over the threshold. "Great, one more thing to fix in this damn rental. Come on Daisy."

She flicked on the lights, locked the door behind her, and froze in front of the entry room mirror. She had several bloody nicks around her neckline and jaw and up both arms. Until she saw them, the sting hadn't been too bad. Now, looking at them, she found they burned. She dropped her coat, stripped off her clothes, and hurried down the hall to the shower.

Steam filled the room, and she squealed each time the warm spray made a direct hit on one of the many wounds, and there were lots. But she figured it was the best way to clean them out.

After she toweled off, she applied antibiotic ointment on all the cuts. "Holy shit, that hurts. Ow … ow … ow!" Hopping around, she panted until the sting receded. Then she held her arms stiffly as she took a good hard look at her wounded reflection. "Damn fucking cat. Why do I need to save the day?" But she already knew the answer. With any kindness paid to her by someone, she felt the need to pay it back ten times, and then some. Otherwise, she wouldn't be able to sleep. And, as of late, no matter how hard she tried, she couldn't get past it.

CHAPTER 7

Richard called seven times the next morning before Maggie went out, and she let every one of the calls go directly to voicemail. She couldn't talk to him, not after yesterday, because yesterday, they'd met at his lawyer's office to discuss settlement prior to the divorce. She had been so worked up before the meeting because of their illicit tryst against the kitchen wall—afraid Richard would bring it up and somehow block the divorce.

She chewed on a piece of nail hanging from her thumb. "Think, think," she said, but try as she might, she couldn't make sense of what had happened in that boardroom as she sat beside her lawyer, across from Richard. The only thing she was clear about was how much she hated that god-awful painting of some ancient battle and resulting carnage that appeared to take up half the wall in that male-dominated boardroom. She remembered not one word of what had been discussed, decided and agreed upon.

Today her head was clear, thank goodness. Maybe this was her wake-up call. While Diane, a state trooper and her friend, hadn't questioned her yet on what had come out of yesterday's meeting, Maggie knew that before this day was over, Diane would know everything.

A branch snapped over to her left. Dressed in full camo gear with a loaded paintball gun in hand, Maggie peered over the log she crouched behind. She stared into the thick brush but couldn't see anything. Then something rustled the underbrush about a hundred yards in front of her. Her hands were damp as she gripped the loaded gun. Her heart pounded in her chest, and the adrenaline roared long and loud in her ears.

Diane had told her when she picked her up this morning that this was exactly what she needed. It would be therapy and so much fun, but crawling around in the dirt and hiding behind a rotted-out log as something tickled her back was not her idea of fun. "Oh, this is just great," she muttered. Branches snapped, and it sounded right in front of her. She peeked over the top of the log just as two large guys approached, all decked out in faded green camo gear. She suppressed the urge to giggle and propped her loaded gun on the log, waiting for them to come closer. Then she pulled the trigger and nailed both of them, *boom, boom,* with bright orange paint dead center in their chests.

"Yeah, yeah, got you! Now you're dead." Maggie held her gun high over her head and jumped up. Then—*what the hell...?* Both the big guys battered her with paintballs. Maggie dropped her gun and covered her head with her arms to ward off the stinging welts as they continued to fire, and she ran.

MAGGIE LIMPED AND YANKED A TWIG FROM HER HAIR AS SHE FOLLOWED Diane, a short, compact woman with a boyish brown cop cut, to her brand new Toyota SUV.

"Jesus, girl, you don't mess around with those SWAT guys like that," Diane said. "They really take it personally."

Maggie said nothing, remembering how Diane had forewarned her that morning about the SWAT guys they were playing war with today. The extra-tough types—the ones you sent into a problem scenario no one else wanted to handle. For some reason, they had taken offense to Maggie hiding under the log, waiting—their quote to Diane—to "ambush them." The SWAT guys had said it was nothing personal when they smiled and sauntered away a few moments ago. *Assholes*, Maggie wanted to yell at them. She stifled the urge when Diane yanked her from the small clubhouse of Sequim's paintball club.

Maggie snorted in disgust and massaged her battered shins while Diane drove out of the parking lot.

"Maggie, how many times have I told you? You don't mess around with guys like that. They operate on their own agenda. They don't believe the same rules apply to them. Remember our little stint? We didn't follow the rules. Lord, when I think back on what you and Marcie did, gathering that marijuana for Dan, you're lucky you didn't end up in jail."

Maggie was aware, but she couldn't honestly remember all the details of how she had helped Marcie get Dan's marijuana. After his threats, it had been the only way to protect her husband and Sam from being framed for some unspeakable crime. She was forgetting a lot of things lately.

Then she remembered the SWAT guys talking this morning about the incident at Waco and the fact that it would never happen to them. Diane translated their meaning when Maggie questioned her as they left the clubhouse after gearing up. Many cops believed that the same rules civilized societies deemed to live and abide by, didn't apply to them. And, even worse, a few of them honestly believed they were entitled to make up their own rules.

"Oh, okay" had been all Maggie could say.

"Are you all right? You know you still haven't told me what happened yesterday."

"I did something stupid," Maggie said, looking straight ahead through the unusually clean windshield.

"Wait, don't say anything yet." Diane pressed the brake and pulled a U-turn on the fairly quiet highway, driving across two lanes and into the parking lot of the Roadside Pub. "I'm pretty sure I'm going to need a glass of wine to hear this."

Maggie said nothing but chewed on that same piece of nail on her thumb as Diane pulled into the empty gravel lot and parked.

CHAPTER 8

"I can't believe you did that." Diane rested her forearms on the small corner table beside the warm fire blazing in the dining room section of the cozy pub. It was mid-afternoon on Saturday, so the dinner crowd hadn't arrived yet. Except for the two guys watching the sports channel above the bar, they were the only ones in the place. "You accidentally took a sleeping pill before going to his lawyer's office?"

"Ah, yeah, that would pretty much sum it up." Maggie couldn't remember Diane's deep brown eyes ever looking more shocked.

"Did you snore? Whoa, wait. What are you doing taking sleeping pills to begin with?"

This was the part Maggie dreaded. None of her friends were aware she'd started taking pills for anxiety during the day and pills to sleep at night. Maybe that was why Richard kept calling. He must have suspected something. "I didn't want to tell you this. I meant to take Ativan for my anxiety, but I mixed up the pills."

"What! Why are you taking anxiety meds, too? Pills! What the hell, Maggie? You know better. After what we've seen out there with drug users and addictions—weren't you paying attention? You know as well as I do that prescription drugs are as addictive as illegal narcotics, and they're just as destructive. Do you really want this lecture?" Diane leaned closer, glancing over her shoulder when the waitress set the table behind them.

Maggie glanced down at her short fingernails, the ones she'd begun chewing down, something she hadn't done since she was an awkward teenager. Diane was staring at her when she looked up. Her lips had paled into a thin line as if ready to launch into a lecture—something scathing that'd leave her poor ears ringing. Maggie held up the flat of her hand and shook her head. "Don't, Diane."

"Sorry. I'm sure the last thing you need right now is someone else coming down on you. But I need to know all the pills you're taking and how long you've been taking them."

"Since I left Richard, and it's just the sleeping pills and Ativan."

"Does Richard know?" Diane lowered her voice so the lingering waitress wouldn't hear.

"No. You're the first."

"Okay, what about Ryley? I mean, has he seen you popping pills?"

"I only take them when I need them. Not that often, so stop worrying. You're making me sound like some irresponsible mother. Ryley's fine. He's with Richard right now, anyway." Maggie picked up her water glass and sipped.

"All right. So tell me what happened with the lawyers." Diane appeared to relax and lifted her glass.

"My lawyer warned me about keeping my cool and playing fair. Well, he got his wish. I didn't say a word. In fact, I had a hard time keeping my eyes open, I was so relaxed. I don't remember what was talked about or what was agreed upon, but I do remember my lawyer nudged me a couple times. And the way Richard watched me..."

"What?" Diane raised both hands in the air.

"I don't know; but I know he suspects something." Her heart ached, and she squeezed a fistful of her brown sweatshirt. "He's going to try and keep Ryley."

"Did he say that?"

"No."

"Well, what *did* he say to you?"

"Nothing. I didn't give him a chance. I left right after the meeting, grabbed a cab. He keeps calling, but I haven't called him back."

This time, Diane's face softened, and her mud-brown gaze reached across the table with a seriousness that only appeared when she was in cop mode. "Maggie, I love you, and I don't want to hurt you, but you need help. You're not being fair to Richard. Call him back. Don't play games. You and I both know he doesn't deserve this silent treatment. No one does."

When Maggie tried to interrupt and defend herself, Diane waved her hand gently in front of Maggie's face before reaching across the table and gripping her wrist to stop her from talking. "No, please let me finish. I think you need to hear this. Remember, I'm your friend, but I'm Richard's, too. I'm the one standing in the background, watching both sides with clarity. You and Richard both suffered a horrible loss no parent should have to endure. But, Maggie, you need to pull it together for Ryley. You seem to be forgetting about him from the little bit I've seen recently. Richard can see how much Ryley needs you guys, and he's pulled himself together. So, right now, maybe Ryley would be better off with Richard. I just mean until you clean yourself up."

Maggie felt the blood drain from her face, and her heart was sliced open as if sharp claws of betrayal were cutting into it. How could Diane turn on her? She slid her chair back, but Diane grabbed her arm again.

"No, sit down, and get that wounded puppy look off your face. As your friend, I'm entitled to set you right. That's what friends are for. We should be able to say anything with love. When you do something stupid and don't see things clearly, good friends are there to help guide you back onto the right path; even if it's a hard kick in the ass.

"You need to call Richard and come clean about the pills. If you don't, I will. Then you need to get some help, counseling. I'll help you find the right person to help you get off those pills and stay off."

"I don't need help. I rarely take them. I'm not addicted," she said. And to prove it, she'd dump them out as soon as she got home.

CHAPTER 9

Richard's brand new one-ton truck was parked in front of Maggie's rental house when Diane pulled into the driveway to drop her off. Richard was hunched under the front end of her car, and he stood up and waved when Diane parked.

"What's he doing here?" Maggie gripped the armrest and squeezed, glancing at Diane only to see a rosy telltale flush on her cheeks. "You called him? When…?"

"When you went to the bathroom. I'm sorry, but I realized you'd put it off and avoid talking to him. So, to make it easier for you, I took charge. I know I eliminated and took away your power, but you need to tell him; and this way I know you're going to talk to him." Diane's face reflected a subtle sternness when her compassionate gaze lingered on Maggie. At this moment, Diane had an inner strength Maggie would have killed to have just a fraction of.

Maggie's hand trembled on the flat handle when she pushed open the door and climbed out. Richard gripped the top of the door, forcing Maggie to skirt around him.

"Hey, Diane. Good to see you."

"You too, Richard. She knows I called you, and she's got something to tell you."

Maggie's face burned when Richard swung his deep gaze like a spotlight down on her. His eyes flared for a moment, just as they used to when he knew she was hiding something. He never blinked or looked away, even after Diane left.

"Okay. Shall we talk here or in the house?" He crossed his arms.

"She shouldn't have called you." Maggie tried to walk past him, but he moved and blocked her escape. "Richard, please."

"After you, Maggie." He didn't touch her but jammed his hands in his pockets as she scooted around him. Her stomach ached, and she felt her chest burn as her heart kicked up a beat. Richard dogged her heels, and she could feel the burning heat of his gaze in her back. Daisy yipped and scratched at the door while Maggie fumbled with her keys. When she popped open the door, the gray weather stripping around the door frame slipped out again and whacked her on the back of the head. "Shit."

Richard pressed the thin rubber strip back in its slot along the doorframe. Daisy whined and demanded all of Maggie's attention, so she ruffled the top of her dog's head and then limped to the back door, letting Daisy into the backyard.

"Did you hurt yourself?"

Her shins, her ankles and her arms ached. She'd rather focus on that—talk about that, than why he was really here. "Diane took me to her cop club for a game of paintball war. Two of the SWAT guys Diane works with took offense to me nailing them, which I did fair and square. Being the bad sports that they are, they had a temper tantrum and unloaded all their paint rounds at close range; thus the limp." Maggie swished her hand at her legs.

"Why didn't you tell me your car broke down? The transaxle snapped, and that old heap of junk is not worth fixing. You could've been hurt or even killed if it broke on the highway."

Had he even listened to her? "What the hell does my car have to do with the SWAT guys?"

He said nothing, but his eyes and his face took on that hard, dark look he had when he got a hold of something and wouldn't let go.

"What are you going to do about it? We're divorced, remember? I'm not your responsibility anymore." Maggie paced in front of him.

"Well, let's talk about that. For one, we're not divorced. We're not even close to being divorced. Get this straight, Maggie: You *are* my responsibility."

She didn't expect that, not from Richard. After Lily was killed, he'd turned his back on her when she needed him most. "It's amazing how you remember that now. You seemed to forget that when Lily—" A lump jammed up her throat, and the never-ending tears glazed her eyes.

"Let's say it all, have it out." Richard jammed his finger in Maggie's face. "I was grieving, too. She was my little girl, and I'm sorry, but you weren't there for me, either. It's a two-way street, baby, and you holed up in her room for days and didn't come out. We both said terrible, cruel things to each other. But Ryley… my boy didn't have either one of us. We lost Lily, and it's tragic, and I'll always grieve for her loss, but life goes on, Maggie. It's been a year, and you need to get past this. Ryley needs his mother and father. Don't you think he deserves that much?"

Well, that was a slap in the face: the same words she'd heard from Diane earlier today, though Diane had been kinder. She shook her head and covered her ears. Deep inside, she felt herself slipping back into that dark hole. Her chest ached, her palms were sweating, and she started to gasp for breath.

Richard gripped her arms and rubbed both hands up and down before resting them on her shoulders. "Maggie, you're shaking."

"I don't want to talk about this right now. Please, Richard, just go."

"No, I'm not leaving yet. Diane said there's something you need to tell me. I'm not leaving until you've told me what it is."

Maggie sighed and peered into his steely blue eyes, wondering if maybe he already knew. "I've been taking sleeping pills. Sometimes. When I have trouble sleeping."

"I see. And?" He said nothing else, and his hands stayed right where they were, as if holding her in place.

"I accidentally took one yesterday before meeting you at your lawyer's office."

"I don't understand how you accidentally take a sleeping pill. Unless you're taking something else, and you mixed up the pills."

Maggie blinked and swallowed the lump that jammed her throat again. Richard's fingers gripped her shoulders, and his eyes widened as if he could read her every thought.

"Maggie? What else are you taking?"

Okay, he really did know. "Ativan for anxiety."

"Oh God, Maggie!" He stepped back and pressed both hands on top of his head. "What are you doing? How often are you taking them?" He was getting louder, more demanding, as he firmed his lips into a fine white line. "Where are they?"

She couldn't speak and stood frozen when he stormed down the hall to the bathroom. It wasn't until she heard him rummaging in the bathroom that she could move.

"Richard! What are you doing?"

He dumped toiletries, bottles, and makeup all over the counter and lined up five prescription bottles. Lifting each up, he read the labels. "Doctor Martin prescribed these?" He glared in a way that, at another time, would have had her taking a step back from the doorway where she stood.

"Richard, I want you to leave. Those are mine. Put them back." Whose voice was that? It was so weak it cracked when she spoke.

But he didn't put them back. He lifted the toilet seat and emptied the first bottle into the toilet. She didn't realize it was her screaming as she grabbed his arm, trying to reach around him to rescue the remaining pill bottles beside the sink.

Richard blocked her. He emptied all the pill bottles into the toilet and flushed, throwing the empty bottles into the trash. She felt every ounce of energy leave her, and she leaned against the doorframe and wept as she slid to the floor. Then he was on the floor, sitting beside her, and he scooped her onto his lap as if she were a child and held her.

She pushed against his shoulder, his arms, but this time he didn't let go. Why hadn't he done this before?

"Shh, I won't let you take these. And the doctor who prescribed these? I swear I'll have his medical license revoked."

Sitting on his lap, she gave in and allowed him to hold her, to rub her back, but none of it eased the knots twisting up her insides. When she jerked upright, she wondered if she'd dozed off. She'd lost track of time. Her heart was pounding in her ribcage, her hands sweaty as if she'd had too much caffeine, only today she'd had none, just a glass of white wine with Diane. She knew the demon had returned. All the signs were there, the familiar anxiety, which soon would give way to panic. He must have sensed what was going on inside of her. After all, he'd know the signs.

"Maggie, you need to tell me: How often were you taking those pills?"

His chin rested atop her head. She could feel his warm breath feathering her hair as he spoke. Could he feel how fast her heart pounded? At one time, he used to know what she was thinking, but things changed, life changed, with all its damn tests. Their foundation was not the solid storybook she once thought, but he was here now. Her breath caught in her throat. If she told him the truth, he'd use it against her to keep Ryley away from her. She pushed his arm down and scrambled to her feet.

"I rarely took them." She wouldn't meet his brutal gaze when he stood.

"Look at yourself. You're already agitated, sweating…" He grasped her chin and tilted it up so she was forced to look at him. "Don't ever forget you can't hide your lying eyes, not from me." He pointed a finger so close to her nose she'd swear he touched her. He narrowed his eyes, and she was sure a flash of lightning passed between them.

She swatted his hand away. "I want you to leave, now."

Richard shook his head and looked away. He held his hands up in what appeared to be surrender, backing up, and then he left.

She heard the door close, his truck start, and his tires squeal as he drove away.

Maggie stood in her dimly lit hallway, alone for what felt like an eternity, trying to steady her racing heart. She slowly crept to the kitchen, but she wasn't hungry. Regret and loneliness were her bitter companion. So were the tears and piles of misery that burdened and weighed her down. Why wouldn't it leave?

She felt a gentle nudge against her thigh. Daisy, so patient, filled with unconditional love, stared lovingly up at her with what appeared to be worry filling her murky brown eyes. Maggie glanced at the open back door. "I'm so sorry, my girl. I forgot about you." She hugged her dog and then followed Daisy out the open door, this time not wanting to see anyone.

CHAPTER 10

"I'm sorry, Maggie. I won't renew this prescription."

If he'd sucker punched her, it would've been kinder. She felt her face heat, and her back broke out in a cold sweat. A lock of hair dangled in her face, and she scooped it back, feeling tangles in her windblown hair. She must have looked a wreck. She'd tossed and turned all night, unable to sleep. At this moment, as she sat stooped in the plastic chair shoved in a corner of the doctor's sterile examination room, she felt old and haggard. It wasn't the pills—it couldn't be. This was Richard's fault and his emotional roller coaster. Why wouldn't he leave her alone?

"I don't understand. You prescribed these for me." She knew her face had to be two shades of red.

"Maggie, I suspect you may be having withdrawals. That's why you're not sleeping. I told you when I prescribed these that they were temporary, to get you through a bad time and help you cope with an unbearable situation."

Dr. Martin's aging round face resembled an inscrutable poker face. Gone were the kind eyes and gentle, caring bedside manner. She realized this was the first time he didn't ask, "So how are you really doing, Maggie?" Leaning against the door with his arms crossed, the short, hefty man darted his eyes across the room. He seemed to look everywhere, just not at her. He pulled out a pen shoved in the pocket of his long white doctor's coat and bent over his desk, scribbling something in her file.

"It was Richard, wasn't it? He called you, didn't he?"

Dr. Martin let out a heavy sigh and clicked his pen, popping it back in his coat pocket before facing her, this time staring at her with a hardness she'd never seen before. "Maggie, look at you. If I'd known you were going to abuse those pills, I never would have prescribed them."

"What?" She gripped the edge of her chair.

He scribbled something on a piece of paper and handed it to her. She ripped it from his hands and stared at the unusually neat handwriting. It was a name, Dr. Sheila Murphy, and a phone number. Maggie blinked and gazed up at him.

"Call her and make an appointment. She's a psychologist, and she can help you." He wasn't looking at her again. "Okay. I think that's all." He gripped the door handle, opened the door, and paused. His cheeks colored a bright pink when he glanced at her, and for a second she was positive she saw something—pity or regret—before he left, closing the door to the examination room behind him.

Maggie opened her mouth, took a deep breath, and stood on shaky legs. She couldn't bear to walk out into the crowded waiting room, past the reception area—past his nurses, because they'd know what he'd said, and she knew they'd think her an awful person. Was there a back door? She wanted to find a way to slink out of here unseen, go home and hide, even though the *doctor* was the liar, not her. He made her feel as if she was someone of no importance. He'd never, not once, told her to be careful with those pills. In fact, he was the one who had pushed them on her. She remembered now, she hadn't wanted to take them. He told her she needed to because her health was more important. She clenched her fists. Damn him to hell. She wanted to make him tell the truth, share the blame.

She swiped at the tears streaming down her cheek, tucked her purse under her arm, and hurried out past the nurse, whose eyes widened before looking away. Maggie scooted out the door of the clinic and reached in her purse for her keys before stopping in the middle of the gravel lot. She blinked and gazed at the half dozen cars. Hers wasn't there.

"What are you doing? You took the bus, remember?" She smacked her forehead with the palm of her hand. Her car was a broken heap in her driveway. She started walking to the bus stop around the corner, and she dug in her purse for the change she needed when her fingers touched the piece of rose quartz she had tucked in the bottom. She pulled it out and clutched the treasured gift. "Why didn't I think of that sooner?" Maggie smiled for the first time in days when she realized who she needed to see.

CHAPTER 11

Maggie spent the last of her spare cash on a cab to catch the two forty-five ferry over to Las Seta. She'd loved this crossing. At one time, she'd loved a lot of things.

There were half a dozen people on the passenger-only ferry as it docked. Sam, a southern gentleman, tall, fit and extremely handsome in his worn blue jeans and jean jacket, and one of the most caring men she'd ever met, was waiting.

Sam grabbed her hand as she climbed over the side of the small boat, and before she could pull back and step away, he pulled her close and hugged her. "Maggie, it's good to see ya."

The southern drawl remained the same thick, musical lilt, filling her with some measure of comfort. He didn't question her, but when he pulled back, he gazed at her with soft blue eyes that reached inside her heart. Maybe he knew why she was really here.

"Marcie's bathing the baby. I will be your chauffeur, milady." He secured his arm around her shoulders and led her up to his black Jeep —the one he had moved to this reclusive island on the barge. Sam's Jeep was most likely the only licensed vehicle on the island.

She wondered how he liked living off the grid on this island with no utilities, no modern conveniences. Love did strange things to people, and she knew Marcie would never live anywhere but her granny's cabin.

They'd come a long way from when Sam first met Marcie; when she was attacked and robbed in the New Orleans airport. Then, while she was recovering from a head injury, Marcie, Sam, Maggie, Richard, and Diane had come together. Unlikely friends, joined, to battle and outwit a cowardly predator and a threat to each of them: Dan McKenzie, Richard's business partner and, at the time, Marcie's lover. He was a man of deception—a man who preyed on the weak and vulnerable. God, how she hated him.

Maggie didn't want to speak; she'd always hated small talk. Maybe that was why Sam was so quiet. They bumped along the rutted dirt road, thick trees surrounding them as they made their way inward to the west side, an isolated part of the island, to Marcie's granny's cabin.

Sam cleared his throat when he pulled down the long dirt driveway. The bushes scraped the side of the Jeep. "You've no idea how surprised Marcie and I were to hear from you. Are you going to stay for a bit?" He parked in front of the cabin.

"No, I need to get back tonight, so I can only stay a few hours. I need to be on the last ferry."

He didn't reply, only nodded before climbing out of the Jeep. Wisps of smoke rose from the chimney. She followed him up the brand new wood steps and inside the quaint log cottage.

Marcie was sitting in an old rocker by the wood stove, humming a lullaby to her five-month-old baby girl. Kyla cooed and giggled as she reached up with tiny fingers to touch her mother's lips. Maggie wiped her feet on the mat and stared at the boots and shoes crammed on the wood shoe rack by the door, trying to steady the unsettled confusion filling her. Sam gently gripped Maggie's upper arms and then skirted around her. Maggie didn't move, but she glanced at the door when the thought to bolt and make her own way back to the ferry appealed to her so strongly it frightened her.

"Maggie, how are you?" Marcie rose from the rocking chair and handed Kyla to Sam. She didn't hesitate as she strode in her long dark skirt to Maggie and hugged her in a way that made her want to weep. "Can you stay for dinner?"

Marcie stepped back, holding both of her hands. Maggie didn't answer. She couldn't, because Marcie was watching her as if she could read her every secret and knew why she was really here.

"You're shaking. What's going on? Come sit." Marcie spoke so kindly. She didn't deserve this welcome, not from Marcie, not after the cruel words she had shouted at Marcie the day of the funeral: *You don't deserve a child after what you brought into our lives.*

Sam stood in the kitchen, as still as a man could be while holding a baby, and stared at her as if he too knew what was really going on.

Maggie wanted to cry, and her face heated with shame. She pulled her hands free from Marcie and shoved them in the pockets of her down coat. When she glanced up, she didn't miss the uneasy look that passed between Sam and Marcie. She fisted her hands to stop the trembling. Her heart was hammering so hard she wondered if they could hear.

"I'll get you some tea. Maggie, come and sit here." Marcie pulled out the kitchen chair and patted the back.

"I'm okay…. I don't need any tea."

"My granny used to say there's nothing better to soothe away your worries than a steamy cup of tea." Marcie filled a teapot from the black kettle on the wood stove. She reached for two mugs on the narrow shelf by the sink and placed them on the kitchen table, pouring the hot tea and placing a mug in front of Maggie before scooting a chair up beside her.

The wood stove heated the kitchen, and love filled this cabin, but it did little to alleviate her overwhelming emptiness. She placed her hands on the table but couldn't bring herself to touch the hot mug.

"It's so good to see you, Maggie. I was just saying to Sam the other day how much I miss you guys. When you called and said you were coming, well … I'm happy to hear from you, but, Maggie…" She stopped.

A few seconds of silence passed before Maggie realized Marcie wasn't talking. She glanced at Marcie, and when she saw her brows furrowed and how her light blue eyes took on a seriousness she'd not seen before, she wondered if they'd ask her to leave.

"We're worried about you." Sam rubbed his daughter's back and stood behind Marcie.

Something squeezed her chest, making it hard to breathe. Her sound reasoning slipped away, and she wanted to scream. They were judging her. She could feel their disdain. She scraped her chair back and stood. "Richard called you, didn't he?" She couldn't keep the bitterness from blurting out.

Marcie started to say something, stopped, and glanced at Sam.

"Maggie, you're in trouble. I don't know what you came looking for, but what you're going to get is help." Sam placed Kyla in Marcie's arms, his hand lingering on her shoulder for just a bit, before stepping around the table toward Maggie. As he moved, the way he watched the mother of his child had Maggie envying Marcie for what she had with Sam. He was a good man. He touched Maggie's arm as if she were a wild horse ready to spook. "Maggie—"

She heard footsteps clambering up the steps. Someone knocked, the door opened, and Richard stepped in. His steel-blue gaze latched on to Maggie, and she knew without a doubt that the shaky tower she'd constructed around her heart had just crumbled.

CHAPTER 12

"You called him. How could you do that to me?"

Marcie flushed and rested a sleeping Kyla against her shoulder. "Maggie, sit back down. You need some help. Look at you, you're shaking. Your forehead's covered with beads of sweat. I bet right now your muscles ache. You haven't eaten anything, have you? You're nauseous, right? Your eyes…" Marcie eased back her chair and stood up beside Sam.

Maggie clutched at her chest through her bulky coat and stepped back until she bumped into the small-framed archway that led into the front room. She needed to get out of here, but Richard blocked the only exit. The way they were watching her was freaking her out, so she shut her eyes. Her ears were buzzing.

"Maggie," Richard called out to her.

She opened her eyes, but her vision blurred from tears she hadn't even known she'd shed. She staggered when the room swayed, and her heart thumped harder against her ribs.

"Maggie, you're not getting any more of those damn pills or anything else. You were taking more than what you told me. Every day. Weren't you?" Richard sounded so angry.

She covered her face, unable to speak past the dryness in her throat.

She couldn't fight him anymore. "Please don't take Ryley away from me," she begged, and she let her arms fall to her side. She didn't have the energy to fight. Her skin felt so irritated. She rubbed her arm as the nausea and sweating worsened. She shoved her hands in her coat pockets, hoping she had an Ativan stashed; even though she'd searched every pocket and purse twice already. She hoped to find a sleeping pill, too. She needed one to take her out of this world to a dreamless void of nonexistence. To erase the pain she still refused to face.

Richard stepped in front of her, blocking Sam and Marcie, and pulled her into his arms, just like yesterday, but this time, they just stood together while he rubbed her back, and then her arms, in slow, even circles, up and down. This time when she leaned into him, something cracked the shaky layer around her heart as a whimper escaped, and she crammed her fist in her mouth to stifle her sob.

She clutched his shirt. "Richard, I hurt…. I'm so tired. I can't stop shaking. I can't fight you."

"Shh, baby, I'll get you through this."

"Damn you, why are you doing this to me? Please just give me something to make this hurt stop!" Unable to keep up the charade, Maggie sobbed and held on to Richard, and, for the first time in a very long time, she realized she wouldn't be alone.

CHAPTER 13

The late morning sun streamed through the cathedral window on this unusually warm winter day. Maggie sat cross-legged on the cushioned window seat in the sunroom Richard had built as an addition onto their house. Maggie sighed as she stared out at the acres of thick forest in Olympic National Park and at Mount Olympus on the horizon.

Maggie couldn't remember ever having been so tired. She shut her eyes as she leaned against the stack of fluffy pillows. After bringing her home, after a rough first night at Sam and Marcie's, it had been a week of night sweats, insomnia, vomiting, and cramping muscles—and Richard had never left her side. She'd begged them, each one of them, for something to ease her ache, but each had been unbending as they got her through that hellish first night. Sam boiled her water to drink and explained the details of how she was dependent physically and psychologically on these drugs. He told her over and over that she needed to understand what her body was physically going through. Her brain receptors had become less sensitive to the drugs, and soon she had needed more and more for the same effect. Her quality of sleep had been reduced, and the next day she'd experience drowsiness and cognitive slowing, like a hangover, which was even worse than sleep deprivation. Marcie rubbed her back and reminded her that she'd be okay. She was strong, and she'd get through this. But it was Richard who never left, and sometimes he even yelled. He was adamant, a steel wall of support, cutting through her foggy reasoning until she let go and leaned on him.

The next morning, Sam and Richard returned on the ferry, taking her home to the Gardiner acreage. Richard held her outside on the deck of the passenger ferry as she vomited over the side at least a half dozen times. Ryley had stayed overnight at a friend's, and Sam had gathered a few of Ryley's belongings and hopped on the first ferry back to Las Seta with him. Meanwhile, Diane had picked up Daisy from Maggie's house in town.

Maggie never would have believed she was addicted to a couple of simple medications many people took every day, but the withdrawals the second day—*wow.* She trembled just thinking back, remembering so clearly in her delirium how she had begged Richard to give her something, anything, to stop her insides from burning, aching. Her nausea had her hanging over the toilet and sleeping on the cool tile floor to relieve the pressure in her head, which was so bad she'd swore her head would explode from the unrelenting pounding. Through the shakes that racked her body, Richard had remained firm as he held her and swore to her at least a dozen times, that if he could get away with it, he'd kill the doctor for giving her the pills in the first place. Richard cleaned her up, bathed her, and rubbed her back while she cried and begged. After three days, the worst was behind her, leaving her so empty and sapped she only wanted to sleep.

Now, after a miserable week, Richard had dared to leave her side. Maggie watched him through the window as he paced back and forth in front of the barn, talking on his cell phone. After what they'd survived, it was hard to believe how he'd become her rock—in a way she'd never expected, even after all the horrible, hateful words of blame she had spewed like venom; which shamed her now as she did her damnedest to avoid thinking about and reliving them.

Richard glanced up as he spoke on his cell phone and watched her as if he expected her to leave. She'd given him good reason, after all. Wasn't it the second night she'd snuck out? Barefoot, with no coat, she'd taken his truck keys and had started the engine before he ripped open the driver's door and yanked the keys from the ignition, pulling her from the truck, kicking and screaming as he carried her back in the house. She knew he was tired, and he'd started hiding the keys. He'd installed deadbolts on both doors, the kind she would need a key to open, and he hid those keys too.

But as she leaned back into the plump pillow of the window seat, she dozed and wondered when Richard had changed. There was something solid and older about him; some wisdom and a nurturing side that had never existed before.

When she opened her eyes, Maggie sat straight up. Richard appeared upset and yelled at whoever was on the phone. Then he shoved his cell phone in his pocket and raised a fist in the air. He stomped toward the woodshed and scooped up an armload of wood.

The screen door hinges squeaked, and Richard's heavy footsteps creaked on the oak floor. Maggie listened to him fill the wood box, stuff more wood in the stove, and close it up. Maggie gazed at her fluffy pink slippers just as she felt him appear in the archway. She looked up into those magnetic blue eyes and saw the familiar concern as he watched over her.

"I need to run in to town. I won't be long. Do you think you'll be okay until I get back?" He hesitated as if holding his breath. Either he'd trust her or lock her in.

"I'm good."

"Okay…" He hesitated again. She noticed the dark circles under his eyes, the day-old beard, and his shaggy hair was a little more mussed than usual.

"Richard, is everything okay?" She slid around and started to get up to go to him, but he shook his head.

"Don't get up, Maggie. Stay comfortable."

"Richard, is something going on? I saw you out there on the phone. You look upset, and I know you're tired."

He flicked his fingers through his hair, spiking it up. He let out a heavy sigh and appeared impatient. "Maggie, I've got to go. I'll call Diane and ask her to come over." *Well, I guess he doesn't trust me after all.*

"No, Richard. I don't need Diane to come and babysit me. Please don't call her." This time she did get up and walked straight toward him. She touched his arm, and she could feel him tighten. Maybe he'd had enough of her problems. "Why won't you tell me what's going on? I can feel it. I know I put you, *everyone*, through a lot. Is this about me? Do you want me to leave?"

"Maggie, you're not leaving. Stop reading something into nothing, and stop asking questions. I don't want to get into it now. I've got a lot on my plate," he snapped, closing his eyes for a second as he let out another heavy sigh.

Why is he shutting me out?

"Richard, please." She shook his arm gently. This time his face softened, and the way he watched her let her know love still lived there, but it was tinged by a lifetime of hurt and pain.

He cupped her cheek, caressing her cheekbone with the pad of his thumb. "I won't be long, Maggie. Stay in the house. Will you promise me?"

"I won't leave." She placed her hand over his, the one touching her face. A second later, he pulled away and left. Maggie stayed where she was as she listened to the door close and realized Richard had paused a few seconds before hurrying down the stairs. She let out the breath she hadn't realized she was holding. He didn't lock the door. Trust was a shaky thing to rebuild.

Maggie wandered into the kitchen, leaned against the kitchen sink, looked through the window, and watched as Richard drove his truck a little faster than usual down the long gravel driveway. Where was he going? Was he meeting someone? Would he tell her when he returned? She hoped so.

She shivered and rubbed her hands up and down her arms. Even though she wore a heavy sweatshirt, she had a hard time staying warm. She grabbed her bulky sweater off the hook by the door and pulled it on as she wandered back into her sunny sanctuary, this time curling up in an overstuffed chair and ottoman, shutting her eyes, and waiting for Richard's return.

CHAPTER 14

attle, rattle, clank. Maggie blinked, needing a moment to wake up. She sniffed the spicy aroma of lamb curry. Her favorite. A moment passed before she remembered where she was as she lolled her head back against the overstuffed cushion. She clutched the patchwork quilt now nestled over her. When had she covered herself? How long had she been asleep? Her eyes widened and took in the shadows of the brilliant sunset filling the room.

Maggie's stomach grumbled, and for the first time in a really long time, she was hungry. She tossed back the blanket and crept across the room in her fuzzy pink slippers. She stopped in front of the wall mirror with the beech-wood frame just outside her sunroom. Her eyes looked glassy, and the skin under them was tinted gray, but at least she had some color in her cheeks. Her shoulder-length curly hair was tangled and stuck up at the roots on one side. For the first time in many years, she worried about how she would look to Richard, even though he'd seen her at her worst.

She ran her fingers through her hair, trying to work out the tangles, and stepped into the kitchen, where Richard stirred something in a pot. Steam rose from another. He glanced up, frowning with what appeared to be concern as he studied her. "You're better," he said.

Maggie felt her cheeks warm and nodded. She shoved her hands in the deep pockets of her brown sweater. Uneasy, she pulled her hands out and tucked her hair behind her ears.

Richard smiled in a teasing way. "You look fine, Maggie." Then he glanced away, distracted again.

"Did your meeting go okay?"

"I didn't say I had a meeting." He opened the refrigerator, grabbed a bowl, and then set it on the counter.

"Okay. No, you didn't, but you said you needed to go out, and you left in a hurry. I know you're bothered by something. We were married. I know when something's going on with you."

"We're still married, so get that straight."

"I realize the divorce isn't final…" She stopped, unsure where to go, and then paused, surprised by the intensity that flared to life in his eyes. He abandoned stirring whatever was in the pot and crossed his arms as he stepped toward her.

"You don't even remember the meeting at my lawyer's, do you? Did you think I didn't know you were on something that day?" His voice climbed with each step he took toward her until she could feel the heat of his body. She opened her mouth to say something, but he didn't let her respond. Instead, he spoke right over her. "You think I'm going to let you go? No divorce, ever!"

She was stunned by his passion, and his caveman "I'm the boss, you'll do what I say" attitude raised her hackles. However, she was still mad at herself for the screw-up with the pills that had turned the entire day into one big blur. She let out a heavy sigh and wiped her palms down the sides of her face. "What did you do?"

"Let's just say all the cards are exposed on the table, and I advised the lawyers, yours and mine, of our rekindled relationship." He was leaning into her, and her jaw slackened as she sputtered, trying to respond with something intelligent.

"We didn't rekindle anything. You fucked me against a wall. It was sex … just sex." Although, and she knew it, the laws of the state were clear in divorce proceedings—no personal relations for a year before divorce could be filed. What a bastard! He had used it. "How could you?"

"Don't look at me like that. I told you the divorce isn't going to happen." He relaxed a bit as he rested his hands on his slim hips, a package that looked darn good in the dark jeans he always wore.

"That's underhanded even for you, Richard."

"Knock it off and drop this nonsense. You're back here now where you belong, so put it behind you. What does it matter now, anyway?"

This was incredible. She blinked at his arrogance. It was a side he didn't show often but one she knew existed. She stomped upstairs, muttering "Arrogant asshole" under her breath. Her hair and disheveled appearance were forgotten as she flung open the closet door in their bedroom, where they had lain together every night since she returned.

She grabbed her overnight bag from the closet floor and tossed it on the neatly made bed. She pulled open the drawers where Richard had put away her clothes, and she yanked them out, stuffing what she could in the small bag.

She froze when she realized what he'd done. How could she forget Richard was a master at deflection? She nearly laughed. After all, she was no longer pursuing his mysterious meeting. So he did have something to hide. She knew it. There had been a meeting. The question was with whom and where? And what had it been about?

Richard was a man of mystery, one of the qualities that had drawn her to him, but facts were facts. He no longer had the right to tell her what to do. She zipped up the black bag and hefted it over her shoulder. "Who the hell does he think he is…?" She jumped as Richard loomed in the doorway. His eyes narrowed as he pushed away from the doorframe, taking slow, predatory steps toward her.

"You're not leaving, so put the bag down."

Her heart pounded, but it wasn't from fear. There was something possessive about him that hadn't been there when she'd needed it most. "You can't tell me what to do."

He stood so close she could feel his heartbeat as he cupped her face and then spliced his fingers through her messy hair. He lowered his head, the tension, the heat filling the space between them. His breath, so warm and sweet, mixed with hers. He leaned closer, watching her, yet their lips barely touched. Her lips trembled until he touched hers.

His message was clear, and she couldn't help herself for leaning into his mind-blowing kiss. His hands slid down her back to her waist, skimming over her derriere, and then he lifted her. As she wrapped her legs around his waist, he walked to the bed. Their clothes disappeared in a frenzy. Richard's possessive hands explored every inch of her in a fast, hurried fury. Then he was inside of her, and it was hot, hard, and fast. She urged him on, begging between their deepening kisses. They came together, both crying out the other's name. His weight collapsed on top of her before he rolled to the side, pulling her tight against him, sated, their legs tangled together, her muscles and her bones limp. She shut her eyes and floated away into the darkness, and she slept.

CHAPTER 15

Maggie rolled over in bed and blinked at the empty spot beside her. She smoothed her hand over the rumpled sheets and stretched as the bright morning sun filled Richard's large master bedroom—their bedroom. A sense of peace filled her belly when she remembered last night. Richard had woken her once when he slid inside her, tender and gentle—a slow ride full of love. He kissed her long and deep and explored every inch of her. This time, a deeper connection had linked them together and opened a hole she had sealed long ago in her heart.

She wiped away the tear that slid down her cheek. Fear licked at the hope she had for something good and strong with Richard. Maggie had buried her pain behind a wall of nothingness for so long that she didn't know whether she was strong enough to take a chance. Where was this going, anyway? She wiped the front of her face with her hands, feeling anger at these cowardly thoughts. She knew her heart would never survive another tragedy or Richard turning his back on her again.

She loved Richard—she knew it in her bones. In fact, through all of this, she'd always loved him. But the ghost of Lily remained here in this house, on this land, and forever between them. How was it possible to get past all the cruel and hurtful accusations, the blame—an obstacle between them? At least it was in Maggie's mind. After merely surviving for fourteen months, she wondered if she was strong enough to expel the desolate emptiness that filled her heart and head. She knew she thought too much—always had. Her stomach rumbled while she lay naked, curled up under the warm duvet. After all, she hadn't eaten anything last night.

Maggie showered and dressed in a peach sweatshirt and blue jeans and then wandered into the kitchen to find it clean and restored to its original show-home condition. Richard was a stickler for keeping everything organized and tidy.

The coffeepot beside the sink was full. Her favorite pink and white mug was sitting beside the pot. She filled her mug with the dark roast blend, and the aroma was intoxicating. She took a heady sip and gazed out the kitchen window at the empty spot where Richard's truck should be, then out over the acres of land and forest on this property. She really loved this place.

Maggie was sitting at the kitchen table, chewing a piece of toast when she heard Richard's truck pull up. Her heart hammered a little harder when she heard both doors open and close and Ryley's incessant chatter. She flattened her hands on the table and scooted her chair back when they strode through the back door together. Richard searched her out, and for a heated minute, his bright eyes connected with hers. She was positive he sensed her need to run. Ryley hesitated only a second before hugging her where she perched on the edge of her chair. And when her little boy—big boy—pulled away, he was grinning ear to ear as he glanced back at his father.

Richard dumped his keys on the kitchen counter.

When Ryley glanced down at her, his innocent eyes darted in a hesitant way as if he remembered something that bothered him. "Dad said you weren't feeling well. You okay now, Mom?"

She and Richard had never discussed the pills, and she didn't know what he told Ryley. She'd never taken them around him, keeping them stashed in the medicine cabinet with all her toiletries. He was only eleven years old; he couldn't know.

"Your mom's still a little tired, so don't push her, Ryley. Okay?"

Richard tossed his tan jacket over the back of the chair and gripped Ryley's shoulders.

Ryley leaned into his dad, an exchange and bond they shared without her that tripped a deeper loss inside Maggie's heart. When had this strong-welded change happened? Ryley had always been *her* boy. They used to share dreams, have long talks, but then she realized she couldn't remember the last time they had sat together as she listened to what he said. Her heart tore at the growing gulf between her and her child—because she didn't know how to fix it.

"Maggie?"

"Huh?" She blinked and gazed up at Richard.

"I asked if you ate. You okay?"

Ryley peeked around his dad, watching her, so she forced a smile for his benefit.

"Dad said he's going to make a big breakfast. I'm starving." Ryley rattled on, and Richard glowed as Ryley wrapped his arms around his waist and hugged him again, and the entire time Richard's eyes were fixed on Maggie.

She picked at her fingernail and then reached for her empty mug on the table. Ryley dumped his red and black jacket over an empty chair and tore out of the kitchen, bounding up the stairs to his room while shouting, "Call me when the sausages are ready!"

He never acted that off the wall with her. He was quiet, watched TV, played his Gameboy, read, and went to bed.

"What's going on in that head of yours?" Richard placed a frying pan on the burner.

She stood up with her mug and walked the long way around the kitchen island to the coffeepot.

"Maggie?" Richard dumped sausages in the hot frying pan and then pulled the eggs from the fridge and a loaf of bread from the freezer. Richard had always been good in the kitchen, and watching him now, she couldn't figure out what to do, where to be, where to stand.

"Richard, I don't belong."

"What are you talking about?" He popped two slices of bread in the toaster. He continued making breakfast, cracking eggs in a bowl and whipping them with a fork.

"I lost Ryley."

He dropped the fork in the bowl and set it down. He stepped around the island toward her. "What are you talking about?"

She couldn't stand still. Her throat burned, and those damn never-ending tears blurred her eyes. "He … with you there … never does that with me."

Richard shook his head. "You lost me…?"

"Then you hugged and joked and talked, and the way he took off, excited, up the stairs, shouting for breakfast … and even the other night, when I left … the way you two were talking, he doesn't do that with me." She couldn't stop the choked sob but shoved a shaking fist to her mouth to try to silence it. *Don't let Ryley hear.* The warning echoed in her head.

"Shit, Maggie, is that what this is about?" He pulled her roughly to him, and she pressed her face into his chest to stifle her sobs.

She clutched at his shirtfront and held tight even when she pulled back. The fresh air from the outdoors lingered with his scent; he smelled so good. She realized she depended on Richard, and he was fast becoming her crutch. And that might not be wise.

"Maggie, I didn't want to get into this now, but you put a wall up with everyone … including Ryley. After Lily died, I wasn't much use, but I pulled it together 'cause I saw how bad our boy hurt. I let you take him. But, Maggie? You didn't see him." Richard held her shoulders, and when she tried to interrupt, he squeezed her gently. "Let me finish. I think it's time this was said. You don't realize how bad he still hurts. Did you know he blames himself for Lily's accident?"

"What! It's not his fault. It was mine!" She covered her mouth with her shaky hand. "Was it me? Did I blame him?" She rested her palms on Richard's biceps.

"Stop the blame. You're going to have to talk to him, and if he says something that hurts, you're going to have to deal with it. No more running away and hiding. You scare him."

She blanched and stepped away. Richard didn't try and stop her. "What?"

"I didn't say it to hurt you. You need to take a hard look at yourself. How long has it been since you stopped living? You popped pills to get through the day, then pills to sleep."

She felt the heat in her cheeks and knew her face must be bright red. She covered her ears with both hands and stepped back again, but this time he stepped closer and pulled her hands down.

"You were so whacked out. You didn't know he gets night terrors, did you?"

Her stomach felt as if the bottom dropped out, like on one of those free-falling rides at the fair.

"I won't let you hide anymore. You're off the pills. You need to start living again. You can't keep hiding and pulling the covers over your head. It sucks big time. We got dealt a shitty hand in this life, and there are still days I curse God for the cruel joke he played on us. You know I even believed God was mad at me for all the sketchy things I did with Dan, and that was our punishment. We lost our little girl. It's horrible, but life goes on. And you know what?"

She was trembling and mesmerized by the tears glistening in his magnetic blue eyes.

"I hurt, too. Every day I see her, but I hold her inside me, and I've learned to go on. Ryley needs me. He needs you. But if you keep pushing him away and wallowing in self-pity and your pain, baby, you're going to lose him for good. And he'll hate you."

The smoke detector beeped. Richard jumped back and hurried to the stove as smoke from the forgotten sausages billowed. He turned off the burner and moved the pan, then disengaged the alarm on the ceiling behind Maggie.

"Dad, Dad!" Ryley shouted while racing into the kitchen. She didn't miss the fear that pierced his voice as he reached for his dad.

"Whoa, it's okay. I just burned the sausage." Richard laughed while he held Ryley tight and rubbed his back. This time when Richard looked over at her, she saw the warning and how fragile her boy really was, and with it came self-recrimination. What a bad mother she was for turning on him. Why hadn't she seen the signs? She couldn't touch him now. He wanted Richard—not her. She was afraid to find out whether he'd push her away, so she stayed safely where she was.

"See? They're perfect, just the way I like them. Why don't you go wash up, and this time I'll start the eggs. They'll be ready to dish up by the time you get back down."

Ryley didn't spare her a passing glance, but she saw how shaken up he was. It wouldn't take much to set him off. Her kid needed help. He carried an awful burden, and she now realized that in all her grief, she'd forgotten about him.

Richard grabbed her arm. "Don't. You're not going to creep away, to take this on, too, and hide out and lick your wounds. Suck it up, Maggie. Talk to him."

She gazed longingly at the door as terror filled her and made her want to run outside and hide. Richard must have seen it, too, because he raised his eyebrows in a way that sent a clear message: He meant what he said.

The toaster dinged, and Ryley raced back in the kitchen.

"Butter the toast, Maggie," Richard said.

She couldn't speak, so she nodded. At least doing something helped her stop thinking. She'd worked herself up so much, she'd become untouchable.

CHAPTER 16

Maggie clutched a damp cloth and scrubbed the last remnant of jam from the round oak table. She had volunteered to clean up after their late breakfast so Richard and Ryley could take off for a few hours on the ATVs. Ryley followed his dad, revving the powerful four-wheeler and taking off, a little too fast, south on an old trail at the back of the property that led onto an old logging road near the state park.

Breakfast had been tense, but Richard had remained vigilant through everyone's anxiety and kept the stilted conversation flowing. She felt like a guest and, through each bite, stared obsessively at Ryley. She knew she was making him nervous when he gawked at her with big startled eyes each time the conversation lagged. Richard covered her wrist with his supportive hand and squeezed gently. That was enough of a reminder to pull it together, but her mind continued to reel, desperately trying to find a way to bridge the gap between herself and Ryley.

The telephone rang, and she dumped the rag in the sink. After wiping her hands on a dishtowel, she grabbed the cordless phone. With a quick glance at the caller ID display, she saw it was a private number. "Probably someone just selling something." She hesitated for one ring, wondering if she should answer. "Hello?"

"Richard…" Static crackled in the background.

"No, he's not here right now. Can I take a message?"

But the strangely familiar male voice was impatient. "No, I'll call his cell."

A rude disconnect clicked in her ear. Uneasiness burned her stomach, and she grabbed the counter to settle herself. *No, it can't be.*

But then the phone rang again—same display, private number.

"Hello, Dan," she said.

"Hey, Maggie. How's it going?"

"What do you want?"

"I'm sorry, really sorry, about Lily. I never got a chance to tell you."

He hadn't changed. For a second, she could almost believe his sincerity as his deep voice took on a soft edge of caring, which made her want to believe, except all his smooth, kind words were a mirage. Because she knew better.

"Um, listen. Richard isn't answering his cell, and I really need to talk to him."

She closed her eyes. She should hang up. "Sorry, Dan. He's not here. I don't know when he'll be back."

"So are you two back together? I heard you split up."

Fight the urge; don't confide. He made it too easy to slip into a false sense of comfort where she wanted to tell him everything. Except that would be dangerous. "I'll tell Richard you called."

"Not going to answer me? I'm sure after everything you've been through, things are pretty shaky between you two. I told Richard the same thing the other day."

It felt like she had swallowed her heart, a heavy lump stuck in the middle of her chest, and instinctively, she gasped aloud. Then she winced, knowing he'd heard. "He didn't tell you? Maggie, I'm so sorry, I didn't realize … I shouldn't have said anything. I just thought … well, I would've thought Richard told you. Why would he keep that from you?"

Damn you, Richard. Don't you be involved with him. "Actually, he did. I just forgot. He raced out of here in a hurry the other day, late. I guess

I just forgot it was you." She wasn't any good at lying. This was a game Dan played well. She really had no business stepping into his arena. A snake, he changed his colors as rapidly as a chameleon and would strike when least expected.

He laughed. "Well, he was late. Okay, so maybe I was wrong."

Oh, fuck! Richard, you stupid idiot. I'm gonna kill you when you get home. "Yeah, can you remind me what the meeting was about? I'm forgetting things lately." She winced.

Dan let out a heavy sigh. "What are you doing? Don't play games with me. Richard needs to be careful with you…. I'm sure he's got a good reason for not telling you, but I meant what I said. I'm so sorry for your loss. It can't be easy for you, and if you ever need to talk … any time, I mean it. I'll bring over some exotic beer, and—"

"I'll tell Richard you called." She hung up and slammed the phone down on the counter. He was slippery with that soothing compassion he could turn on and off. She trembled because she scared herself with how much she wanted to confide in him, even knowing what he'd done to her, Sam, Marcie, and Richard. What was wrong with her? "Richard, you stupid idiot. What the hell are you doing, bringing him back into our life?"

She punched his cell number into the phone, but it went right to voicemail. "Hi, this is Richard. You know what to do."

"Call me as soon as you get this, Richard. Dan called." Maggie knew that, when Richard was in range and listened to her message, he'd come home. What worried Maggie was what business Richard had slipped back into with Dan.

CHAPTER 17

Several hours passed and still no Richard. Maggie paced the kitchen and then the living room until she was sure she'd worn a path in the hardwood floor. Unable to wait patiently like a good little girl, she searched Richard's office—the spare room just off the living room—and rummaged through each drawer of his big mahogany desk and the bookshelf. When she yanked the top drawer of the file cabinet, it was locked, and she searched everywhere for the key. All she'd been able to find were receipts, invoices, and work orders, nothing that would give her a clue as to what Richard and Dan were involved in. With Dan, it would be something not quite legal.

"What's this?" Maggie slid out a folder from the bottom drawer of the file cabinet. In it were insurance papers for a new Chevrolet, full-size, extended-cab truck, registered to Dan McKenzie. "What the hell's this?" She scattered the file on Richard's desk and jumped a foot when the phone rang beside her. "Hello?"

"Maggie, I just got your message. We were out of cell range. We'll be home in ten."

"Richard, what are you doing with Dan?"

"Maggie… don't. If he calls again, don't talk to him. We'll discuss this when I get home."

"Richard, you know better than to get involved with him. I found insurance papers for a truck with his name on it. Why do you have this?" She clutched the papers and waved them in the air as if he was standing there and could see them.

"You searched my office?" Richard snapped.

"You bet I did. Last night you tried to—"

"I'll talk to you when I get home." He hung up. The dial tone buzzed in her ear.

Maggie stared at the phone in disbelief just before she heard the roar of two ATVs. She dropped the phone on the desk and hurried to the kitchen door just in time to see Richard and Ryley drive into the barn. Richard ruffled Ryley's helmet hair, and he hugged his dad and then ran to the huge sand pile beside the barn where his large Tonka trucks were piled.

Richard smiled at his boy and then faced the house as if he knew she was watching. His smile disappeared as he stared at her with a look that had her taking a step back. Richard yelled something at Ryley before heading straight for her. He leaped up the stairs and yanked open the screen door.

"No more lies, Richard. No changing the subject. No blowing me off. I want to know the truth." She shoved papers in the air. "What's this?"

"Dan's registration. He signed it over to me."

"Why?"

He let out a sharp breath, and she knew his patience was thin. "Maggie, leave it alone."

"No. Not this time. By God, you'll tell the truth. Is he dragging you back into business with him?"

"No. There are some things you don't understand, and I'm asking you to please trust me and leave it alone."

"Richard, that's a lot for you to ask of me after what he did."

"No, I don't think it is. I'll tell you this, though. There's stuff going on I don't want you involved in. Sometimes there are things you *don't* need to know. It'll be all right. I promise you."

Sometimes when Richard decided on something, it was as if he erected a steel wall, one she couldn't budge. Why was he shutting her out? Was he protecting her? She didn't know, and it didn't calm her by any means. In fact, her unease increased.

Richard brushed past her and hung his light brown coat on a hook by the door. "Ryley wants pizza for dinner. Can you order one, and I'll go pick it up?" He changed the subject so neatly, walking away with the registration. She was about to follow and demand answers, but when she glanced out the screen door, Ryley looked up and smiled at her. She stepped closer, pressing her hands against the screen, and what he did next nearly brought her to her knees. He stood up and waved.

CHAPTER 18

"We're investigating a stolen truck reported by a Dan McKenzie seven days ago in Seattle. A search and rescue team discovered the truck at the bottom of Buckhorn Lake when flying overhead during training. This morning, a team of divers went down and discovered the truck fits the description of the stolen truck. The serial number matches."

Maggie stood in the open doorway, facing two Sequim deputies. "Come in, please." Her heart raced, and her hand trembled as she held the screen door open. *Richard, what are you doing?* She wished he were here, because right now she was fighting the panicked urge to ramble. But he wasn't, because he'd driven Ryley to school while she was getting dressed this morning.

"Richard's not home right now. I'm not sure how I can help." *Call Diane.*

"What can you tell us about this stolen truck?"

Maggie felt her face heat, and she knew her eyes widened. Both officers glanced at each other. *Why don't you just tattoo the words* She knows something *on the middle of your forehead and be done with it?* She closed her eyes to shut out that voice.

"Ma'am, if you know something and withhold evidence, you can be charged as an accessory."

"I don't know anything." She cringed and wondered how pink her face was.

"Where did you say your husband is?"

"He's not my husband. We're divorced." This was not their business. She wanted to take a step back. She wanted to pinch herself, anything to stop her mouth. Both officers glanced at each other again. One opened his notebook and scribbled something down. The sound of Richard's truck pulling in should have made her breathe easier, and she was calmer, sort of, if she could just get her damn hands to stop trembling. She jammed them in her back pockets.

Richard hurried up the steps, and both officers turned in the doorway. Richard glanced once at her, his hard eyes giving nothing away as he walked around the officers and slid his arm around Maggie's shoulders. "Why are you talking to my wife?"

The cute young deputy with the million-dollar smile and sun-streaked blond hair crossed his arms. "Well, she said you're divorced."

Maggie wanted to kick the arrogant deputy, who grinned again.

"She's confused. We're back together, and we're not divorced." Richard spoke to the deputy but glanced down at Maggie with a look that said he was done with this subject. This was the second time he had said they weren't divorced. She wanted to clarify and find out everything, because she couldn't believe he'd told the lawyers they were back together and they'd simply believed him.

"Mr. McCafferty, that's obviously a bone of contention between the two of you and does not concern us. We're here about a truck reported stolen by Dan McKenzie, yet the registration appears in *your* name, sir."

Richard dropped his arm from Maggie's shoulders and somehow moved her away from the deputies. "Maggie, can you please excuse us?" He didn't ask—he dictated again.

She wanted to refuse outright. She even crossed her arms and opened her mouth to say so, but instead she beamed up at him and batted her eyelashes, "Why, absolutely, darling. I'll just go powder my nose like a good little girl."

Richard stiffened and glared at her. She knew she'd be hearing about it later. One of the deputies smirked. The way the other watched her let her know he'd do anything to talk to her alone. She hurried up the stairs and leaned against the wall outside her room where she could hear everything, but Richard, that sly bastard, must have known, because the next thing she heard was the screen door slap closed as the men went outside. Maggie raced to Ryley's room at the end of the hall and stepped over his pile of clothes scattered on the floor, glanced at his unmade bed, and leaned over the cluttered desk against the window. Richard stood with the deputies beside their cruiser. He was talking, motioning a couple times with his hands as if to emphasize something. He shrugged and shook his head a couple of times. She would give anything to listen in.

What was Richard up to? What was he hiding?

She darted out of Ryley's room and grabbed the portable phone from the narrow hall table. She dialed as she raced back to the window and peeked out from the side. It went right to voicemail.

"You've reached Diane. I'm not here, so leave your name and number, and I'll get back to you."

"Diane, it's Maggie. I really need to talk to you. Can you call me back? I'm at Richard's." Why did she keep saying that? This was home. Wasn't it? She hung up the phone. She knew with her head clear, she really needed to address several things, her house in town, and her and Richard—but first things first. What was Richard up to with Dan?

The car doors slammed shut. The deputies were leaving. Maggie blinked and looked down as they pulled away. Richard was watching her. Maggie hurried down the steps, determined to get some answers. He was good at avoiding. Why, even last night he had managed to evade her questions about Dan.

Maggie raced into the kitchen just as Richard grabbed the phone and turned to leave. "Richard, what's going on? First Dan calls, now the cops show up here about that truck. What are you doing?"

He reached out to cup her cheek, but she smacked his hand away and stepped back. "No way are you going to distract me or change the subject. Just so you know, my head's clear, so start talking."

He breathed deeply and gazed briefly out the window as if

deciding something before meeting her gaze. "You've been through a lot, babe. I don't want to put this on you. I'll handle it."

"No, Richard, you need to talk to me and tell me what's going on."

He firmed his lips and shook his head. "I need to go out. I'll pick up Ryley from school on the way home."

She felt her jaw slacken and held up both her hands in disbelief. "Richard, I'm not some mindless ditz. You don't trust me. That's it, isn't it? After everything we've been through, how could you not trust me?" She stepped back and pressed both palms over her chest.

Richard shut his eyes and appeared to clench his jaw for a second before he spoke. "I trust you with my life, Maggie, but there are some things I don't ever want you to know. I'm cleaning up a mess. So stop worrying." He didn't move. In fact, he didn't try to touch her.

"No, Richard. I won't let you brush me off. You need to tell me. I expect no less, or else I'm walking out that door and going home."

The way he glared and stepped toward her, she wondered what he was about to do, so she stepped back again until she bumped the fridge. "I took care of your house in town. You no longer have possession. I had all your things moved out."

"What! You can't do that. I rented that house. It's in my name."

He closed the distance between them. "You're not leaving. This is your home. This is where you belong, so get it through your head."

"Then I'll stay in a hotel. You'll not dictate or tell me what to do. You want to share a life with me? Then you need to be honest and share everything: what you think, what you feel, and if you've done something wrong."

He tried touching her again, but she pushed him hard with both hands flat on his chest. "Don't touch me. This is your last chance, and then I'm leaving."

He crossed his arms in front of him. Maggie sighed and slipped past him, grabbing her coat off the hook and shrugging it on, rummaging her pocket for keys, but they were empty. She touched her forehead with her fingers. She didn't have her car. It was a broken heap in her driveway, the driveway that wasn't hers anymore. So where was her car? She refused to look at him as she walked around the kitchen island and pulled out the telephone book from the kitchen junk drawer and flipped through the pages.

"What are you doing, Maggie?"

She did her best to ignore him and punched in the phone number for the town taxi. It rang once before the telephone was ripped out of her hand. "Stop. Maggie, please stay."

She wanted to cave. She loved him, she really did. But some strength poured from inside, and she knew trust was more important. She couldn't have it any other way. "Will you tell me the truth?"

His answer was another wall of silence.

"I'm calling a cab. I'm leaving, and you can't stop me. I'll walk if I have to."

He must have sensed her unbending resolve. "No, you're not taking a cab. I'll drive you."

CHAPTER 19

She'd always loved Richard's truck, and she nestled in the soft leather seats while the whisper of jazz hummed from the CD player. Richard had stashed her overnight bag behind his seat. He had convinced her only to pack essentials. With his sunglasses hiding his eyes, she was unable to read him through his stony silence. He had a way of blanking out what he was thinking. He'd always been a mystery, one of the many things attracting her to him.

Richard cleared his throat before pulling into the parking lot of an ocean-side restaurant specializing in chowder. "Humor me, Maggie. I'm hungry, and you need to eat."

She shook her head and gazed out her window. This was so like him, deciding everything all the time. "This needs to stop, Richard. I have a mind of my own. I realize over the last little bit I was in trouble, and you helped, but you can't make decisions for me."

"Please, Maggie, it's just lunch."

Maggie wanted to bang her head against the glass to knock some sense into herself because, against her better judgment, she opened her door and stepped down. She needed space and distance from Richard. She'd hidden for so long behind a chemical haze that numbed everything so she didn't have to face up or deal with anything.

Richard stopped in front of his truck and took off his shades, tucking them in his front coat pocket.

Maggie hesitated a minute. "Just lunch, and then you promise to take me to a hotel?"

"Lunch and hear me out. Then I promise, if you still want to go, I'll take you to a hotel for tonight." She wanted to reach up and touch the faint lines on his face that made him so damn good looking. He must have seen it, because something softened in his rock-solid features. Vulnerability? Maybe.

"Fair enough." She walked ahead of Richard, but he was so close, in her personal space, that she could feel his heat. There was a time when this would have been all she wanted.

She chose a seat away from other customers at a small window table for two. A skinny young waitress brought them menus and promised to return in a moment to take their order. Maggie stared at the menu, determined to stand her ground with Richard because she knew all too well his powers of persuasion. They didn't speak. The waitress returned, took their orders and menus, then promptly returned with coffee for her and a beer for Richard. She tapped her fingers on the table, gazed at the ocean, and then lifted her cup and sipped.

"I don't want you to leave."

She set her cup down. "Ah, Richard, look, I told you—"

He reached out and touched her hand, the one resting on the table. "Maggie, please, just hear me out." His voice softened as he squeezed her hand tenderly. "Please."

Maggie finally looked up at him, and what she saw melted a bit of her resolve.

"I'm trying to protect you. I feel like I let you down, because I never knew you got hooked on some pills. Then, after that last week, watching you through that sick and hurt, getting that crap out of you, I swore I wouldn't turn my back on you again. I love you, Maggie." He pulled her hand closer and linked his fingers with hers.

"I love you, too, but this isn't why I'm leaving, and you know it." She pulled her hand away.

"We're barely holding it together to create a sense of balance for

Ryley. What do you think this will do to him, you taking off? You may have an issue with me and my need to protect you, but you mark my words. You scared the hell out of Ryley. He knew you were taking pills. He told me he found them in the bathroom. We talked about it last night. I told him you were off them and home for good. His heart was broken from what happened to Lily and then being ripped away from his home, his family torn apart. If you leave, you're not taking Ryley. I won't let you, and he won't go with you now. You two are on shaky ground. Your focus needs to be on repairing the relationship you have with Ryley. You two used to be close; he was a mama's boy. But you terrified him. He couldn't reach you." Richard tapped his index finger on his head. "Did you know during one of his night terrors, he tried to wake you when you were living in that god-awful rental in town? He couldn't. I have no idea how long ago this was. He never told me. Not until last night."

She shut her eyes and squeezed her fists. This was not what she wanted to hear.

"Maggie, open your eyes. I'm not saying this to hurt you. You need to understand what Ryley saw. You just did things. He'd ask you something, and you wouldn't respond. How many times did you forget to pick him up at school and leave him to walk home? Do you understand what I'm saying? Your anger at me is going to hurt Ryley."

She shivered as if ice water flowed through her veins. Her determination to stand up to Richard evaporated, because he was right. She hadn't begun to repair her bond with Ryley, and leaving wasn't the answer—even for one night.

"I need to think, Richard … alone, without you around," she said. The waitress delivered their sandwiches, and they ate in silence. After a few bites, she pushed her plate away. "I need to take a walk on the beach. Can you let me be for a bit?"

"I'll wait for you."

She slid out of her chair and started to leave, but she stopped and looked down at him, and when he reached for her hand, it felt different, more caring instead of his usual possessive manner.

"Maggie, I didn't say this about Ryley to confuse or trick you. I don't want to involve you in my crap, and I'm asking you to let me handle it. Ryley and you are the most important things in my life. He needs us both. I'm asking you to stop running and help me… to focus on Ryley. He's not okay, and I think you know that. Don't make me go home without you, not again. Don't do that to Ryley."

She pulled her hand away and slipped out the door.

She wandered the gravel beach in front of the restaurant and gazed out over the waves rippling and splashing against the shoreline. The tide had changed and was higher today. She shoved her hands in her wool coat pockets as the wind whipped her dark hair around. Richard was hiding something, but to force her point and leave would hurt Ryley. He needed his mother. She'd only made baby steps in reconnecting with him. Damn Richard, he was right. But she still needed to know what shady scheme Dan had dragged Richard into this time. She turned away from shore, picked her way cautiously over the big rocks, and paused when she spied Richard standing on the bank, watching her.

Richard popped on his shades as she climbed back up the narrow path, and he held out his hand as she stepped up beside him on the grassy hillside. "What have you decided?"

"Let's go get Ryley."

Richard smiled and appeared to relax as he let out a heavy sigh. But that wasn't all Maggie had decided. After they were home, she was going to make some calls and find out what mess Richard had gotten himself into.

CHAPTER 20

Diane tossed a ball across the grass. Daisy raced for the ball, picked it up in her mouth, sauntered back, tail wagging, and dropped it at Diane's feet. Richard parked the truck beside Diane's SUV and glanced at Maggie before hopping out. "Diane, what are you doing here?"

Diane raised the brim of her dark ball cap and lifted her sunglasses, peering first at Richard and then Maggie.

"I called Diane," Maggie said. Daisy barked and yipped with her tail wagging and trotted toward Maggie, bumping her leg and hand, demanding her attention. She bent down and scratched behind her ears, smoothing her hand over her thick coat and hugging her around her neck as she covered her face with doggie kisses. She didn't realize how much she had missed her dog. "Thanks for bringing Daisy back."

Ryley had been so quiet in the back of the truck that she never heard him approach, but Daisy did. She pushed past Maggie, making a beeline straight for Ryley, greeting him as if he was long-lost kin, and when Ryley bent down to the dog, something in his face lightened.

"Ryley, can you grab Daisy's dry food from Diane's car and take it inside? While you're there, fill a bowl of water," Maggie said. Ryley didn't move. He looked to his dad as if he needed his okay, and the air twisted inside her stomach as a cloud of defeat threatened to close in. She felt helpless, so she glanced away, struggling to hold it together.

"Ryley, your mom asked you do something, and I don't see you moving," Richard said. Maggie turned back at the sharpness in his tone.

"I wasn't sure if you wanted the dog, Dad. I know you don't like the mess."

"Daisy's my dog, Ryley, and she's staying. Your dad understands that. Don't you, Richard?"

He looked away with just a hint of a smile flickering at the corner of his mouth. "The dog stays, Ryley. Now go do what your mom asked."

Diane opened the back door of her blue SUV. She lugged out the bag of dry dog food and placed the bundle in Ryley's arms. "Can you handle the bag, or do you want me to take it in for you?"

"Nah, I got it. Come on, Daisy."

The dog appeared unsure when she focused on Maggie as if to ask, *Another new home?*

Ryley called her again, but Daisy waited for Maggie's okay. "Go on, Daisy. Go with Ryley." The dog hesitated for a moment until she clapped her hands, and then Daisy limped up the steps, following Ryley inside.

"So we have a dog now? Diane, are you sure you can't keep the dog?" Richard joked.

"She's my dog, Richard, and she stays with me. Get used to it." Maggie was still irritated that Ryley wouldn't listen and had required Richard's intervention.

Diane crossed her arms and leaned against her SUV. She remained quiet as she appeared to study both of them. "What's going on, Maggie? Your message sounded urgent when you called earlier. I phoned, but there was no answer."

Richard glared at Maggie. "When did you phone Diane?"

"When you were talking to the two deputies."

Richard pressed his lips together so hard they formed a thin white line, and by the way he shook his head, Maggie knew he was irritated.

Diane slid off her dark glasses and squinted at Richard. "What's going on, Richard?" she asked in a way that was all cop.

He held up his hands. The alpha he-man refused to be cornered. "Nothing for you to get involved in, Diane." It was amazing to watch him lock up the stony wall around him.

"Richard, tell Diane the truth," Maggie said. She stepped forward, closer to Diane. "*Dan* called yesterday. Then I found a truck registration in Dan's name signed over to Richard. Then two deputies showed up this morning about this very same truck being reported stolen by Dan from Seattle—yet, somehow, it was discovered at the bottom of Buckhorn Lake. They sent divers down and they said it's the same truck. And Richard also said we're not divorced, but the divorce was already done up, just waiting to go before a judge… before we met in his lawyer's office to finalize details, even though I don't remember. He took it upon himself to move my things from my house and give the key back to my landlord. How can he do that?"

Her breathing had escalated to heavy pants during her rant. She closed her eyes for a minute to slow her breathing. Had she made any sense? When she opened her eyes, she brushed her hair back from her forehead and realized both Richard and Diane were staring at her as if she'd lost her mind.

Diane shook her head and studied the ground as if trying to figure out what to say. When she looked up at Maggie, she opened her mouth to speak and paused. She turned to Richard. "I didn't realize Dan was back in town. When did he get back, Richard?"

"A few weeks ago."

Diane nodded. Her arms remained crossed as she continued to lean against her SUV.

Maggie stared at Diane and then at Richard. Whatever had passed between them, Maggie was dying to be let in.

Diane relaxed her arms and stepped away from her vehicle as if nothing unusual had happened. "Maggie, how about a cup of tea and some girl talk?"

"What? That's it, just tea? Diane, aren't you going to question Richard about what he's doing with Dan?" She jabbed her entire hand at Richard in disbelief. What was Diane doing?

"No, I'm not. I'm more concerned about you, and I'd like a cup of tea." Diane put her arm around Maggie's shoulder and directed her inside.

Maggie hesitated and glanced over her shoulder at Richard. His face held not a flicker of emotion. He was a master of secrets.

Maggie yanked open the screen door, Diane on her heels, an unsettled Daisy hurrying to her side before turning to paw at Diane.

"Is Dad still outside?" Ryley slumped in a kitchen chair.

Before Maggie could answer, Ryley jumped up and fidgeted as if he'd been caught doing something wrong.

Diane squeezed Maggie's shoulders and spoke up. "Hey, champ, why don't you go hang out with your dad? I'm going to have some tea with your mom and catch up." Diane ruffled his hair as he darted out the door, snatching the coat he'd dropped on the floor and looking a lot like a boy given a reprieve.

"He's scared of me," Maggie said.

"Who?" Diane set her shades on the counter.

"Ryley. Didn't you see how nervous he was? He can't stand to be in the same room with me."

"Maggie, you need to give it time. You're just starting to rebuild your family, and you have to know you weren't there for him when he needed you."

Maggie lowered herself in the chair Ryley had abandoned. "Richard said the same thing."

"I didn't say it to hurt you. You've overcome some major hurdles and lived through ugliness no one should have to. Right now, this is about all of you. You know you checked out on Ryley, and he knows it. You need to give Richard some credit. He pulled it together and saw what was happening to his kid. I tried to tell you, Maggie, but you wouldn't hear me. Richard did." Diane rummaged through the cupboards as if she owned the kitchen. "Give it time. You all need to ease up on each other. Why don't you start by giving yourself some credit for what you've done? You moved back home and got off those damn pills."

Diane lit the burner and set the kettle on the flame. She then sat in the chair across from Maggie, reaching across the table to squeeze

Maggie's clasped hands. "Six months ago, I read the riot act to Richard. He was in the same place you were. But he opened his eyes and sobered up to be the support Ryley needed. And don't forget, Maggie —Richard's the one who came through for you, too. So why are you still harping on this divorce?"

"Well, it's because I don't know what happened at his lawyer's office. Richard said he told them we reconciled. I haven't heard from my lawyer, and I don't understand how he can dismiss my motion for divorce just like that, as if—"

Diane waved her flattened authoritative hand in front of Maggie's face. "Stop right there. You were whacked out on prescription meds, and I applaud Richard for having the foresight for whatever he did. He stepped up to the plate, Maggie, and he was there for you, and he loves you. I know you still love him. Look me in the eye right now, Maggie, and tell me you don't."

Maggie crossed her arms and sat up straight. "You don't understand, Diane. He's deciding everything for me."

Diane leaned her head back and laughed. "He's always been such a frickin' strong alpha, and it's nothing new, honey. Let's be honest: You needed someone to decide and step in."

When Maggie tried to rebut, Diane waved her hand in her face again. "Don't interrupt. Look, why don't you call your lawyer right now and find out exactly what's going on? If in fact your divorce is still on the table, you need to decide what you want, Maggie. Do you want to divorce Richard? 'Cause I can tell you right now, if you go ahead with it, Ryley will never forgive you."

She'd been so focused on Richard's high-handed behavior, she didn't stop to look at the bigger picture. "I don't know what I want."

"Well, that's honest, at least. Call your lawyer now and find out where things stand."

"Do you think he's still there? It's after four."

"Only one way to find out. Dial the phone, Maggie."

Maggie rose on shaky legs and strode to the phone on the kitchen counter. She hesitated a second. She didn't know why. She let out a heavy sigh and dialed.

"Peter Sullivan's office, Marissa speaking."

"Hi, Marissa. It's Maggie McCafferty. Is Peter in?"

There a short pause on the other end. "Hold on. I'll check and see if he's still here."

The local radio station filled the dead air as Maggie waited. She kept her back to Diane and watched Richard through the kitchen window as he walked toward the large shed with his arm around Ryley. The bond between father and son flowed. What kind of person would come between that?

"Maggie, how are you?" Her lawyer's deep voice sounded hesitant.

"I'm good. Listen, I wanted to find out what's going on with the divorce, I mean, after that meeting—"

He cut her off before she could finish. "Maggie, that meeting was over two weeks ago, and you fell asleep. You don't remember any of it, do you? Did you take something?"

She winced at his candor. "Umm, I'm embarrassed to say I don't remember the meeting. I did something stupid. I accidentally took a sleeping pill right before I met with you."

"How do you accidentally take a sleeping pill?"

"I mixed it up with one I take for my anxiety." She could feel her face heat up, knowing Diane could hear everything.

"Ah, I see. Are you still taking them?"

"No. Richard helped me get off them."

"Hmm. Well." Sullivan took a breath. "I'm glad for that. Are you back with Richard?"

"I'm staying back at his place, I mean, on the acreage." She winced. Why did she keep saying that?

"Have you resumed marital relations?"

Her spine stiffened. "How's it your business if we've slept together?"

He chuckled on the other end. "Maggie, Richard announced that you had reconciled while you were sleeping. The laws are clear. In order to file for divorce, you're required to remain separated for a period of one year—with no relations. Since you're now back home, living together, you can't apply for divorce again until you separate for one year."

"But Richard moved all my things out of my house in town and cancelled my lease and—"

"What is it you're trying to accomplish, Maggie? Do you want a divorce, really? I'm an honest lawyer, and I believe if you remain honest and do the right thing, you'll reap the benefits. You could go and hire any other lawyer out there, and they'd gladly take your money and file your divorce, not caring whose lives they ripped apart. You two suffered a horrible loss, and add to that your drug addiction, which, by the way, I do know about—I've seen it before, Maggie. It sounds to me Richard's trying to look after you, and the advice I'm going to give you right now is to take a step back and evaluate what you really want. What will make you happy, and what about your son? If being single is what you really want, call me. But I warn you, you'll have to start all over again. Take some honest time, which means not a couple days but a few months. Get some help, therapy, and honestly look at your life. You're angry. As a family lawyer, I've seen the ugliness in divorce battles. Don't go that route unless this is truly what you want. And ask yourself one more question: Do you still love Richard?"

"Okay, thanks, Peter." Maggie hung up the phone and then turned slowly around. Diane leaned back in her chair and stuck her booted feet out in front of her. "Well, where do you stand, Maggie?"

"Back at square one," she replied.

CHAPTER 21

Maggie soaked in a steaming bath and gazed up at the skylight in her en-suite bathroom. Diane had left a little over an hour ago after staying for dinner. Before leaving, she had slipped outside with Richard, far enough from the house that Maggie couldn't hear. But when she came back inside and hugged Maggie goodbye, she told her to let the stolen truck and Richard's involvement with Dan drop. Of course, Maggie didn't let it drop; she glanced at Richard and followed Diane to her SUV. Diane had yelled at her to stop asking questions, which startled Maggie. She wondered what Richard had told her.

The telephone rang, and Maggie didn't move. She heard Richard answer the phone downstairs before his heavy footsteps hurried upstairs and he pushed the bathroom door open. "Jean's on the phone. Do you want me to take a message?"

She lifted a damp hand out of the water. "No, I'll take it."

Richard's finger touched her hand, and then he bent down and kissed her before handing her the phone. He left the bathroom, but this time, left the door open as he went back downstairs.

She leaned over the side of the bathtub. "Hi, Jean. How're you doing?"

"Maggie, I'm so sorry to call so late, but when I called your home number, it was disconnected. I was so worried I called Richard, only to find you two have reconciled."

She sighed. "I guess we have."

"Oh, that's wonderful. I'm kind of hesitant to call, but Angie's in trouble. She needs to find a place to live. The guy she was involved with, well … she's gotten herself into a messy situation. Long story short, he's her landlord, and now he's throwing her and Sammy out."

"What! How would she find herself in a situation like that?"

"Well, this guy's a piece of work. After her divorce, she had to move, so she rented a house from this guy. He apparently showed up every night and wooed her with his charm, like he was her knight in shining armor, and started a relationship with her. She followed him around like a love-struck puppy. She said this guy's been playing games with her for so long, she didn't know if she was coming or going. He's taken so much from her—her money, her time—and profited off her. She's being stubborn and doesn't want to move. She said it's like her first real home, but she also said she suspects he's got grow ops going in a few of the houses on the property where she lives."

"Sounds to me like she needs to get away from this guy, get a lawyer and sue his ass for what he owes her. Jean, what the hell is Angie doing with a guy like that, anyway?"

"In her defense, I think he played her good. Hasn't every woman been there at one time? When you get as emotionally attached as she has, well, she doesn't want to move. That's why I was hoping you'd come with me and talk to her. She keeps everything bottled up inside and carries her pain so she won't burden others, but this guy really hurt her. She was in love with him. I just went over to her place, and you should see what she did with that place, what she did for him. This guy … well, I can see he's up to no good. I just don't know how to talk sense into her. She needs to get away from this guy. Emotionally, she's a mess right now."

"Of course I'll go. When?"

"Tomorrow morning? I can swing by and pick you up."

"Sure, how about nine thirty? Who is this guy, anyway?"

"Dan … something. What was his last name? Started with Mc or Mac, some Scottish name."

Even though the water she soaked in was still warm, Maggie shivered. "Tell me it's not Dan McKenzie."

"That's it. How did you know?"

"Let's just say you need not say more about this guy, because I have a real clear picture of what he's up to, and it's no good. We need to get Angie as far away from him as possible. Or farther."

Long after she said goodbye and dumped the phone on the floor, she stayed in the bathtub until the water cooled. She couldn't believe how Dan McKenzie had evaded jail and charges of trafficking when he'd gotten her and Marcie to get his marijuana for him—from all the marijuana gardens he wooed Marcie into growing for him—by threatening to set up Richard and Sam with some unspeakable crime. He was dangerous, and here he was screwing around a mom with a special needs kid. A mom she knew well and who by no means should have been mixed up in his craziness. "What are you up to, Dan? First my husband, then Marcie, and now Angie. Whatever it is, I'll stop you. I'll find a way."

CHAPTER 22

The last time Maggie had been on Dan McKenzie's property was the night she and Marcie delivered the marijuana to Sandra.

Jean picked Maggie up after Richard left to take Ryley to school. Of course, Maggie hadn't mentioned where she was going this morning. She knew he'd stop her. Seeing Dan's property in daylight, from the front passenger seat of Jean's Ford Escape, filled her with an unsettling sense of oddness and dread she hadn't felt in a long time. The driveway was just as she remembered, but instead of pulling into the small house built onto the shop, they drove past it to the next driveway. It belonged to a large, two-story house, surrounded by beautiful gardens, rockwork, and forest.

Angie must have been watching because the front door popped open as soon as Jean pulled in beside a small Dodge minivan. The gray van appeared quite worn but still in good shape. Maggie stepped out and looked around, half expecting to see Dan or Sandra walk out of his shop—the shop and house she could see through the opening in the crop of trees.

"Thanks, you guys, for coming." Angie appeared thinner but still quite attractive. There was a tightness in her face, making her appear to have aged since Maggie had seen her at school a few weeks before, after Mrs. Johnson's tirade. Angie's long brown hair was tied back, highlighting her apple blossom cheeks and big blue eyes. Maggie realized, as she stared at her friend, that if you put her beside Marcie, they could have been cousins, with those country-girl looks. She nodded her head and swallowed hard. Exactly Dan's type: innocent, naïve.

"Did you do all this work yourself, Angie?" Maggie gave her a quick hug and then gazed in amazement at the acre of green grass, the rockwork, and the gardens filled with perennials and bushes all ready to bloom at the first hint of spring.

"I moved in over two years ago. This place wasn't like you see it now. It was run down. The outside resembled a gravel pit and junk yard. I renovated the inside of the house and landscaped the entire yard."

"I guess I'm a little confused. You were *renting* this house from Dan McKenzie, yet you're having a relationship with him?"

Angie looked down at her clasped hands as she stood shivering in a beige sweatshirt and old faded blue jeans. "I went through hell with my divorce and trying to find a place to live. I work hard and have never bounced a check and always pay my bills, but I couldn't find a place to rent because I'm a single mom. I found this house, and Dan offered it to me on the condition I do the repairs, which I gladly did because I needed a place to live. I did everything here, painted the entire house, repaired all the broken cupboards, doorframes, re-grouted the shower and bathtub, re-mortared the chimney, and rebuilt all the brickwork inside. Of course, I also cleaned the place, as it looked as if it had never been swept. Then I started landscaping and dug every rock from the dirt so I could put in seed grass. And the rockwork you see? I built it with every rock I dug from the ground. It took me almost a year because I fell in love with this place and Dan. When I first moved here and started the work, Dan showed up every night. He knew just what to say, and I thought he was my Mr. Right. He seemed so concerned with my daughter; he knew exactly what to say to me, as if he read my mind." She sighed and then continued.

"I don't even know how to explain our relationship. I slept with him. Then, after I was so in love with him, all the weirdness and his games started. He knew my insecurities. He'd say to me he'd let me know if he saw other women. I thought I could change him. And all through this, I'm paying him rent. It felt odd and made me feel powerless, as if I was less than him. The whole time, I continued to believe we'd have a future together. I'm sure you think I'm stupid for believing all his promises. For the last year, he kind of disappeared and then came back as if nothing had happened."

She wanted to shake Angie and ask her to wake up, but she couldn't shake the bitter feeling that crawled throughout her. Hadn't he played the same game with Marcie? And while he was with Marcie, he'd been with Angie, too. She gazed at the red-rimmed eyes of the lovely lady and at Jean, who watched her like she hoped Maggie had some answers. "How about some coffee, Angie?" Maggie asked.

She followed both Jean and Angie into the light cedar house. As the women climbed the inside stairs to the kitchen, she lingered at the open front door and stared at the small bungalow attached to the shop, half expecting the blinds on the kitchen window to move.

CHAPTER 23

Maggie stared out the passenger window at the miles of heavy forest.

"Penny for your thoughts?" Richard brushed her arm lightly with his hand as he drove home after picking her up from a coffee shop in town, where she and Jean had stopped after meeting Angie, mostly to decompress.

"Do you know Angie Mueller, one of the special needs kids' moms at school? She lives on Dan's property."

Richard took his eyes off the road for a second and squinted at Maggie. "Small world. I met her after she moved into Dan's house. Didn't put two and two together. She's the same Angie you've talked about? She did a lot of work to his big old house on the property, landscaping. It was amazing what she accomplished as a single mom."

"Did you know Dan was sleeping with her and playing daddy to her kid?"

Richard focused straight ahead, but Maggie could tell he was angry by the way his lips tightened into a thin white line. "Yeah, I knew he was banging her. She was head over heels in love with him, too. He's not a nice guy when it comes to women. We've established that. I warned Marcie. So why are you bringing her up?"

"Jean phoned yesterday, remember? She took me to see Angie. He's throwing her out of his house after she stood up to him and all his crap, his bullying, and belittling her. She wouldn't allow him to take advantage anymore, and she set boundaries. So he served her with eviction papers, said he's moving in a relative, the only way to get her out."

Richard shook his head. "She's better off getting away from him. Far away. Whether she knows it or not, he's doing her a favor."

"It's the way he's going about it. You don't rip apart someone's basic foundation like this. Don't you think he owes her?"

"For what?"

Maggie slid her bottom around on the leather seat until she faced Richard. "All the work she did. He never paid her but filled her with promises she would have her own place and, she believed at one point, a relationship with him. He did pretty much the same thing to Marcie, and he was sleeping with Angie at the same time as Marcie."

Richard did a double take toward Maggie. "Dan sleeps with a lot of women at the same time. He fills all their heads with promises. That's who he is. Whatever he told them, he lied to each of them. And he's stolen something, profited in some way, from each of them. You know this. Stay out of it. You don't need to take this on. You're too fragile right now."

"I'm not fragile, Richard, and I'm not staying out of it. That cowardly prick has got some other woman, a thug, he's sent to deal with Angie. And this person has been harassing her for weeks. She even sent a letter saying Angie's not allowed to contact Dan anymore, that she has to go through her to pay rent or have repairs done; any repairs Angie does, this woman will decide whether she gets reimbursed for any of it. Then she phoned her and said she's Dan's friend, and he wants no more contact with her. He did this only after she finally stood up to him, no longer allowing him on the property or around her daughter. She asked him to call first, and they would leave if he needed to come by. She wanted a contract signed by him to protect her and her child's rights while they remained there. He retaliated by evicting her and taking away her home, something she had made hers.

"He had stoked that fire and was responsible for encouraging and making her believe, that with their relationship, this was her home. What makes it worse is that this 'woman friend' showed up with Dan and gloated to her that he was establishing his rights as a landlord and that Angie had no rights. This treatment is unconscionable. This is not okay, Richard! There should be laws to protect women from this type of violation. What country do we live in? Aren't there human rights, civil rights that protect her?"

"Who's the woman?"

"What?"

Richard turned down their driveway. "The woman who's representing Dan?"

"Janet Slugg."

Richard parked, turned off the engine, and put his arm over the back of the seat when he faced her. "Janet Slugg's married to a guy named Hank. He's a friend of Dan's, does all his dirty work. Stay away from them. They're only interested in what benefits them, and they'll play dirty. Angie had best move."

"Well, she needs to sue Dan and make him pay for all the work she did. He stole from her, he profited off her. She can't let him get away with it. He's going to do it to someone else. Richard, you could help her."

"No." Richard climbed out and slammed the door.

Maggie had felt some of Angie's pain just from being in that house and seeing what she'd done, and she understood where it came from. The threat of having your basic foundation, the roof over your head, ripped away could tear a person apart. The fury that boiled through her bubbled up and had her yanking on the door handle and kicking the door open. "Oh, don't you dare walk away from this." She ran after Richard. "Richard, please. This just isn't right, what he's doing to her. She reminded me so much of Marcie and all the same pain he caused her. He keeps doing this to vulnerable women, and nobody stops him. Look at what he got away with. No jail time for his role as a drug dealer. How does he keep getting away with it?"

Richard stopped and turned so abruptly that Maggie ran into him. "One, he had the best fucking attorney there is. Two, the cops screwed up their own investigation. Three, there was a bug planted in Marcie's granny's cabin by Lance Silver, so they heard every fucking thing and turned the tables. Four, Dan had a link to some cop on Sam's team. Still does, I'm sure."

"Well, you could help her. She's going to sue him to make him pay for all the work she did. He owes her, and you could make Dan pay her what he owes or give her a truthful statement about Dan that she could use."

"No."

She cupped his shoulder and flattened her hand across his heart. "That could have been me. I understand how she could have been manipulated. I don't think there's a woman out there who hasn't been exposed at one time in her life to a predator. It hurts. I don't understand why you won't help."

He sighed and then covered her hand with his. "Maggie, if she sues him, there's a very real chance it could freeze my assets."

She tilted her head when a screw-like feeling tightened her shallow breath to a thin whisper. "I don't understand."

"Dan and I are still partners," he said.

CHAPTER 24

"How are you still partners?" Maggie had a sick buzz in her head. She moved back two steps, really looking at Richard, trying to understand what he had said.

Richard rubbed the base of his hand across the center of his forehead.

"Oh, for God's sake, Richard!" she yelled, gripping her fist and stepping toward him. She hit his arm hard and swore again. "You tell me everything right now. You want us back together? There has to be trust. I'm not some weak woman who's going to melt into hysterics. I need to know right now. What the hell's going on?"

He turned his back and raised his fist in the air before facing Maggie. "We still own the property together, and, if you forgot, I dumped a large chunk of cash into that development project."

She opened her mouth to respond, but only a squeak came out. She looked down at the ground and struggled to grasp some intelligent words from her brain over this betrayal.

"Don't give me that wounded pride thing of yours, Maggie. This is the real world, and I can't make him disappear."

"Why didn't you sell?"

"How am I going to sell when the market's in the toilet? Tell me, huh, cause I'd sure like to know." Richard leaned in toward her with a fiery energy that had Maggie considering maybe there was more to it than he let on. "He owns half the property. He won't buy me out. I already tried. Do you honestly believe I'd intentionally stay in business with him? Come *on*, Maggie, do you *really?*"

She felt tears burn her eyes and felt horrible. What burdens did he carry? She looked at him with fresh eyes. He too struggled, but Richard always did it in a way that sheltered her. He handled, he dealt, but she couldn't let him do this anymore. "Why didn't you tell me?"

"Look at you." He grabbed both her arms and ushered her up the steps and into the house. Not once did she fight him as he placed her a few inches from the wall mirror in the dining room. "Do you see those gray circles under your eyes? You're still tired, and each day you fight your way above water to regain a simple thread of sanity. I watch you. And every day, I see you struggle to not sink back into that pit of nothingness. Two weeks ago, you functioned on pills to get you through the day, then more pills to put you out of your misery at night, to shut out those voices, judgments, recriminations and doubts. The thought that you should've, could've, or would've done something, anything, different that horrible day.

"You relive the nightmare of our little girl being ripped away over and over again, so much so that you couldn't even be a mother to Ryley. You existed. You cooked. You cleaned. You went through the motions of living, but you were dead inside, and you never saw Ryley's pain or mine. Now why would I tell you my problems when you were oblivious to anyone around you? Come on, Maggie, explain it to me, because I'd really like to know how I could have counted on you to confide in." He lowered his voice to just above a whisper, and there was no mistaking the punch in his words. "Would you have used it against me?"

She closed her eyes. His warm breath brushed her cheek as he stood behind her and held her tight. "Oh, Richard, I'm sorry." It took every ounce of courage she could muster to raise her eyes and meet the scrutiny reflected back. "You're right. I was too wrapped up in me and the ugliness. You brought me out of the darkness. You sat with me. You took over handling everything. Maybe I wasn't capable of dealing then, but you need to let me in now. I still ache, and that nightmare still finds a way in when I least expect it, but I won't slip back and hide. I promise you and Ryley. I'm pulling me together. I won't break, and I need you to be able to trust me and talk to me."

"You didn't answer my question. Would you have used it against me?"

Sadness lurked in the deep blue eyes reaching her through her reflection. Tears slid and traced a single path straight down her cheek. "Yes," she said.

CHAPTER 25

"I need to pick up Ryley." Richard backed up and put distance between them.

"I'll go with you."

"No, I need some space." Hurt and something vulnerable seemed to hover over him. How had she missed it? She grabbed his arm and held tight when he tried to walk away.

"I'm being honest with you, Richard. I was so out of it, I would have used anything as I fought to keep my head above water. It wasn't intentional. I was in survival mode, and I wanted to hurt you."

"I guess that's where you and I differ, Maggie. I would never have considered using that against you."

"Richard, you played dirty. You cancelled my credit cards, cleared out the bank account. You took my SUV. I had to fight to get what little I had."

Richard reached down and lifted her hand off his arm. "I was trying to freeze you up so you would come home. That was different."

"No, Richard, maybe in your eyes, but not mine."

He squinted. She was sure he'd respond, but then his mouth tightened and he shook his head. He backed away and pushed open the screen door. "I've got to go. Ryley's waiting."

This time, she didn't push her case. She stayed right where she was. Richard was intense at times, and he kept all those hidden dark feelings bottled up inside and stashed away in some secret alcove. Their trust, faith, and belief in each other had been fractured. Maybe she shouldn't have told him the truth. Of course he didn't trust her not to use whatever connection he still had with Dan against him, to get what she deserved in the divorce. It hurt beyond anything imaginable to have that ugly truth dumped between them. So now what? How could she break through the steel wall and rebuild the trust they had once shared?

She wandered through the kitchen and caught sight of a doe grazing in her bed of winter kale. Then a fawn trailed after her. She gazed at Maggie through the window. Those bold brown eyes widened, blinked, and in a flash, she darted back into the forest with her baby. It was pure instinct when she picked up the phone and punched in the familiar number. It was answered on the first ring.

"Hey, sugar."

"I think Richard's in trouble. Dan's back." She squeezed the receiver, breathing in the stony silence that rippled across the line.

"Where's Richard now?"

"He went to get Ryley at school."

He let out weary sigh. "I'll come as soon as I can, Maggie."

"Sam," she said, "thank you."

CHAPTER 26

"Great dinner, Mom."

"Yeah, Mom, good job." Richard winked from where he sat across the table as he shoved a forkful of spaghetti and meatballs into his mouth.

Richard had remained distant when he arrived home with Ryley. He had hovered in the background with his son, but now he appeared to have shaken off the unease that lingered. How had he done that? Maggie was the opposite; she had a hard time shaking off anything hurtful. Her heart ruled her head, so it was no wonder she struggled to let things go.

"While you guys were out having fun, I made blueberry pie for dessert."

"From scratch?" Richard asked like an excited boy.

"Mm-hmm," she replied.

Their eyes appeared to fill with pleasure. After discovering the frozen berries buried in the bottom of the deep freezer, the thought of making one of their favorite pies had struck. Now, as she thought about it, it was her peace offering. The softness filling Richard's heavenly blue eyes was a small step in their reconnection. She had to glance away when an awkward feeling of nerves hit, as if she and

Richard were dating, so she grabbed her empty plate and started to get up.

"Ryley, come on, bud, help me with the dishes," Richard said, resting a warm hand on her shoulder. "Sit, have some tea. We've got this." He leaned in and touched her lips with his, leaving Maggie breathless as she sank back in her chair.

A vehicle rumbled down the driveway. Richard lifted his head and wandered to the back door, but Ryley beat him to it.

"Hey, Dad, look! It's Diane."

"Maggie, did you know Diane was coming?" The way Richard watched her made her think he was suspicious.

"No," she said. She pushed away from the table and followed Richard to the door. Diane's blue SUV was parked beside Richard's truck. She climbed out and waved just as Sam and Marcie came out of the passenger side. Sam reached into the backseat and pulled back out, holding Kyla.

"Hey, guys. Nice surprise. Didn't know you were coming." Richard started out the door.

"Richard, how's it going? We're completely invading you guys. Hope it's all right." Marcie sounded a little breathless as she led the way, her long brownish hair hanging in waves over her heavy wool sweater.

Richard wrapped his arm around Maggie's shoulders and pulled her close to him. She glanced up; his gaze lingered on hers for a few seconds. The teasing spark there moments ago had vanished. "You're just in time for dessert. Maggie made a pie. Got some leftover spaghetti too, if you're hungry."

"If you have enough spaghetti, we didn't have dinner yet, and I'm starved." Sam snuggled Kyla in his arm and hung a diaper bag over his shoulder.

"Maggie, how are you?" Marcie, in scuffed hiking boots, stepped in front of her and pulled her close. Richard moved aside. Arms linked, Marcie led her friend into the house.

"Ryley, you're doing dishes in here all by yourself? Come over here. Give me a hug." Marcie didn't acknowledge his awkward hesitation when he froze. Instead she walked right over pulling him into a strong bear hug, rubbing his back. Stepping back, she held both of his shoulders and studied him, making Ryley beam. "You've gotten so big, and you're becoming as handsome as your father. Your dad said there's some leftover spaghetti, and I'm starved. Lead me, please."

Marcie had a way of breaking through Ryley's awkwardness—the awkwardness that had him appearing to blend into the background and then quietly slip away. Maggie could feel annoyance bubble up because it should have been her putting Ryley at ease, not Marcie. Right now, Ryley was happy to help her, so much so that he was beside Marcie, heating up the spaghetti. The screen door clattered shut as Diane, Sam, and Richard wandered in.

Diane sniffed the air. "Don't heat any for me. I already ate."

Sam and Marcie ate while everyone crowded around the table. Finally the pie was served, and Ryley gobbled down his slice. He slipped away from the table so quietly Maggie didn't know he was gone until she spied his empty spot and dirty plate as she heard the soft click of his door upstairs. She wondered when he'd started this. She rose from her chair to go after him, but Richard laid a gentle hand on her wrist. She looked down into his watchful gaze. He knew.

"Leave him be."

Maggie felt like such an outsider. She was his mother and she couldn't shake the fact he'd erected a wall to keep her out.

When she glanced across the table at Sam and Marcie, they were watching her with such sympathy that she wanted to kick something.

"You're looking really good, Maggie. I'm proud of you for how far you've come. You've climbed mountains and persevered over obstacles most people don't endure in a lifetime. Give yourself a break." Marcie took another bite of pie. "And this is really good."

"So what brings you and Marcie over from your little island?" Richard inquired. "Shopping, supplies?" He leaned back and threw his arm over the back of the Maggie's chair, nudging his dirty plate away with the back of his other hand.

Sam never hesitated when he inclined his head. "Let's skip all the politically correct small talk, shall we? We're here to butt into your business. We heard Dan McKenzie's back, and you're still his partner."

CHAPTER 27

"Dammit, Maggie." Richard slammed his fist down on the table, the small plates and utensils clanking. "Did you phone Sam?" He didn't try to keep his voice down as he leaned toward her, his face just a few inches from hers.

"Yes, I did, Richard. And I won't stop pushing until I know what's really going on. Please let me help. You need to get him out of your life… all of ours."

Richard pushed away from the table and stalked toward the door.

Sam was quick as he gently passed a sleeping Kyla to Marcie, and he jumped up to go after Richard. "Richard, don't walk out. We're here to help, that's all. Look, come back here. This is us, and we *know* there's something going on. Maybe you're jammed up, or he has something on you. Whatever it is, we can help."

Richard circled back away from the door and leaned heavily on the kitchen island, focusing his hard, unforgiving glare on Maggie. "I still own the property with Dan. I've tried to get him to sell me his half, but he refused. Then I tried to get him to agree to put the entire property on the market. He again refused. He has plans, he said. He expects to create a steady stream of income from this property and have a nest egg. We build small affordable houses, sell them to those who wouldn't otherwise be able to afford a house, and rent the land to them. Ready-built homes, similar to a manufactured home park, but they're houses. He sees this endless stream of income year after year. So no, he won't sell. So I offered to sell him my half, and he refused outright. But the next day, he came back with a ridiculous offer of five cents on the dollar. I have a lot of equity tied up in that property, and he knows it. So for now, I'm stuck."

"Richard, just give it to him. We can start over," Maggie said.

He frowned and waved his hand in the air as if he was frustrated he couldn't get her to understand a simple problem. "You don't get it, Maggie. We'll lose this house, this property, and I won't do that. I had to put a second mortgage on our home. The money we would've made by building and selling those homes would have been our retirement. It wasn't that much of a gamble when we bought it, but the housing market crashed, so until we finish building and sell all the homes, I can't walk away."

"How many houses have you built, Richard?" Sam paced the far side of the kitchen.

"So far, ten. We have five more to go. And of those ten, we still have five to sell." Richard's face appeared to darken.

"Richard, is the property legit? You and I both know anything Dan does has some twist for being not quite legal. This whole project of yours sounds off. How can local zoning allow you to build a house and sell just the house, then charge a pad rent? It isn't a mobile home park. You can't move a house if he suddenly gets mad and evicts the homeowner." Marcie shifted a cooing Kyla in her arms, keeping her voice even and calm. She didn't bother to look at Sam, but he appeared to be well versed and on board with her assessment.

"It's all in the construction. By using different framing, we can fit within the definition of a modular home. Dan did get the designs approved by local zoning."

Maggie didn't miss the way his eyes shifted. The heaviness in her heart tightened. "You're lying," she said. She had everyone's attention now. "You think I don't know when you're hiding something? I know you, just like you know me. What the hell are you doing, ripping off innocent people now?"

He didn't say a word; he just walked out the door.

Maggie searched out Sam, who stood behind Marcie but was watching the door. "Sam, he's not telling the truth. That line is something Dan would say. What am I going to do?"

"Maggie, I'll go talk with him. There may be something else going on, and he may not want you to know. Sometimes a man's pride and natural instinct to protect his family clouds his good judgment."

Maggie stood, prepared to follow.

Diane grabbed her wrist. "Maggie, listen to Sam. He's right. Let him talk to Richard alone. Besides, there are some things we need to talk about. One of them is your friend Angie and your interest in helping her."

CHAPTER 28

Diane had a way of disappearing into the background, the silent observer who read people and situations. At times, Maggie found this quite unsettling. A silent communication passed between her and Sam, one of comrades who understood the other's role. They'd been the perfect partners at one time. But that was when Sam was with the DEA, and they'd investigated Lance Silver.

Sam was now what you'd call an independent investigator working with the Sequim Detachment and the Feds in a new role of watchdog. He brought together all departments and local jurisdictions. He tied all of the investigations that crossed boundaries, including white-collar land fraud, criminal misdeeds toward children, and the special needs community, all of which could include drug trafficking. He handled those unusual cases falling in the gray area of unclear jurisdiction.

Sam didn't linger. He went after Richard. Diane patted Maggie's shoulder, and Marcie initiated the conversation.

"This friend of yours, Angie, who lives in Dan's house, you were out at her place today." Marcie lifted her chin as she spoke.

The blood tingled on its way down from her head. How did Marcie know?

Marcie's smile was vibrant. "I already know, Maggie. I didn't then, but he was sleeping with her when he was doing me. She's another of his innocent victims, and he really took advantage of her. I don't envy her position, but for the record, she has some real balls to stand up to him. He's a fool to take her on."

"How did you find out? Are you having me followed?"

"Nobody is having you followed, so stop being paranoid. Richard phoned Diane, and Diane told me. Besides, Angie notified state and local authorities on his bylaw infringements on that property. Every time a charge is levied against a property owner for whatever infraction, Sam's notified because of his new position. So, because of Angie, Dan's under investigation for too many houses on his Gardiner property, which also brings in the state, which regulates the wells. You're not allowed to have that many houses on one well. Because of the illegal dwellings with no permits, and no permits for a septic system installed for two houses, he has pending environmental charges against him, basically minor fines."

Diane busied her hands and stacked the dirty plates on the table, scooping the crumbs with her hand onto a plate and then wiping her hands.

"I like Angie," Maggie said. "She has a special needs kid; it's not okay what he's done to her. Now that she's stood up to him, he's throwing her out. How can he get away with that?"

Diane rested her hand on Maggie's wrist. "You can't help her. Your friend shouldn't have called you. It'll be a battle for Angie, but if she stays honest and presents her case, Dan will have to pay her for all the work she did. She's seen a lawyer and filed a claim against Dan with the rental board. She has photos. He can't lie his way out of this one. As far as the eviction she's trying to fight, she won't win anyway. Landowners have always had the law on their side, even when they've lied. The best thing for Angie to do, is to get as far away as possible from Dan. She may not see it now, but he did her a favor by evicting her."

When Maggie looked up, she saw a hint of pain shadow Marcie's baby-blue eyes. "Are you okay knowing all this?" she asked.

Marcie released a heavy sigh and gazed down at her baby girl. "Well, of course. But I'm still human, Maggie. I'd be lying to everyone if I said it didn't hurt to find out about yet another betrayal by Dan when we were together. Don't misunderstand. I love Sam and what we have, but you can't erase your past. When someone hurts you as badly as Dan did me… well, in some ways I feel responsible for what Angie has suffered and wonder how many other innocent women he's fleeced. Did I do enough to stop him from hurting others?" Marcie frowned. "You know me, worrying about what else I could have done to jam Dan up sucks me back into him, which is what he wants. He wants me to obsess over him, and I can't do that. I won't give him that. Sam's watching the investigation, and he started his own a while ago. I've asked for help from other sources." She raised her hand above her head.

Maggie watched the confidence spill forth from Marcie. Her belief in a higher source was at times inspirational, but, logically, Maggie had trouble understanding what could be gained from such faith. "What's Sam investigating on Dan?" she asked.

Diane shared what appeared to be a conspiratorial wink with Marcie before announcing, "Fraud."

CHAPTER 29

"What about the marijuana grow ops Dan's running again? He's always got one or more going somewhere, usually at one of the houses on his property. Why not go after him for drug charges?" Maggie got up and pulled on a thick corded sweater. She carried the dishes from the table and then started loading the dishwasher.

"He's too cagey, Maggie. He moves it. It's as if he knows trouble's coming or the cops are going to show, because his grow op suddenly disappears. He's one slick operator. And besides, Sam's done a lot of research. What Dan's done on paper is going to bury him. He's manipulated state funds, bylaws, telling a different story to each state and municipal authority on land use, wells, septic, and all with environmental impacts. Don't forget undeclared income, tax evasion. Forget the drugs, he's too shrewd, but everything else is still a big deal. Do you understand?" Marcie spoke with such confidence.

Something light and fluffy tingled inside Maggie's tummy. She matched the crooked smile that lit up Marcie's face and the subtle wink offered by Diane. "He just screwed himself, didn't he?"

Diane grinned. "Yep, and we're going to nail him."

CHAPTER 30

Richard paced the shop that filled one side of his oversized barn. Instead of animals, the barn was littered with all sizes of power tools and metal storage chests. It was every man's dream of a place to build, create, and come to peace with his lot in life. He sanded the cedar chest he'd made for Maggie two years ago. Until now, it had been left covered by a sheet in a corner of the shop. Engraved in the lid were their children's names, Lily and Ryley. It had become a source of solace now for him to finish it.

The shadow that drifted in his light irritated the hell out of him. There were times he needed to be left alone, and now was one of them. "Walk away, Sam. You don't want to talk to me right now."

"That's a nice piece of work. You're good with your hands. How long did it take to make?"

He tossed the sandpaper on the ground and paced over to his workbench. He didn't know what he was looking for as he stubbornly rummaged through the steel carpentry tools littering the dusty wood top.

Sam's boots scraped across the cement. With each step, his shadow stole a little more of his light. He didn't like being cornered, nor did he want Sam anywhere near his business. He threw him a warning glare, but Sam wouldn't back away. Instead, he perched himself right against the workbench and crossed his arms.

"Richard, please listen. Right now I have Dan under investigation for land fraud and possible tax evasion. He has an order against him from the state water board for environmental contamination for an improperly installed septic system. He's violated local zoning with his illegally built houses, as he sold the two mobile homes on his private land, which is not zoned for a mobile home park, yet he managed to convince some state agency it was a mobile home park with fraudulent papers. Then there's the matter of the marijuana grow ops we know could pop up at any one of the illegally built houses on his property. Of course, he moves them just before we get in there. I'm tying all of it together, and I'm going to nail the bastard. So tell me, how much of this are you already aware of?"

"All of it." He knew darn well Sam was condemning him by the way he stared at him. "Don't you dare judge me. You just don't get it."

"Then help me get it. Tell me, what kind of trouble are you in?"

"Look, Sam. This is how it is. Not one of those small infractions has amounted to jack shit. He's gotten away with pulling this kind of stuff for years, and there's more you don't know. There was actually a group of locals who took him on when he subdivided, and they went after him with the argument that the original land zoning prevents him from building all those homes. Then they went after him once he put the septic system in and dragged in the first of the two mobile homes. That would be the environmental part, where he didn't have the paperwork completed and the approvals in place for the installation beforehand. Do you know what happened?"

Sam crossed his arms and appeared to hold his breath.

"Nothing. No charges, no fines. Nothing. The local authority said it didn't have the resources to pursue the matter. The state didn't give a shit; they had bigger fish to fry. But this was after he managed to embellish his hard-luck story and spin quite the tale with one of the broads he was dealing with at the state water board. I think he even met her for drinks. Anyway, long story short, Sam, it went away. That group of locals was stuck with a huge legal bill; and one of them suddenly had their property taxes jacked up—when no one else's in the area had been." He began to pace as he continued.

"Harvey, the organizer of the group, had two of his cows butchered and left disemboweled in his driveway: a message delivered, and he got it loud and clear." He picked up a wood scraper and then dropped it. "I sincerely hope you're able to make things stick this time. I do, Sam. But I've no idea what you expect from me."

"What does Dan have on you? I'm trying to help. You can't go at this alone. You know him, what he's like. Do you honestly want to stay in business with this guy? Why are you protecting him?" Sam yelled.

Richard stepped closer to Sam. The tightness strained his back as he fisted his hands. "Look. You have no idea how tied up I am. He won't sell. The only thing I can do is sell the houses, finish building and sell my share—at a loss. With the money out of those houses, at least I won't lose this place. I took a mortgage out when I bought the property with Dan five years ago. I took a second mortgage out right before the market crash to build the houses. I have no equity left."

Sam's face appeared to soften.

"Don't pity me."

"Hey, this isn't pity. I do understand. But I have to ask: The property you have zoned as a mobile home park: How is it you can build a house and sell it and charge a pad rent? Don't give me this crap about different framing. You're ripping innocent people off."

Richard couldn't hold back the sarcasm as he laughed so hard his stomach ached. "You're kidding, right? You know who the real crooks are. The municipality, for allowing Dan to find this loophole in their official community plan. The state, for having legislation that conflicts with rural municipalities. You've already seen it; no one works together. They're not sharing information. Unless it's black and white and falls within their rules, they don't care. Dan's smart. He put this together. Actually, he had some broad put this amazing proposal together. By building on site, the loophole was in the construction. If he used smaller framing, he could make it fit as a manufactured home. And you're right, it's not, but those government people bought it."

"So when someone who buys one of these homes pisses Dan off, he can evict them at any time, and then they have to find a way to move a house; a house they can't just up and move to any mobile home park? Sounds like people being screwed to me."

Richard felt the heat rise in his face. For some reason, he'd managed to block out the faces of people. Actual people. He had taken the personal out of it, but Sam had just ripped open that wound and was not allowing him to quietly sit by on the sidelines. "Fuck, Sam, what do you want from me?"

"Can you honestly tell me you'll be able to sleep at night knowing you're responsible?"

"I'm not responsible. I didn't set out to screw people. I'm just trying to get my money back and protect my family. And sleep? I haven't slept since my little girl was mangled on the road in front of my house." His voice cracked, and he turned his back on Sam to pull it together. He focused on the shuffling behind him as Sam cleared his throat.

"Richard, if you sit by and allow a bully to hurt innocent people and do nothing to set the record straight, you're just as guilty as Dan."

He didn't turn around as Sam's heavy footsteps echoed across the concrete and out of the barn. He balled his fist and then slammed it into the cover of the electrical panel. "Fuck!" he yelled, shaking his scraped-up knuckles. Why did Sam have to put this on him? Rage seeped through him, and with one angry sweep of his arm, he sent a handful of tools flying off the workbench. He yelled and pounded the electrical box again and stumbled against the wall, sagging to the floor with no choice but to face the truth.

CHAPTER 31

Maggie stood alone on the dark porch as Diane left with Sam, Marcie, and a sleeping Kyla. When Sam returned from the barn, his face held an edge she hadn't seen since first meeting him at the hospital after Marcie's accident.

Sam didn't reply when she asked him if he'd found out what was going on with Richard and Dan. He only nodded and then packed Marcie and Kyla up, gesturing to Diane in their cop-talk way of knowing what the other was thinking.

As she watched the light drift out of the barn, she understood Sam's frustration. Richard could be a stubborn jerk. He'd always been a secretive and selfish bastard who never shared when it came to handling his problems. Those were the words he always used, "his problems." He'd never ask for help—ever. Even when something came back to bite him in the ass, he still wouldn't ask for help.

She went inside and closed the door. It was after nine on a school night, and Ryley should have been in bed. She kicked off her shoes and treaded over the Berber carpet in the hallway and stairs. As she approached Ryley's closed door, her heart was pounding so hard she found it difficult to breathe. She stopped and peeked at the light flickering from under the door, and then it suddenly went dark. *He knows I'm standing outside his door.*

She shuddered through her fear and made herself knock softly. Without waiting for him to answer, she opened the door and stared at the huddled form snuggled under the quilt. "I saw your light go out, so I know you're still awake."

He didn't answer.

"I love you, Ryley. I just came to say goodnight."

"Where's Dad?"

It hurt, his need for his father. She wondered for a moment if he hated her. He didn't want to be alone with her. What had she done to him? "He's in the barn; he'll be in soon. Do you want me to have him come up and say goodnight?"

"No." He released a loud breath as if he'd been holding it, something that sounded too much like relief. Maggie started to close the door. "Mom? Goodnight."

Her blood tingled and bubbled up through her heart as she shut her eyes, offering up a silent thank-you. Maybe all was not lost after all. "Thank you, Ryley. Have a good sleep."

She left the door open a crack and treaded back downstairs. This time, her steps felt lighter, as if she'd overcome a major obstacle.

Richard rummaged through the fridge and pulled out a beer. She never gave him a chance to twist off the cap. She walked right up and wrapped her arms around his waist, burying her head against his chest. The soft cotton of his T-shirt smoothed against her cheek. She listened to the clank as Richard sat the bottle on the counter and held her.

"He said goodnight to me." Her voice cracked as she tilted her chin up and rested it against his chest.

"Who said goodnight?" Richard appeared confused and distracted by her response.

"Ryley. He said goodnight to me."

Richard swept his fingers through her hair. The hint of a smile broke though the heavy strain visible on his face.

"Do you really want that beer?" She traced her hands lightly up the front of his chest and then back down over his waist. His eyes filled with a whisper of light, and his touch promised closeness with maybe a moment to put aside their differences.

He shook his head as he reached for her hand and led her upstairs to their bedroom.

CHAPTER 32

The cool sheet drifted over her bare skin and slid down to her waist. Richard's heavy breathing remained uneven. Maggie knew he couldn't sleep. His body remained tight against her. His arm rested above his head, and she instinctively reached out and linked her fingers with his. She kissed his bare chest. He must not have known she was awake, because he touched the back of her head and caressed her in a tiny circle.

"Where are you?"

"Hmm?"

Even in the darkness, she could see the distraction in the lines that pulled around his face. "Go to sleep, it's late," she said.

He slid his hand away and roughly ran his fingers through his hair. His wall. At one time she had believed it was to shelter her and the children, but now she knew it was meant to keep her out. She rolled to her side, rose on her elbow, and placed her hand on his rigid chest.

"Stop pushing me away. What happened with Sam tonight?"

"What did he say?" He rolled toward her in a demanding way, and she sensed he was worried about what Sam might have given away.

"Well, that's the thing. He didn't say anything. He came in, gathered everyone up, and left. He seemed off."

Richard sighed as he dropped his head down on his pillow. It almost sounded like relief to her.

"Richard, please don't shut me out. At some point, you need to trust me again. I'm standing here by you. And yes, I called Sam because I know you're in trouble and because you and your stubborn pride refuse to ask for help. I love your strength, but dammit, sometimes you make me so angry with this arrogant attitude; like you believe you can do anything. And if you have a problem, only you can fix it. By yourself. You won't—"

He pressed his hand against the back of her head, pulling her close and capturing her lips with his. His tongue teased her bottom lip. He pressed her back and followed her down, holding his weight above her. When he slid his hand over the curve of her hip, she slipped a little further before bracing both hands flat on his chest and pushing him away.

"Stop it. You're not going to distract me this time. I need to know what's going on."

He rolled away and sat up. His back stiffened.

Before he could leave the bed, she grabbed his arm. "Don't run away. Please, Richard. I'm trying here, but you keep blocking me. Whatever it is, whatever you've done, it doesn't matter. I won't leave you. I won't turn my back on you. You stood by me, if it wasn't for you…"

He lowered his head like a defeated man. "Maggie, what do you want from me?"

"The truth," she said.

He didn't turn around, but as Maggie leaned against his naked back and slid her arm around his waist, he covered her hand with his. "Okay."

CHAPTER 33

It was eight thirty the next morning when the car horn honked in front of the house. "Ryley, your ride's here," Maggie said, handing him his backpack and hurrying him out the door, waving at Mrs. Bellman in her small red sedan. Her daughter was in Ryley's grade, and sometimes they shared a ride. "Don't forget, I'm picking you up from school today."

"I *know*, Mom." He didn't linger, hopping into the backseat of the idling car. She waved again as they drove away and hurried back into the house. Richard was loading the breakfast dishes in the dishwasher. She touched his arm and then reached around him for her mug of lukewarm coffee.

"I called Sam," Richard said. "I'm meeting him in Sequim this morning at his new office. It's next to the state trooper detachment, so if it doesn't go well, I won't have far to go when I'm arrested."

Maggie instinctively rubbed his arm. "Sam won't turn you in. You were railroaded by Dan."

"No, Maggie, it was of my own free will. I chose to help him for money. It may have been his idea to dump the truck in the lake and collect the insurance money, but I went along with it. He owed me the money, and it was the only way he was going to pay me. I was in a real bind when all the loans came due."

She didn't say anything. She was grateful he had opened up to her last night about the stolen truck and why the sheriff had appeared on the doorstep. Dan owed Richard a lot of money for his share of the building materials purchased for the final homes they were building on the Gardiner property.

"You know what I can't figure out?" Richard closed the dishwasher. "How does he appear to be doing so well? He screams he's always broke, but then he somehow suddenly comes up with money for other things. It's a game with him. He hoards his money, lives like a pauper, but then all of sudden he has cash to throw around."

"He's growing dope again. So why hasn't the sheriff caught him?" She dumped her cold coffee down the sink.

"Because he's too smart. He shuts it down when he gets a whiff of trouble and moves it, most likely to some lowlife friend in the area." Some of the hardness in his face lifted, maybe because he had finally shared his burden. "I better go." He hesitated until she stepped toward him, and then he slowly leaned in and kissed her, holding her close for a few seconds before leaving.

She flattened her hand on the counter and tapped her fingers when Richard slipped on his black leather jacket. "Are you sure you don't want me to go with you?"

"No. Stay here. I'll leave you the truck so you can pick up Ryley. I don't know how long I'll be." He went out to the barn and, a few moments later, came out with his Harley. He fired up the engine and pulled on his helmet. She lingered on the porch, wearing just a navy sweatshirt and worn blue jeans. She leaned against the smooth porch railing. He didn't wave, nor did he look back when he drove away. She couldn't help but be amazed at the mountain he'd appeared to have overcome since last night after he finally shared the hook Dan held on him. She'd been speechless but forced herself to listen without judgment… even though she wanted to jump up and down and yell.

He hadn't told Diane the full story about the truck, only enough for her to realize it was best left alone. Dan couldn't sell the truck, so he was going to collect the thirty-thousand dollars of insurance money on it. After they dumped the truck in Buckhorn Lake, Dan had filed a report that the truck was stolen outside of a Seattle hotel. If she thought about it, what were the chances of a search and rescue team accidentally discovering a truck in that deep lake? When the divers went down and matched the serial number to the stolen truck, one of the biggest questions was how the truck had gotten all the way back here if it was stolen on the mainland. The problem now was that Dan had signed the truck registration over to Richard without telling him; and had passed him the registration the day before the sheriff arrived. Ownership questions now dangled in the wind, and that created a very big problem. With no insurance money paid, under the current investigation, it was now unlikely to be forthcoming. Because of Dan's stupidity, Richard would be the registered owner, and Richard's insurance would technically pay for the truck. The problem was Richard didn't have insurance on the truck, and registration papers hadn't been filed at the DMV.

When the sheriff spoke with Dan, he had concocted a story similar to the facts but thoroughly massaged for his own benefit. He played the bad boy, confessing to the officers that they'd caught him. He owed Richard money, and Richard had forced him to sign the truck over to him—but had then taken the truck from Dan. Then Richard had demanded cash and forced Dan to file a report saying the truck was stolen, which Dan thought it had been, since Richard had told him the truck was missing. He said he was just trying to help Richard out because Richard didn't have the vehicle insured yet. Richard was his business partner, but Dan had no idea what he had done with the truck. After Richard took the truck, he hadn't seen it again.

The question in Maggie's mind was whether the sheriff had believed Dan. Such a brilliant liar. Confess to a smaller crime, and it was apparently enough to sway the officers to look harder into Richard's financials. When Richard spoke to the officers, he told them he never had possession of the truck. He did tell them Dan had given him the registration the day before the officers appeared to question him. He urged the sheriff to check with the DMV. The fact that he hadn't registered the vehicle in his name or insured it should have told them Dan was not disclosing all the facts. Richard had pointed out he wasn't the one who filed the stolen vehicle report and then said nothing further to the officers.

This morning, Richard was going to tell all of this to Sam to get his help. At this point, it didn't look as if Richard would see the money from Dan unless he took Dan to court; and Richard wanted to steer clear of court. Too many spotlights would shine directly on his own financials. Add in Dan's ability to spin a tale and think quickly on his feet, shifting a story to benefit his cause. It was enough to make Richard take a step back and reevaluate.

Maggie could see Richard was scared. The heat Angie had managed to stir up in Dan's direction had shaken Richard because the attention was focused on Dan and all his properties… including the one he owned with Richard. Richard didn't want any investigator looking too closely at the applications, let alone the approving officer who'd overlooked many of the details.

Sam was right. All the innocent people buying these homes didn't know that if they pissed Dan off, he could legally evict them with little notice. They would be required to move their homes; which they'd discover was not as simple a task as had been implied. They'd be forced to walk away and lose their homes—because, of course, those homes were on Dan and Richard's property. Dan and Richard would once again own the homes. Richard was unsettled with the sloppy homework done by the property lawyers and the realtors, who hadn't picked up on this minor detail. Nobody appeared to look at all the pitfalls anymore. A good lawyer could make a case for fraud if they put the time and effort into it. The fact that Richard had ever gone along with this scheme to begin with was problematic, if one looked at the polished version of the land deal: Two guys own a piece of land and have it rezoned as a mobile home park. They apply to the community zoning board for approval for twenty-five manufactured homes with a twist; built on site to spec, they get themselves an edge in the market.

For a moment, she wondered if it might not be better to just walk away from everything and start over fresh with no ties to Dan. But it would mean no money, bankruptcy. She would have to say goodbye to their home, where her children had been born and raised—and where Lily had died. As she breathed in the ache, the reality of the situation sank in. She wondered for a moment about the choices Richard had made for all of them, whether she too would be able to sacrifice what they had left.

CHAPTER 34

"Nice digs. Don't you find it a little unnerving, being parked this close to the sheriff?" Richard lounged in one of the worn second-hand office chairs in front of Sam's desk in his dingy, tiny office with outdated brown paneling and one small window.

Sam wore a five o'clock shadow, obviously having had no time to shave that morning. "It has its perks," he said, watching Richard meticulously with a hardness that failed to loosen even a little.

Richard couldn't remember the last time someone had made him squirm. "You're not going to give me a break, are you?"

Sam twirled a pen between his thumb and index finger. "You called me, remember?"

"I need to know something, Sam, before I tell you anything. Will you use it against me?"

Sam appeared to soften as he dumped his pen on the desk and leaned forward, resting his forearms on the pile of papers scattered across his desk. His eyes lightened with sympathy. "Richard, I told you last night I'm trying to help you. I'm pretty sure you didn't kill anyone and now need my help to relocate a body; or do you?"

"No, I didn't kill anyone."

Sam opened his hands—an invitation to start talking. "Well, then, fill me in."

"You need to know first, what I did … I did to protect my family. When you're in a partnership with Dan, it's like making a pact with the devil. Try breaking that tie, and it's damn near impossible. He's got me over a barrel, Sam. He's slick, and I was so wound up in my grief, and Maggie…" He stopped and looked away.

"I know what you went through and why your head was out of the game. There's no judgment from me. Talk so we have a place to start."

Richard nodded. "Okay. Three months ago, the line of credit was pulled by the bank. I had exceeded the limit too many times, and I was late with the payments. Dan had stopped paying the subcontractors and suppliers and had stuck me with all the bills, which, over the past year, amounted to 350 thousand dollars. I tried to not pay for a bit and then to only pay my half, except no one could find Dan to make him pay. Since I'm the partner who's here, legal action was threatened solely against me. They only needed to make one of us pay. Whatever I'm out, I need to take legal action against Dan. But you need to serve him, and he's such a cagey bastard that he won't give out his address. He has no landline, only a prepaid cell phone, no internet, and no permanent residence, so find him first. He's almost invisible. He knows how to live off the grid.

"He knew I'd be stuck, so I made the payments myself. I took out a second mortgage on my property. I've no equity left anywhere. The five houses that sold last year, I only got half the money. The lawyer handling the proceeds from the beginning set up two accounts to divide half of each sale. One half is placed in my account, the other in Dan's. Because we shared our land lawyer, he couldn't represent me and take action against Dan to get my money back. I had to get another lawyer, which went nowhere because we were unable to find Dan and serve him until three months ago, when he showed up crying the blues. The lawyer I hired did a quick check on his bank accounts. He has no cash floating around, and his equity in his rental property is minimal. My lawyer's advice was to negotiate and work out a deal. That was after I couldn't come up with another fifty-thousand for his retainer.

"When Dan finally showed up a while ago, he met me for a beer. After a couple, he offered me his new truck. He said he couldn't make the payments on the truck, but an insurance settlement would net him about thirty-thousand, which he'd sign over to me as a partial payment. But first he had to make the truck disappear. So *yeah,* I helped him. We took the truck up to Buckhorn Lake and drove it in. Dan left for Seattle, spent the night in a downtown hotel, and then reported his truck stolen to Seattle PD. He filed an insurance claim, and with the replacement cost on his fairly new truck, he was expecting an insurance settlement, after the lien was paid off, for more than thirty thousand dollars. It turned out the insurance company has a vehicle theft clause, so they have up to ninety days to hold the claim and await recovery of the vehicle."

Sam scrubbed the flat of his hands up and over his face, and Richard knew he was struggling to hold his tongue.

"You, um, sure you want me to continue?" he asked.

Sam said nothing but gestured with his hand in a sharp circular motion. His face was flushed, and his eyes took on the haunted look of a man trying to absorb the content of an unbelievable tale.

"Several days ago, search and rescue flew over the lake looking for some lost teens. What they discovered from above was a truck submerged at the bottom. Divers were called in to check for a body. They pulled the serial number to find out who it belonged to and discovered it was Dan's missing truck. After they called Dan's cell phone, which was on the police report, the sheriff requested his presence and questioned him on the validity of his report. You see, someone from Seattle PD decided to do his homework. A detective went to the hotel Dan listed on the police report where the truck was supposedly stolen. According to their folio, there was no truck. He had to provide a plate number of his vehicle for security, and there wasn't one. He tried to tell the sheriff he forgot to put it down. When the front desk manager was questioned at the hotel, she said that would be impossible because the security officer matches up all the plates nightly with registered guests as he does a walk-through of the lot. Any vehicles parked in the lot and not listed are made note of and towed before morning.

"Dan phoned me several days ago in a panic. He told me divers were going back in, and the truck was scheduled to be pulled out the next morning. I told him I was done. He said I'd never get my money otherwise, and he'd make sure I lost everything if I didn't help him get rid of the truck, so I did. Dan borrowed a big boat. When we got to where the truck was, he dove down and attached a line to the frame of the truck, and we dragged the truck into the middle of the lake and dropped the line. The lake is a mile deep in the center and filled with caves and caverns, so when the two deputies showed up at my house, it was before they realized the truck was no longer visible in the lake. One of the deputies told me something quite interesting. Dan had changed his story and pointed the finger at me, said he owed me money and I forced him to sign the truck over. He said it was me who told Dan the truck was gone, and that I had made him file a report to get the insurance money. That's what he does, and he's good at it. If you confess to something smaller, the cops believe you."

Sam leaned back in his squeaky swivel chair and locked his hands behind his head as he appeared to contemplate the whole story.

"Diane already knows about the truck. She told me not to say anything else to the cops since the truck's now gone. They may decide to drop it."

Sam shook his head. "Diane's right. But fuck, Richard. You shoulda called me."

Richard was tempted to get up and walk out. "Is this all I'm going to hear today? Recriminations, how badly I fucked up? I don't want to hear what I already know. I didn't come here to be hassled." He hefted himself from the chair and could feel his temper going from zero to sixty.

"Stop right there with that sanctimonious bullshit. I should be able to speak honestly to you. You fucked up big time. Now would you come back here and sit down? Please." Sam jerked his hand toward the empty chair. Richard leaned against the doorframe in the open doorway, uneasy with the way he kept flying off the handle.

"Sorry, I didn't mean to jump down your throat. This thing ... it's getting too hot, Sam. Maggie and I ... you already know. I've just gotten her back. And Ryley, his whole world's been rocked. I don't know how much more I can take. It would make my life so much easier if… if Dan was dead."

"Whoa, stop right there. You're talking about killing the man, and that threat alone can get you locked up."

CHAPTER 35

"How was school, bud?" For a moment, as she walked beside Ryley to the truck, lost in her own thoughts, Maggie realized he failed to answer her. She touched his slouched shoulder and gently shook. "Are you all right?"

A tear slid down his cheek when they reached the truck. He climbed in the passenger side. She glanced back at the crowd of kids and parents, who all hurried onto buses and into cars. She climbed in the driver's side and shut the door before facing him.

When he turned his face toward her, tears filled both his eyes. "The kids at school were mean today. One of them said Dad's a thief and you're a drug addict, and that God punished us and took Lily. That I'm next."

She froze and was positive her mouth gaped. She didn't think—she reacted. She grabbed Ryley's hand and dragged him out of the truck and into the school office, pounding like an insane woman on the front glass of the reception window.

The pert school secretary slid open the glass. "Mrs. McCafferty, what can I do for you?" The short, squat woman sounded irritated.

"I need to see Jacob. Is he still here?"

Another teacher who lingered behind the secretary peeked in

Jacob's office. "Nope, not in right now. Hmm, I know he's around somewhere. Oh, there he is." She pointed brusquely to the gymnasium behind Maggie.

She turned around, her hand still clasped around Ryley's; and with each fury-filled step, she all but dragged Ryley alongside to where Jacob chatted with Mr. Harris, the gym teacher.

She didn't wait for him to finish. She took in his thoughtful glance in her direction and rudely interrupted his active discussion. "Jacob, I need to speak with you."

"Mr. Harris, would you excuse us?" Jacob must have sensed Maggie was about explode, as he placed his arm around her shoulders and guided her and Ryley to his office. He shut his office door and said nothing until she was seated beside Ryley.

"Something obviously happened that has gotten you quite upset. You're shaking, Maggie. What is it?" He perched on the corner of his desk right in front of them.

"Ryley, tell Mister Peterman what you just told me."

Ryley's face appeared stricken. He yanked his hand from hers and stared into his lap. His voice was hesitant. "I don't want to get my dad and mom in trouble."

"What? Why would you think that? I don't—"

Jacob reached out and squeezed her shoulder. "Maggie, would you let me talk to Ryley alone? I'll see if I can get to the bottom of whatever's going on." He didn't wait for her reply. He helped her up and guided her out of his office to a chair in reception. "Just give us a minute. Sometimes it's best if the parent isn't there. You have my word this won't go anywhere."

She sat, shunned by her own son, as the door clicked closed. The big industrial clock mounted on the wall above her head ticked on while students and staff bustled in the office and past the glass window. Ten minutes slipped by before Jacob's office door popped open and he poked his head out.

"Maggie, come in."

The executioner's song played in the back of her mind as she slinked back in and scooted her seat beside a solemn Ryley. He wouldn't look at her. Instead he kept his eyes down and twiddled his thumbs until Jacob sat across from him. He then shifted a hopeful glance at Jacob, not her.

"Ryley and I had quite a talk. I understand why you're so upset. I've explained to Ryley that I will be contacting the parents of this other child who said those hurtful words. We have no tolerance at this school for what was said to Ryley. It was malicious, and I'll be taking this on." Jacob gently touched the top of Ryley's head. "I explained to Ryley how proud I am that he came forward. This is in fact bullying and will *not* be tolerated. Ryley, give your mom and me a moment, please." He patted Ryley's back as he slipped past him. Her heart hammered in her throat when Jacob closed the door and sat beside her in Ryley's chair.

"Maggie." He reached for her hand and gently squeezed. "Don't panic. Just let me say, I know you and Richard have gone through hell. If you ever need anything, don't hesitate to pick up the phone or drop in and see me. I know you're upset, and I don't want you to get mad at Ryley, but you should know you scared him."

"How did I scare him?"

Jacob squeezed her hand. "Maggie, it's not about today. I already suspected you were taking antidepressants, but I didn't realize you were in trouble. Ryley told me you didn't function. You took pills to sleep, and he couldn't wake you at night, and you took pills in the morning. He said he would try to talk to you, and you wouldn't hear him." She tried to interrupt, but Jacob held up his hand to stop her. "Maggie, please, just listen. I'm not lecturing you. I do understand that what you've gone through is any parent's worst nightmare. I already know whatever you and Richard have done now, you're doing the right thing. You've pulled it together. Most parents who've suffered the kind of loss you did—don't. But you have, and I understand you and Richard are back together, giving Ryley stability. You're putting your family back together. I'm just telling you the kind of fear Ryley's lived with will impact him; but the decisions you make now will determine his outcome. I do need to ask you a question about something Ryley commented on about his dad. Is Richard in trouble? Is he under investigation for theft? Before I call these parents, I'd like to know everything."

Her mind whirled, her tongue thickened, and her words stuck in her throat. "Richard's not a thief. He's a good man. I don't know where this accusation came from, but there are no criminal charges against my husband." She flushed from Jacob's scrutiny.

His face then closed down as he let go of her hand, slipped out of his chair and opened the door. "As I said earlier, I'll not let this matter drop. I'll be in touch. Ryley, here's your mom. I think you two should stop at the beach on the way home. Ryley, my door's always open. Everything's going to be fine. Remember, your mom's a fine person. You guys have come a long way together, and your mom really loves you." This time, Jacob didn't touch her. He excused himself, went into his office, and shut the door.

Ryley trailed her out of the school, a step behind as if afraid he was in trouble. She too wanted to slink away as that old childhood rhyme chimed in her head: *Liar, liar, pants on fire.* She imagined Jacob was singing it now.

CHAPTER 36

"How did it go with Sam?"

Richard poured himself a glass of red wine then leaned across the kitchen table and refilled Maggie's glass. "Productive, enlightening. But I don't know what Sam thinks he can do. Dan and I have a contract. A good lawyer could null and void its existence, but I don't have that chunk of change to pay a good lawyer's retainer. Sam's tying together a few different angles. Hopefully I'll be able to use them to cut ties and obtain at least enough money back to keep us afloat until I can find a way to sell that property."

Maggie sipped her wine, wondering if she should tell Richard what had happened at school. He must have seen the worry etched in her forehead, because he traced his finger across her brow and down her cheek.

"Something's bothering you. What is it?"

She didn't want to look at him. He read her so well.

He reached for her hand. "Maggie, come on, no more secrets."

She swirled her glass of wine. "Something happened at school today. Please don't get mad."

He pulled his hand away and leaned one arm over the back of his chair, placing his other on the table. It was his way of preparing himself, and he would most likely launch himself out of the chair and pace when she told him. "Just tell me what's going on."

She stared at the red liquid in her glass, wondering how to tell him a cleaner version of what Ryley had heard. "Something happened at school. A kid told Ryley I'm a drug addict, you're a thief. That God was punishing us by taking Lily away."

She was right. He launched out of the chair, which tilted back on the floor with a loud crash. "Where would some kid get that kind of information?"

She shook her head and sipped her wine as her husband paced, fisting his hands.

"Who is this kid? Who're his parents?"

"Richard, I spoke with Jacob. He's handling this. I don't know who the kid is. I didn't find out."

Richard stalked out of the kitchen. "Ryley!" he shouted.

"Yeah, Dad?" he replied. Maggie could hear the tremble in her son's voice.

"Come on down here now! Did something happen at school that you forgot to tell me about?"

Maggie abandoned her wine and wandered into the living room, where Richard stood at the bottom of the stairs motioning for Ryley to hurry up. Her boy appeared to wobble with each step. Even she was wary of the control her husband wielded. He was the head of this family, and he made that clear time and again.

Ryley appeared to shrink as he stood before his father.

Richard placed his hand on Ryley's shoulder and looked down upon his son. "Come on, Ryley. If there's one thing you and I do—we tell the truth. Don't start hiding things from me now."

Ryley peered solemnly up at his dad and said nothing.

"Let me help you out, son. Did some kid at school verbally attack me and your mom?"

Ryley nodded. "She said some bad things, Dad, about you and Mom. She knew about Mom taking pills and said you were a thief. But you're not. Why would she say that?" Ryley's voice trembled.

"Who is the kid who said these things? I want a name, Ryley."

"Mister Peterman said he was going to handle it, and he thought it might be better if I didn't say." Ryley's voice cracked, and he really was shaking.

Richard took a step back and planted both his hands on his hips. His mouth parted when he breathed out his rising temper. "Let me tell you something, Ryley. Jacob Peterman does not have a voice in my house or over you, for that matter. I asked you to name this kid, and that's exactly what you're going to tell me now."

Maggie covered her mouth and flattened her hand against her lips. Ryley glanced over at her as if pleading for help. "Your dad's right. Jacob had no right telling you to keep this from us. You need to tell us who this child is."

Ryley pursed his lips and stubbornly shook his head, a smaller version of his father. Richard raised his fists high in the air and roared. Ryley jumped back, and this time she hurried to his side and pulled him close.

"Richard, stop this madness! You're scaring us." She turned her back on him and, with both hands on Ryley's shoulders, she peered into blue eyes that appeared too old to be a child's. "Why won't you tell us this girl's name?"

"Because I don't want Dad to get in any more trouble."

She was confused as she stared at Ryley and then realized why he was worried. "Ryley, do you think your dad is going to go over there and confront this child's parents or fight with them?"

He shook his head in response.

"Then what is it?"

"I'm scared Dad will get hurt once he knows. She's the daughter of a congressman. Kids at school have said he could hurt you and Dad."

She locked eyes with Richard and frowned because they both knew then who they were dealing with.

"Fred White, our elected congressman," Richard said. "His family lives here. It's his daughter, isn't it, Ryley?"

Ryley gazed up at his dad. "Yes, and her name is Rhonda."

Richard shut his eyes as if he'd heard the worst news possible. This time when he looked at her, his face was filled with regret. "If the rumors are true about him, he's a dirty player in politics, has a way of digging up everybody's skeletons. But why is he focused on us?"

CHAPTER 37

The banging on the front door, along with Daisy's growl and bark, shook Maggie awake. The bedside lamp clicked on and filled the dark room with a hazy orange glow. "Is someone at the door, girl?" She rolled over and blinked.

Richard pulled on his pants. "Stay here; I'll see who it is."

The pounding sounded as if someone were trying to break down the front door, and Daisy was now growling and scratching at it. Maggie bolted out of bed and yanked on her thin purple housecoat, trailing after Richard. Car headlights flooded the living room window.

"Hold on, I'm coming!" Richard shouted.

"Open up!" Someone shouted again. Richard yanked open the front door and bent over, holding Daisy by the collar. Bright headlights blinded her as she darted down the stairs. What looked like three large men loomed in the doorway, and it wasn't until she reached Richard's side that she realized they were uniformed officers.

"What's going on, Richard?"

He jumped when Maggie touched his arm, his whole body annoyed by her presence. "I don't know yet. Hey, fellas, it's the middle of the night. What's going on?" Of course, coming from Richard, it sounded sarcastic.

"Mister McCafferty, we're going to ask you to come with us."

"Maggie, take the dog," Richard said. She grabbed Daisy's collar and dragged her into Richard's study, closing the door as Daisy barked and scratched.

She raced back, and Richard was shaking his head. "No, I'm not going anywhere until you tell me what's going on."

"Richard McCafferty, please turn around and put your hands on your head." One of the officers roughly turned him around and shoved him bare chested against the open door as the other deputy read him his rights. She tried to stop the officer from cuffing him, but the third officer grabbed her roughly and shoved her back into the house.

"What are you doing? You can't just show up and arrest my husband! For what? You haven't told us why!"

"For murder, ma'am. Your husband is under arrest for the murder of Dan McKenzie."

CHAPTER 38

Maggie reacted as any woman would, watching her husband handcuffed and led away, barefoot in blue jeans, in the dead of night, told nothing that made any sense.

Richard had been stuffed into the backseat of a police cruiser and had yelled, "Call Sam! Diane, too. Tell them to get me a lawyer. Don't talk to these guys, Maggie, just—"

The deputy slammed the back door so she couldn't make out what else he said.

She raced barefoot after one of the officers, stumbling blindly over the hard ground. "Where are you taking my husband?" She tried to reach out and touch the officer's arm as he hurried behind the others.

"To the Sequim Detachment. Please step back, ma'am." He held out his arm to brush her back as if she were a common criminal—a woman of no importance.

Maggie placed her hands against the window of the cruiser, where Richard stared back. The cruiser pulled away, forcing her to leap back.

Now, as the sun peeked over the mountains, she raced out of the house with Ryley in tow, locking an anxious Daisy in the house. She leaped into Richard's big diesel truck. "Ryley, come on."

She ground the starter when she forgot to push the button to prep the diesel. "Dammit." She slapped the steering wheel and this time waited for the ding before starting the engine. Ryley just closed the passenger door when she shifted in reverse and backed up, right over the bike he'd forgotten to put away.

She glanced at Ryley. He said nothing as he peered at his crumpled bike in the side mirror. She hit the gas and sped down the driveway, knocking over the newspaper box staked on the road as she cut a sharp right. She wasn't used to driving Richard's large one-ton, and being stressed, tired and damn near freaking out, she probably shouldn't have been behind the wheel. Ryley appeared small in the passenger seat beside her. His hair was flattened on one side and stuck straight up on the other.

Richard's cell phone rang on the seat beside her. One handed, she held the cell phone to her ear. "Hello?" Her voice trembled.

"Maggie, it's Diane. I just got your message. What the hell's going on?"

She had been so freaked out after the officers left that she couldn't remember what message she left Diane. "Richard's been arrested. They said he killed Dan. The officers took him to the Sequim Detachment. That's your detachment, right?" Her voice was breathless and filled with urgency, and she was driving too fast.

"Maggie, where are you right now?"

"I'm on my way to Sequim, to where the cops took Richard."

"Turn around and come to my house. Do *not* go to the precinct. Listen to me. You're the last person who should be walking in there right now. You'll only make it worse for him. I'll see what I can find out. Do you hear me, Maggie? Go to my house. Meet me there!" Diane yelled, which was so unlike her.

"Diane, I want to see my husband. I need to get him a lawyer. I've called Sam too, but he didn't answer his cell phone. I don't know how many messages I left. Why can't you guys answer your phones?"

A loud beep cut through the line. Maggie pulled the phone away and glanced at the number on the screen. "Diane, Sam's on the other line. I gotta take it."

"Okay, okay. But don't go to the detachment. Meet me at my house. Do you understand? Maggie!"

"Yes, okay, I will." She clicked off before Diane could say any more, before she missed Sam's call.

"Maggie, it's Sam. What the hell's going on? I've got twelve messages from you that Richard was arrested."

"Oh, Sam, they showed up an hour ago and took him away in handcuffs. They said he killed Dan. I need to get him a lawyer."

"Where are you, Maggie?"

"I was on my way to Sequim, to the police station where they took Richard, but I just spoke with Diane, and she doesn't want me going there. She wants me to go to her place."

"She's right. I'll take care of a lawyer for Richard. You just go to Diane's, and if by any chance the police try to question you, don't talk. Ask for a lawyer."

"Sam, I don't know anything. What the hell's going on? Is Dan really dead? When would Richard have killed him? None of this makes any sense."

"Maggie, I don't know, but I'll find out what's going on. Go to Diane's."

"Sam, which ferry are you coming over on?"

He hesitated. "Marcie and I are already here."

CHAPTER 39

Diane wasn't home when Maggie pulled in. Ryley said nothing as he frantically clutched the seat belt across his chest. Maggie leaned back and really looked at Ryley, with his pale face, staring like any frightened child whose world had been rocked again.

"Ryley, I know you're scared. So am I. But Diane and Sam are going to help."

He turned only his head to face her. "Did Dad kill Dan?"

The way his innocent yet worldly gaze searched and pleaded for her honesty, she knew if she lied, their shaky bond would be forever severed.

"I don't know anything, Ryley, but your dad wouldn't do something like that. I'm being honest with you. I don't know how long Diane's going to be. Do you want me to take you to one of your friends'?"

He shook his head. "I'm not leaving. I want to know what's going on."

Maggie nodded and sucked her lower lip between her teeth. She couldn't shelter Ryley. She touched his arm. "Let's go in and wait."

Maggie dug out the spare key hidden under the big rock in the flower garden and had just shoved the key in the lock when Diane drove in, spewing gravel and dirt. She jumped out of her SUV dressed in her uniform and slammed her door.

"Diane, what did you find out?"

Diane wiped her damp forehead as she stepped onto her front porch and glanced at Ryley.

"He needs to hear what's going on, Diane," Maggie said. "I promised Ryley I wouldn't keep the truth from him."

Diane slid open the door and motioned them in. She flicked on the kitchen light as the sunrise didn't quite fill the dim room. "Right now, Richard's being questioned. I couldn't get in there, and I was called into my boss' office and ordered to stay out of the investigation. They know we're friends. The IPB's been called in to investigate my link with Richard. This happened so fast it doesn't make sense. I did find out, before I got my hand slapped, that a call came in early this evening to 911. Untraceable number. No idea who called, just that it was a woman. She said Dan McKenzie was dead. She gave the operator Richard's name as the man who killed him, and she said he did it at the last house built on Richard and Dan's property, the one just dry-walled. When the police arrived, there was blood everywhere. Two nine-millimeter slugs were found at the scene, and there was enough blood for it to be ruled a homicide."

"I don't understand. You just said 'enough blood.' What about Dan?"

"There was no body. The detectives assigned have concluded the body was moved."

"Diane, that makes absolutely no sense. If there's no body, how can they say Dan was murdered? Maybe it's not even his blood."

Diane waved her hands in front of her face to stop Maggie's rant. "Look, Maggie, they've built cases with far less. The crime scene technicians will type-match the blood to Dan's from his medical records. They'll reconstruct the scene. But from the 911 call, the woman identified Richard as the one fighting with Dan and said Richard pulled out a gun and shot him. That's all I know." Diane turned away, grabbing her coffeepot and then filling it with water. "I'm going to try and get a hold of that tape."

"My dad was at home all night with us," Ryley piped up in a voice determined to challenge.

Maggie pivoted to face her eleven-year-old boy. Why hadn't she picked up on that? "Ryley's right. Richard was home with us. He didn't go out. I'm his alibi. Call them, or better yet, let's go down there and I'll tell them. They'll have to let him go. It'll clear this whole thing up."

Diane gestured for her to stop when all she wanted to do was bounce out that front door. "Slow down. We will, but it'll be with a lawyer."

Maggie tapped her forehead as if just remembering something. "Sam said he would take care of a lawyer for Richard. Sam and Marcie are already here."

Diane hesitated and opened her mouth to say something, looking like she felt strangely out of the loop. She yanked her cell phone from her belt and turned away from Maggie as she dialed and pressed the phone to her ear. "Sam… yes, Maggie's with me. Why are you in town?"

Maggie crossed her arms and paced in the bright, airy kitchen.

Diane sighed and faced her. "We're on our way down now, Sam. Maggie's Richard's alibi. Okay. Okay, we'll meet you there." She clicked off her cell phone and clipped it to her belt. "Let's go. Sam's just retained Harper Lee. They'll meet us down at the Sequim Detachment."

"Harper Lee? I thought you guys hated him. You called him a blood-sucking, slimy scumbag of a lawyer. Why would Sam call him?"

Diane's face remained hard when her gaze shifted to Maggie's. "Because when the shit hits the fan, he's the one lawyer you want representing you. He's good … slimy, but he's really good. Let's move it and see that Richard's home in time for breakfast."

CHAPTER 40

Breakfast was exactly what *didn't* happen. What they walked into when they entered the front doors of the Sequim detachment was trouble. Sam and Harper Lee were nowhere to be found, but Diane's boss was at the front window and refused to allow Maggie and Ryley access. Diane was buzzed in through one of the brown locked doors, and Maggie was told to sit and wait in the small sterile entryway that had locked doors and sealed glass.

After an hour, Maggie tapped the reception window. "Excuse me, I'd like to see my husband, Richard McCafferty. Your officers brought him in hours ago."

The dark-haired cop behind the glass had a pot belly and glasses. He slid open the glass window. "Sit down, ma'am." He pointed his pen sharply at the empty plastic chair beside Ryley. She gripped the counter, and the cop jabbed his pen in the air, pointing toward her chair. "Ma'am, either sit down or leave."

So she returned to her seat and patted Ryley's hand.

"Mom, why is this taking so long? Why won't they let us see Dad?"

She shook her head and stared at the cop behind the glass. "I don't know, Ryley."

The front door opened, and an elderly couple walked in. A very different smiling cop slid open the window, greeted them, and laughed at something the white-haired gentlemen said. The cop handed the elderly man a piece of paper. He thanked the cop, and the couple turned to leave. The woman's eyes widened when she glanced at Maggie and Ryley, and she hurried with her companion out the door.

Maggie looked down at the worn blue jeans and heavy black coat she normally wore out in the garden. She brushed her tangled hair back with her fingers. She probably looked as if she'd spent the night in jail. Maggie strode to the window again and tapped the glass when the cop ignored her.

He slid open the window. "Ma'am, I'm going to ask you one more time to take a seat."

"No. Where's Diane? I want to see Diane."

The cop leaned back to take a look around the corner.

"What about Sam Carre and Harper Lee, my husband's lawyer? I understand they're both here. Or let me talk to your boss. I've been waiting over an hour—"

"Hey, if you don't sit down, I'm going to have you and your kid thrown out of here!" he yelled and then picked up a phone as if to call someone.

She had no time to do anything before the side door flew open, and Sam and a short balding man wearing designer gold-rimmed glasses hustled out the door from the inner sanctum of the detachment.

"Sam, where's Richard? What's going on?" She grabbed his arm and didn't notice the officers who followed him.

"Maggie, this is Harper Lee. He's the lawyer I retained for Richard."

Harper thrust his large hand toward her, a gesture that seemed a little formal under the circumstances. Nonetheless, she accepted his cool touch and was somehow hustled out the front door, his hand draped across her shoulder, aware that Sam followed with Ryley.

"Wait, where are we going? Where's Richard?"

"Keep walking, my dear. We'll talk in the parking lot, not within a police station where they're listening in." Harper was her height, and he let go of her shoulder when they reached the middle of the lot, where she'd parked Richard's truck.

Sam somehow got Ryley to sit in the truck and wait for them. Harper removed his glasses and rubbed the bridge of his nose. He looked tired.

"What is it? What's going on?"

"There will be an arraignment this afternoon … a bail hearing, at which time I'll attempt to get the charges dropped."

"I don't understand. Richard was home all night with me and Ryley. I'm his alibi. We just need to tell them and they'll let him go." She stared at Sam and then Harper. She couldn't understand why they weren't jumping all over this. Instead, their faces appeared grim.

"Your alibi is unlikely to hold any water. I already presented that argument, but the DA has information on your drug history, sleeping pills and anxiety medication, both of which destroy your credibility as a reliable witness. They're contacting Children's Services to have Ryley removed from your care because of your drug addiction, and his primary caregiver, Richard, is in jail."

She placed her fist against her mouth to stay quiet. All she wanted to do was scream, so she blinked back the burning tears that wouldn't allow her to suck it up and stay strong. "I'm not taking them anymore. Sam, you know. A doctor prescribed them to me. I'm not an addict."

"Maggie, you need to listen to this guy. He's good. He's telling you the facts, and this is what we have to work with. They were ready for us when we walked into the precinct. The DA was already at work with the detectives, hammering away at Richard before we got there. He said nothing, but someone's been building up a case against Richard for some time. They have details on your suspected addiction to prescription medications. Someone had already investigated you to destroy your credibility. So far, they're one step ahead of us. Richard apparently told them he was home all night, to ask you, and one of the detectives made a snide comment, 'You mean with your junkie of a wife? That won't fly.' He punched the officer, and by the time we got there, Richard was cuffed to the interrogation room table."

Harper cut in. "Look, I shut it down. They can no longer question Richard without my presence, but now we have the additional charge of assaulting an officer. This detective has had numerous accusations of police brutality and harassment, so I'll attempt to get that charge thrown out or at least reduced. Children's Services? Nothing may happen there, so let's not panic. I will be preemptive and contact them on your behalf. Let's at least flush out that threat. They receive hundreds of complaints daily, and rarely do they result in removal, even in the most extreme cases. You have supportive friends, so we'll tackle that issue if they contact you. But I prefer to be prepared and cover all bases. Do you have family or friends who can take Ryley if the situation arises?"

She felt hollow inside while panic rose from the threat of losing another child. She gaped at Sam. "Sam, help me. I can't lose another child. I'm just getting him back. My mother could … but she's traveling right now, visiting John."

"Worst-case scenario, Maggie, Marcie and I'll take him. He'll stay in the family." Sam gripped her shoulder and held her as if she needed support to stand.

"So what now?" She pressed her hand against her chest to settle the ache expanding there like a balloon.

"Go home. Get ready for the hearing this afternoon. Wear a dark suit. Put on some makeup. Presentation's everything. This is a battle of wits, and we're going to force them to show their hand and flush out who this 911 caller is." Harper dug in his pocket for a set of keys.

"What about the body? Diane said there's no body. How can there even be a murder charge? For all we know, Dan's holed up in some back-road motel, laughing over the trouble he's caused." She didn't want to leave without Richard. Surely there had to be something they hadn't thought of.

Sam and Harper shared a look that raised the hairs on the back of her neck.

"Maggie, there was a security camera installed outside the house. It shows Dan McKenzie being dragged out, tossed into the back of a pickup truck, and covered with tarp," Harper said.

Sam continued. "The last frame of the video shows the man's face when he turns toward the camera. Maggie, it's Richard."

CHAPTER 41

"Hear ye, hear ye. All rise for the honorable Judge Malcolm."

Maggie's legs shook when she stood in the gallery, directly behind the empty defense table. Sam, Marcie, and Diane flanked her. The packed courtroom was filled with unfamiliar faces of loved ones awaiting their turn.

"Who's next on the docket, George?" The judge was old, appeared weary and wore silver-gray bifocals perched on the tip of his nose.

Documents were handed to the judge by the court clerk, and the charge was announced along with Richard's name. Richard was led in, wearing blue jeans and a faded T-shirt, by two deputies. He had a second to glance at Maggie before Harper Lee pushed through the gate with his briefcase and joined Richard at the defense table.

"Mister McCafferty, the charges are murder in the first degree and assaulting an officer. How do you plead?"

"Not guilty, Your Honor."

Harper Lee stood a foot lower than Richard, wearing a black Armani suit that looked to have been tailored just for him. "Your Honor, we respectfully request these trumped-up charges be dropped immediately. My client has an ironclad alibi: He was at home with his wife and son all evening. In fact, this entire charge of murder is completely circumstantial. We don't know for sure if a crime has even been committed. There is no body. No physical evidence has been presented to us that shows my client was even there, though yes, he owns this property.

"As far as the assault charge, we have evidence the detective involved is a hothead with a history of repeatedly provoking suspects, numerous claims of brutality. His own sergeant has had to discipline him on more than one occasion because of his violent temper. He attacked the character of my client's wife, calling her a junkie. My client reacted without thinking, but he was nonetheless protecting his wife's character, character this detective crudely and inappropriately maligned. They have tried to destroy this poor woman's credibility when instead they should be giving her a medal.

"Just last year, her severely disabled child was murdered right before her eyes, and her own doctor prescribed her anxiety medication and sleeping pills—a common practice in the medical community. For the police, and even my fellow counsel, to even hint at a possibility that Maggie McCafferty is a drug addict is morally reprehensible. Let's set the record straight: She is no longer on any prescription medication."

"Your Honor, Missus McCafferty is not on trial here," offered the district attorney.

"Yes, Mister Lee, enough with the theatrics." The judge peered at Harper, his face free of emotion.

"Of course, Your Honor. My apologies."

"Your Honor, we have evidence that puts Richard McCafferty at the scene," asserted the DA. "We have a security video from the scene which clearly identifies Richard McCafferty dragging the body of Dan McKenzie out of a house, tossing him into the back of a truck, and covering him with a tarp. The DA sympathizes with the McCaffertys' loss, and we agree the detective's comment was not appropriate, but Richard McCafferty has a history of being unable to control his temper, and he proved it when he struck the detective." The DA was slim, light-haired, handsome, and very much in control.

The judge held up his hand when Harper went to speak. "Okay,

okay, you two, stop your bickering. I'm going to drop the charge of assault. That was an inappropriate remark, and you know it, Counselor. But I'm going to hold the murder charge and hold it over for trial. I assume you'd like bail, Mister Lee?"

"Your Honor, my client has deep roots in this community. He has a wife and a young son. They suffered a tragic loss a year ago and have just pulled their family together. Mister McCafferty has a business here. He's an upstanding citizen. We respectively request release on his recognizance."

"Your Honor, that is absolutely absurd. Richard McCafferty has a violent temper, and he is close to bankruptcy. There is nothing holding him here." The DA jabbed a finger at Richard as if he was ready to take him on in a fight. "We request remand."

"Well, of course you do, Counselor, and nice try, Mister Lee. I'll meet you both halfway. Bail is set at two million dollars, and your client will wear a monitoring bracelet."

The gavel echoed through the air of the courtroom. "Next case," the clerk said before announcing the parties. Richard was led away by the deputies and, in the chaos, managed only a brief glance at Maggie.

"Hang tough, Richard! We'll get you out!" Sam shouted as he leaned over the rail. Then a strong hand on Maggie's back propelled her into the aisle and out of the courtroom.

Stopping in the busy hallway of the bustling courthouse, Sam, Harper, Maggie, Marcie, and Diane circled together. "Can you come up with the money?" Harper focused his impersonal intent on Maggie.

"I don't know what we have. Everything's in Richard's name. I can't access anything."

Sam piped in and placed a steady hand on Maggie's shoulder. "We'll come up with the deposit for the bondsman. When Richard gets out, he'll pay us back."

Marcie remained silent as she lifted her chin, watching Maggie in an unreadable way. She crossed her arms as if holding on to something. "Sam, we'll put up Granny's property. That should be more than enough to get Richard out." She didn't look at Maggie again.

Harper shrewdly held up the flat of his hand, a motion to get moving. "You two, hurry and meet up with the bondsman. Bail needs to be posted within the next hour, or Richard is here for the night."

"Maggie, go with Diane," Sam said before hurrying away, holding Marcie's hand. Maggie couldn't shake how off Marcie seemed, almost as if she no longer wished to be involved. Maybe she believed Richard was guilty. But why?

CHAPTER 42

Children's Services was waiting outside Richard and Maggie's when Diane pulled in. The young deputy that accompanied the social worker flushed and mumbled an uneasy hello to Diane.

"What's going on here?" Diane stepped in front of Maggie and approached the deputy.

He gestured toward the social worker. "Diane, you know the drill. Don't interfere."

A matronly woman wearing a knee-length navy skirt and a vibrant sweater stepped around the deputy. "We're here to pick up Ryley. I have an emergency order to remove him from your care, Missus McCafferty. A hearing date will be set to determine your fitness as guardian to your son. At that time, you'll be able to argue your rights."

"You're not taking my son. I've done nothing wrong. How can you just show up here? Diane, how can they do this?" She bunched her fists and bounced around Diane, demanding the woman leave her property.

"That's what I wanna know. Cal, whatever's going on, you know this ain't right. No formal investigation's been done." Diane's voice deepened, the way it did when Maggie knew she was angry.

His face hardened. "I'm not a judge, Diane. You've done this enough times to know. You don't have a choice on enforcement. Now where's the boy?"

Another officer stepped out of the house. "The kid's not in here."

Daisy bolted out of the house and started growling and barking.

Maggie gasped. "What the hell are you doing in my house? Get off my property." She bolted toward the officer, but a hard yank on her arm stopped her.

"Don't, Maggie," Diane whispered. "This is what they want. Don't give them anything to use against you, too. Remember Ryley. Isn't he with your mother, visiting friends in Sandpoint? They left just before the hearing. They were driving, right?" Diane stared at her as she spoke. She didn't blink but raised her eyebrow at Maggie when she didn't respond.

Maggie forced the words past her dry throat. "Yeah, that's right."

"Grab Daisy," Diane said.

Maggie clapped her hands and called her. When Daisy came to her, she grabbed the dog's collar.

The social worker *tsked* as if reading the situation for what it was. "You can't hide him. We'll find him, and the judge will hear about this stunt." The social worker pulled a pen and paper from her bag, "I heard what was said. Where is your mother taking Ryley? I need the address."

Diane turned to face the social worker, her defiant arms crossed as she pulled in a deep breath. "No, I don't think so. You can contact Maggie's lawyer if you have any further questions. Harper Lee's his name, and he's in the phone book. Since you already know Ryley's not here, I'm going to repeat what Missus McCafferty already said to you. Leave. Now." Each word was perfectly and clearly enunciated. The two officers were taller than Diane. When passing her, one uttered something Maggie was positive was a veiled threat.

Maggie didn't move until both vehicles pulled away, leaving a small trail of dust.

Diane bolted up the steps. "Maggie, get in here."

"Go on, Daisy," Maggie said. Daisy followed Diane. She hurried as best she could in her black pumps, clutching her long pleated skirt with one hand. "Diane, why did you say Ryley went with my mom?"

But Diane was pacing in Maggie's kitchen, already talking with someone on her cell phone. Daisy whined and trotted through the dining room and living room, sniffing the air.

"They were *waiting* for her when we got back. They want Ryley. What the hell's going on? I've never, in my thirteen years of being a state trooper, seen Children's Services show up without an investigation and take a child, except in the most extreme cases where the child is in imminent danger. Who the hell ordered this?" She yanked out one of the wooden kitchen chairs and placed her foot on it, dropping a pad of paper on the table and digging a pen out of her coat pocket. She scribbled something and then clicked her pen. "Well, you find out. In the meantime, are you sure they won't find him?"

Whoever Diane was talking to must have offered the right reassurance, because she appeared to breathe a sigh of relief as she squeezed the back of her neck and then let her hand drop.

"Well, that's good news. Thanks, Sam. See you soon." She pocketed her cell phone and rolled her shoulders as if working out a kink before facing Maggie. "Richard made bail. He's on his way home."

CHAPTER 43

"Just remember that with this ankle bracelet, there's a GPS attached. You have restricted approval of where you can go as outlined with the program administrator. No side trips. Remember, the monitoring station records all your activity, and it will be reported to the court. Any unauthorized activity, or detours, will result in immediate revocation from this program, and you'll return to jail to await your trial." Two men from the Electronic Home Monitoring Program fastened the transformer to an inside wall by the back door. "This receiving device reports directly to the monitoring station through the phone line. Any tampering with the phone line or with the device will signal an alarm. Do you understand how this works, Mister McCafferty?"

Richard stood off to the side in the kitchen. He hadn't shaved, and a day-old shadow speckled with white stubbly hair made him look dangerous. But the deep lines around his eyes showed Maggie how tired he really was. Sam stood beside Richard and nudged him with his elbow. "Yes, I understand," Richard snapped.

Daisy barked from the study where Maggie had locked her up.

One of the men looked up from his clipboard, recognizing attitude when it was dished up. For a moment, Maggie wondered if the small man was going to continue humiliating Richard.

Sam stepped in front of Richard and over to the one holding the clipboard. "Are you almost done? Richard hasn't had much sleep, and I'm sure he'd appreciate a shower before his lawyer arrives." Sam checked the face of his watch and then tapped the front. "Actually, Mister Lee should be here in a few minutes."

Obviously, the two men understood his meaning. Everyone new Harper, a definite badass, and the cops hated him. To them, there wasn't a scumbag he hadn't managed to get off, and he enjoyed spotlighting the screw-ups of law enforcement personnel.

The one attaching the responder to the wall stood up. "We're done."

The other one handed Richard the clipboard and pen. "Sign at the bottom."

Richard was tired, and, to his credit, he held it together long enough to scribble his name at the bottom of the page and pass it back. The two men left. The screen door clattered, and a strange silence lingered. No one made eye contact, and no one spoke.

Richard uncrossed his arms and walked out of the kitchen. "I need a shower."

Maggie looked at Sam and then at Diane. "Have you talked to Marcie? Is Ryley safe?"

Sam swiped his broad, handsome face with the flat of his hand. "Don't worry, Maggie. They won't find him. She's taken him and Kyla to stay with Sally, her teacher, just until we clear up this mess."

"Did you find out who ordered this?"

Sam was sympathetic when he placed a hand of support on Maggie's shoulder. "Harper's working on it. He'll be here soon. We should order in some food. Has anyone eaten?"

Through the chaos of this day, Maggie had survived on little more than a few cups of coffee, which now burned the tender lining of her stomach. "I could make something." She didn't know what but was grateful when Sam shook his head. He then rifled through the phone book that sat by the telephone. "How about pizza?"

"Order from the new place that opened on the corner of the highway," Maggie said.

Diane pulled out her cell phone when Sam showed her the number. With Sam and Diane focused on ordering dinner, Maggie slipped out of the kitchen in her stocking feet and hurried upstairs. She opened her bedroom door, and steam from the open door of the en-suite wafted out. She leaned in the doorway of the bathroom as Richard shut off the shower and popped open the glass door. She handed him a towel. She could usually read him, but today, when their eyes met, something appeared like a shadow between them. He didn't smile, and he didn't offer any words of encouragement as he dried himself off and then cursed at the black bracelet surrounding his right ankle.

She still wore her long skirt, although she'd exchanged her black blazer for a heavy wool cardigan. She perched on the edge of the bed while Richard dressed. "We need to talk about Ryley and what to do," she said. After Diane called Sam, he'd raced to Diane's with Marcie, where the sitter was looking after Ryley and Kyla. He'd put them on the first ferry back to Las Seta.

Richard pulled a T-shirt over his head. "Ryley's safe at Sally's. Marcie won't let anything happen to him."

Maggie couldn't shake the worry—a worry only a mother gets when her child's in danger. "Richard, why are they attacking us? I'm not an addict. Where did that come from?"

"Who?"

"Children's Services. What do they have to gain? I love Ryley. How can they believe he's in imminent danger? You and I both know there are so many kids out there, in this area alone, living with drug dealers and thugs, who are being abused, and they're in imminent danger. These social workers know who they are, too."

The bed dipped when Richard sat beside her. He linked his fingers with hers. "Maggie, there's something more playing behind the scenes. We'll find out…" Voices downstairs distracted him. "That's Harper. Let's go."

He helped her up, and they walked hand in hand down the stairs together. Sam stood in the open doorway, paying the pizza delivery man.

Harper Lee addressed Diane as he draped his dark blue Armani jacket over the back of the kitchen chair and dumped his briefcase on the table. "Richard, I'm sure you're glad to be home. Now the real work starts." Harper rubbed his hands together and then pulled notes and a pad of yellow lined paper from his briefcase.

Sam plopped the pizza box in the center of the kitchen table. Maggie squeezed Richard's hand and then strode to the cupboard to grab five pale green plates.

"Maggie, you have napkins?" Diane hovered next to her.

"In the drawer beside the sink, there are cloth ones."

Harper passed on the pizza, but everyone else dove in. "Okay, first thing, Children's Services. The way they handled this situation is a bit unusual. I've contacted the district supervisor, who was uncooperative and terse, to say the least. Not at all forthcoming. But she did remind me an emergency hearing has been set for the day after tomorrow, and they're demanding you produce Ryley. They're not buying that he's with your mother. If they find your mother and call her, Maggie, is she going to speak with them? It doesn't look good for our case if we start out by lying to the judge. And two, since time's not on our side, we need to find out why the urgency and where this information against Maggie came from. Sam, Diane, I'm leaving that to you since you both have volunteered your services."

Maggie knew Sam was helping, but when she looked over at Diane and the way her jaw stiffened, she sensed something was up—and not in a good way. "Diane?"

She pushed her plate away and tapped the table. "I'm on a leave of absence until this situation with Richard's settled."

This seemed to pull Richard out of his melancholy. "Are you in trouble because of me?"

Diane leaned back in her chair beside Richard and placed her hand over his. "No, my friend. There's a conflict of interest, as pointed out by my boss, and I was advised it'd be better if I took time off. If I didn't do it voluntarily, he'd have forced me. I think they're worried about this case. All I was able to find out was that there was pressure coming from somewhere to push this case against Richard. It's all too neat. Even one of the detectives I'm friends with said something about this evidence not jibing. When I questioned him further, he wouldn't talk to me because we're friends."

"I'm sorry, Diane." Richard wiped his bloodshot eyes.

"Okay, let's move on," Harper said. "We've got a lot of ground to cover. As of yet, the DA has failed to provide me with the evidence. I'm most interested in the video tape. As soon as we get it, Sam, I want you to go through it. Let's find out how Richard's face ended up on that video when he was at home all night." Harper scribbled on his notepad.

"My kid is more important to me than this murder investigation," Richard said. "I don't want him thrown in some foster home. I've seen some of these people who milk the system. To them, the kids are just another check. Harper, I need you to make sure they don't take Ryley. Appoint Marcie and Sam as guardians in the interim if we have to."

Harper peered through his gold-rimmed glasses. His expression was so focused that it was unreadable. "I doubt very much we'll have to go there, but it's a back-up plan, and the court should have no hesitation about approving that. A note of caution: One thing I've learned over the years is that the state legal system is fraught with inconsistencies, and there are no guarantees. Being prepared for the unexpected is what we're going to have to tackle, along with poking holes in all the state's evidence. At this point, we need to control the evidence, so we are not going to introduce anything new. Let's let their own evidence work against them. Now…" Harper smacked his hands together. "At the emergency hearing, I want to make sure Ryley is *not* available."

Everyone looked at each other.

"A second ago, you said not to piss off the judge." Richard braced his forearms on the table, and Maggie leaned closer to her husband.

"Yes, I did. But we also don't want Children's Services to be able to snatch him, and they will. Once they have him, it'll be difficult to get him back."

Harper jabbed his pen in the air toward her. "Maggie, call your mother. Make sure she's on board, that she had Ryley and he's now with Sam and Marcie. I'll have a letter of guardianship done up in the event we need it, giving temporary guardianship to them. Hopefully, we won't have to use it. Now, Diane and Sam, that's where you come in. You need to find out where the information against Maggie came from. She was on prescription medication prescribed by her doctor but is no longer taking it. One, due to doctor–patient confidentiality, they don't have access to your medical records. So how did they find out? Also, Maggie, I'm going to get you to provide a urine sample to a private lab I use. Those clean results will shoot down the state's claim you're still taking them." Harper paused and removed his glasses, staring hard at Maggie. "Just so we're clear, I need to ask. You're clean, aren't you? Will anything show up?"

Maggie felt everyone's eyes burn into her, and she wanted nothing more than to crawl away and hide.

Richard must have sensed how this was ripping her up inside, because he slid his arm around her when she tried to pull into herself. "Whoa, back off. Don't go accusing Maggie—"

The famed pit bull, as Harper was known, launched back at Richard. "Stop right there. When I ask something, you give it. Get used to it if you want me to save your ass and keep your family together. I want every deep dark secret, and you will provide what I ask for in detail. I'll not be blindsided by anything. Do I make myself clear?" Harper propped his elbow on the table. His dark eyes flashed how serious he was as he looked at each person sitting around the table. "If for any reason I find out you withheld information from me or lied to me, I'll walk away, and you can find yourself another lawyer to represent you."

"I haven't taken anything." Her heart pounded as she scooted her chair closer to Richard.

Everyone stared at her.

"You haven't taken what?" Harper was direct, but this time when he addressed her personally, there was a hint of compassion.

"Since Richard got me off the pills the doctor prescribed, I've taken nothing—not even an aspirin."

That appeared to satisfy him, as he offered a simple nod before he continued attacking each issue, good and bad. Close to an hour later, Maggie excused herself and slipped into Richard's office to call her mother.

Her mother was groggy when she answered her cell phone. Maggie glanced at the clock; it was after nine. Maggie quickly filled her mother in on what had transpired: Richard's arrest, Children's Services trying to take Ryley, and Diane's lie.

"Oh, Maggie, you know I can't lie! I'm no good at it. Any judge asks me, and you know I'll stutter, my face will turn red and I won't be able to look at them. Your dad always said I was not the person to have in a car if you were ever stopped by the police because I'd start confessing small details; that he was speeding or a brake light was burned out. You remember?"

Maggie smiled fondly over her dad's frustration. That was many years ago, and he had long since passed on, but their mom had been painfully honest. At times, none of them wanted to be out with her in public for fear of what she might say.

"I understand, Mom, but we need your help. If Children's Services gets a hold of Ryley, it'll be hard for us to get him back, and who knows where he'll end up."

"Maggie, whatever you need. I'll take Ryley if I have to, to make sure those people don't get him. Do you want me to come and get him? I'll bring him back here to John's. They won't find him down in Florida."

Maggie smiled for the first time in days. "Thanks, Mom, but just in case a social worker or someone calls you, remember, you had Ryley."

After she hung up, she went up to her room and changed into her sweatpants and slippers before returning to the kitchen. Richard looked up when she strode in. "I just spoke with Mom, and she's agreed to go along with the story. She offered to come and get Ryley to take him back with her."

"Where is your mother now?" If anything, Harper was extremely efficient, covering all bases.

"She's in Florida, staying with my brother."

Harper's focus appeared to instantaneously shuffle and compile all information provided to him. "Unless the state has exclusively dedicated a team of detectives to track down your mother, I'm pretty sure her testimony and her whereabouts will be unable to be corroborated. In the eyes of the judge, with Sam and Marcie now caring for Ryley and the fact he was apparently with your mom when Children's Services arrived, it should be a moot point."

At eleven fifteen, they finally packed it in for the night. All agreed to meet back at the house the next afternoon. Everyone except Richard and Maggie had a lot of work to do in order to prepare for the hearing on Thursday. How much they'd be able to uncover in that short amount of time would be a miracle. Time was not on their side, and the emptiness of one child lost would be amplified by the absence of another. Maggie wondered for a moment if it was possible to die of a broken heart, and this time she didn't know if she could go on.

CHAPTER 44

The dead air in the box-like room of Courtroom 101 in Sequim rivaled that of a dry summer day. Maggie recognized the social worker and deputies who'd been at the house to take Ryley sitting in the courtroom. Harper whispered to her and Richard that the chief counsel for Children's Services was Cliff Roberts and that the proceedings had been facilitated by that department.

The court clerk announced the docket and the arrival of the judge. Both Richard and Maggie stood beside Harper Lee and faced Judge Cooper, a woman with long dark hair threaded with gray, possibly in her early fifties.

The judge scanned the room with a dour expression. "I have in front of me a motion to take the said child, Ryley McCafferty, into custody. Are you the parents?"

Harper spoke for them. "Yes, Your Honor, these are Ryley's loving parents, Richard and Maggie, and they are horrified by the unfounded allegations by Children's Services."

"Your Honor," said Roberts, "Children and Family Services has a duty to protect children, and we fear if this child is not taken into custody, his health, safety, and welfare will be seriously endangered. We do have reasonable grounds to believe Missus McCafferty's dependence on anti-anxiety medication and sleeping pills has left her unable to adequately care for this child. With the father recently arrested for murder, that household has the potential risk of imminent harm to the child.

"We have an affidavit signed by a Missus Johnson, Ryley's school counselor, that she witnessed on more than one occasion Missus McCafferty forgetting to pick up her child. Ryley's behavior and lack of social connection has diminished to the point where the child has days of complete depression. The death of their unsupervised daughter, who was a severely autistic child, was caused by the parents when they left an eight-year-old boy in charge of her supervision. She was struck down and killed—leaving a prominent school educator with questions as to the parents' suitability as responsible role models."

Maggie squeezed Richard's hand when tears pushed to the surface. Those cruel words were the ones she'd accused Richard of and then herself, over and over. If only they hadn't asked Ryley to watch Lily, would she still be alive?

"Your Honor, as I stand here today, I'm truly horrified Children's Services has the audacity to blame these outstanding parents for their daughter's death based on the mere gossip of a malicious busybody."

"Objection, Your Honor."

"Sustained. Is this the affidavit from Missus Johnson, the school counselor?" The judge peered over papers she perused after slipping on her reading glasses and addressed the social worker directly.

"Yes, Your Honor, it is."

"Your Honor, I too have an affidavit," Harper said. "Mine is from the district principal of the school Ryley attends. He attests to the fitness of both Richard and Maggie McCafferty, addressing the devastating loss they suffered. He also attests to their character and to how they were model parents, fighting and advocating for their disabled child's rights. They suffered a terrible loss and struggled through a parent's worst nightmare. In the end, they kept their family together, always working *together* for the best interest of both their children. After the loss, even in their grief, their decisions now have been made for the best interest of Ryley. Also, Your Honor, I have two affidavits from two other parents with special needs children who have the courage to speak about the credibility of Missus Johnson. She has been known to bully parents and has refused to meet their children's unique needs in school. She gossips about parents and frequently casts doubt and judgment upon a parent merely based on her opinions. In essence, these parents attest that Missus Johnson has in fact been a hindrance to their children's progress at school."

Maggie wasn't sure when they'd sat down. Her head was still spinning from listening to that man say such horrible things about her. She'd known Mrs. Johnson didn't like her, but this? What she really wanted was to slink away, pull the covers over her head, and try to brush this nightmarish day away. Richard must have known, because he squeezed her hand.

"And, Your Honor, these unfounded allegations that Missus McCafferty is dependent on prescription medication are a slanderous accusation created for no reason other than to destroy a godly woman's credibility so she cannot speak the truth of her husband's whereabouts in a criminal proceeding," Harper continued. "In fact, I have lab results, urine and blood analysis just obtained from Maggie McCafferty, to prove to this court that there are no barbiturates or traces of any drugs in her system." Harper passed a copy of the lab results to the court clerk and offered one to Children's Services.

The courtroom door whisked open. Sam strode to the rail directly behind Harper and snagged his attention, whispering something only Harper could hear.

"Mister Harper, are you still with us?" the judge asked in an irritated fashion.

"I beg the court's indulgence, Your Honor. It has just been brought to my attention that these false allegations to destroy Maggie McCafferty's credibility came from political interference."

Maggie gasped and covered her mouth as she looked at Richard and then Sam. The judge removed her glasses and stared at Harper with a look that was far from pleased. Richard leaned over the rail toward Sam, and Diane slid closer, her face mildly registering her surprise.

"Do you have proof of these serious allegations?" the judge said.

"Your Honor, we have proof that Fred White, local congressman, made statements about Richard and Maggie McCafferty before these allegations were ever made by the state. We also have just received information that Fred White directed the executive director of the DSHS to investigate and remove Ryley McCafferty from my clients. His apparent quote from the DSHS reads, 'Maggie McCafferty is a junkie, and Richard McCafferty is a thief.'"

"Mister Roberts, is it true what Mister Lee has alleged? Did political interference from our local congressman, Fred White, result in these allegations against Maggie McCafferty?"

Mr. Roberts and the frumpy social worker appeared to shuffle their stance.

Busted.

"Ah, Your Honor, in fact, most allegations arise from a complaint, but I can assure you our filed petition for the dependent child Ryley McCafferty is valid. We have determined that if this child is not taken into custody, his health, safety, and welfare will be seriously endangered. We have reasonable grounds to believe from affidavits, and, yes, from the congressman, that a risk of imminent harm has been demonstrated. This lab report shows us she didn't take anything for forty-eight hours, which will not prevent Maggie McCafferty from leaving this courtroom—"

"Your Honor, I must object to this witch hunt. First, Children's Services has no evidence of any drug abuse. Nothing has been provided, and I request that this be stricken and that this petition be dismissed without merit."

"I tend to agree with Mister Lee," the judge said. "What I've heard here today does not lead me to believe that young Mister McCafferty is in any immediate danger. But with Children's Services, we take seriously all allegations—especially those of drug abuse. I would like to talk to this minor child, who is of an age to offer me a clear understanding of what's really going on. I'll be able to determine if this child is in fact at risk. I would like to meet with Ryley McCafferty in my chambers without the parents." The judge raised the flat of her hand when Mr. Roberts started to say something. "And no, Mister Roberts, Children's Services will not be allowed to attend the meeting.

Shall we say two this afternoon in my chambers?" The judge scribbled something on a paper in front of her.

"Your Honor, that brings us to another point. When the social worker arrived to take Ryley McCafferty into custody with the sheriff, he was not present but was told he was with his grandmother out of state—"

"Your Honor, Ryley McCafferty will be in your chambers at two." Harper was slick, the way he cut in. The social worker was apparently thrown by the ruling, as her eyes flashed, and she pursed her lips and then whispered angrily, like a child who didn't get her way. Mr. Roberts brushed his hand down in a gesture to hush her.

"Thank you, Mister Lee. I'll see young Ryley, and then you'll have my decision. We'll reconvene tomorrow morning at nine, and I'll give my ruling at that time." The fiery, stern judge smacked the gavel down like a gunshot and left the courtroom, her clerk following.

Harper reached past Richard and touched Maggie's shoulder. "It's not over yet, but it went well. Let's meet back in my office. I'll head over there now. Let's get Ryley back here, and it would be best if I met him first. Then I'll bring him over to meet the judge."

Sam clicked off his cell phone. "Marcie's on her way. She'll meet us at your office with Ryley."

Maggie staggered on shaky legs out of the courtroom behind Richard, saying nothing. She climbed into the truck and slumped back in the leather seat. "It went well, didn't it, Richard?"

He jammed the key in the ignition and then dropped his hand. He didn't look at her, but he did link his fingers with hers. All that fiery energy of his melted just a little, allowing a tiny hole through which she could enter.

They shared a comfortable silence as Richard drove. When they arrived, they rode up the elevator to Harper's private, quiet office and walked into the lavish conference room with mahogany walls and rich blue carpeting. Diane, Sam, and Harper were already there. Less than an hour later, the elevator dinged. Marcie, carrying a sleeping Kyla in her car seat, arrived with Ryley. Both of them were dressed in blue jeans and winter coats.

Richard didn't allow Ryley to go anywhere in the room except right into his arms. He held his boy tight.

"Dad, I can't breathe," Ryley muttered. Maggie touched the top of his head. When Richard released him, he hesitated only a second before taking a step toward Maggie and hugging her. She closed her damp eyes, holding on to this moment. It was a giant victory; she wanted to jump up and down and shout her joy to everyone, but she held it together for Ryley. Her glassy eyes locked on to Richard, and his handsome face softened with the connection. The love flowed from and into her heart—she loved him so much.

"Okay, everyone, grab a seat. June made coffee, muffins, and there's fruit. Help yourselves." Harper waved toward the back of the room as his secretary plunked down a tray on a large credenza that appeared to be dedicated for buffets, considering the food displayed. It was obvious this law firm didn't scrimp on anything. Maggie shuddered as the thought of who was footing the bill struck.

"Ryley, you and I'll be going to see a judge this afternoon," Harper said. "She wants to talk to you alone." He hurried to the head of the table and dumped his expensive dark jacket over the back of the thick leather chair.

Ryley's eyes widened. "Why does he want to talk to me? I don't want to talk to a judge."

Richard wrapped his arm around Ryley. "Hey, bud, it's okay. This judge is a she, and she's not buying this crap the social worker are trying to dish out. She just wants to ask you about these rumors going around about your mom taking pills and you not being looked after."

"But, Mom, Dad got you off everything. You're not taking anything anymore."

She wanted to go to him, but something held her across the table from him. She accepted the cup of coffee Diane poured for her. "You're right, Ryley, but those were pills the doctor prescribed after Lily was killed. I wasn't sleeping, and I was scared then. Now your dad and I are here. We're a family, and no one is going to separate us."

Harper sat at the head of the table, notepads and files stacked beside him. "Ryley, I want to go over a few things with you before you talk to the judge. She is going to ask you if we prepped you or tried to sway you in what you tell her. You just need to tell the truth about how your mom and dad love you and they look after you. Have they left you alone?"

"No. Dad's always doing something with me. And Mom, now that we're home, she's there… she sees me now." He blushed as he peeked over at her like he was wondering if she'd get mad at him for what he said. She offered him a smile of reassurance that appeared to ease some of his stress, as he breathed easier and his shoulders relaxed.

Harper put down his pen. "This is where we could have a problem, Ryley. I need to ask you about when you and your mom lived in town, after your parents split up. What happened? Did your mom leave you alone … forget to pick you up?"

Ryley's face colored and shifted his gaze down. "I don't want to get Mom in trouble."

She could only imagine how bad it was. Those days for her were a blur. It had taken everything inside of her to get out of bed, to get off the couch, to function. If anyone asked her to recall the details of the days after losing Lily and the months that followed, she wouldn't be able to tell them. Her face was wet, and she could barely see Ryley through the film of tears that coated her eyes. "I'm so sorry, Ryley."

An arm surrounded Maggie. Marcie's head touched hers.

Harper's voice cut the fog of pain that had cast a shroud over all of them. "Unfortunately, there are times during a loss that we lose our focus. I can only imagine the pain you must have all endured, but I need to make something clear here. Everyone needs to hold it together because someone out there is trying their damnedest to paint a picture of complete neglect. Someone knows details they shouldn't. Maggie, you took prescription medication, which is widely prescribed by doctors during times of stress. It's prescribed like candy, but that information is confidential. And, Maggie, this is not a time for recriminations, but we need to hear everything from Ryley before he goes in to see that judge. Maybe it would be best if I spoke with Ryley alone? Richard, Maggie?" Harper had a way of looking at her that had Maggie wanting to snap to attention.

She dried her face and scooted up her chair, looking across the table at Richard. His eyes softened, and he reached across the table, linking his fingers with hers. "No, Harper, we've come a long way. We can't hide from what happened. Ryley, your mom will be okay. Won't you, Maggie?"

She held tight to Richard and wiped her nose with her other hand using a tissue Diane handed her. She breathed deeply, finding her voice. "Ryley, don't be afraid. I don't remember much from those days, but I love you and always have. Losing Lily the way we did, it took something out of me. If it wasn't for you, I don't think I would have wanted to go on. Those pills drowned my pain. I cooked for you, cleaned the house, did your laundry, and I know now I was just getting through the day. We never talked, and for that I'm so sorry."

"It's okay, Mom. I knew you were sad. But you scared me. I had a bad dream, and I went into your room to wake you up. I even shook your arm, but you wouldn't wake up. My teacher knew I was upset at school, and Missus Johnson would come in and talk to me. She was really nice. She talked to me a lot after Lily died."

Maggie couldn't help the way her spine stiffened. Richard must have known it by the way his face hardened.

"Ryley, did you ever tell Missus Johnson your mom was taking medicine?" Richard asked. Ryley slumped in his chair the way a boy does when he thinks he's done something wrong.

"It's okay, Ryley," said Maggie. "I understand you needed someone to talk to, but it's really important for you to tell us everything you said to her. We won't get mad." She didn't know where those rational words came from. The hesitant glance Ryley fixed her with let her know he wasn't sure she really meant what she said.

He stuttered and then swallowed. His big eyes still held a touch of innocence she hadn't managed to shred. "I told her you took something to make you sleep, that you were always taking some kind of pill but I didn't know what it was."

"Ryley, how often did Missus Johnson pull you aside and talk to you?" asked Harper.

He shrugged his shoulders. He was just a boy, and he hadn't hung on to those important little details the way an adult would. "I don't know. Lots, I guess."

"Are we talking less than five times or more than ten?"

"I think more. Why does that matter?"

Harper simply laughed in exasperation. "I have a boy your age, and I forget sometimes what it was like to be a boy. Not much sticks in your head, and you sure don't remember details, do you?"

Ryley looked confused and furrowed his brows as if he was worried he was about to get in trouble.

"Relax. Now let's see how much I'm able to squeeze out of that head of yours. I bet I'll get lots." Harper surprised all of them with how animated he could be when he squeezed his hands around an imaginary head and slipped his tongue out the side of his mouth.

For the next thirty minutes, Harper dragged all kinds of details from Ryley's memory, and what they realized was that what he had said to an adult in the school, who should have known better, had been twisted. Ryley had told her about the police involvement before Lily was killed and how cool it had been to have police officers and DEA agents at their house. He said Mrs. Johnson had asked many times why they were there; were his dad and mom in trouble, did they have a greenhouse, what kind of things did they grow, were there guns in the house, did he know about drugs, and who were his parents' friends? Maggie blinked, and her gaze never left Richard's as she tried to absorb this absurdity.

"She asked me if I always had to look after Lily, and what were Mom and Dad doing when I had to watch her? If they left us overnight, how often, and did they leave me alone with Lily? When we were in her office one day, she said she knew Dan and his family. She also knew friends of his, one lady named Sandra. She asked if we had ever met. I didn't know her, but it was cool when we got to talk about Dan and how much fun he is."

Maggie wondered if the strangled sound she had made was just in her head. No one looked at her except Richard, whose eyes flashed as he made a tight fist with the hand he rested on the table. Harper snagged her attention when he got up and walked over to the door and opened it.

"Marcie, there's a great coffee shop on the main floor. Why don't you pop on down there with Ryley and just give us a minute here."

Harper was direct and didn't wait for an answer as he held open the door.

"Sure. Come on, bud. Let's see if they have something with chocolate." Marcie guided Ryley out, and Harper shut the door. Thankfully, Kyla was still sound asleep in her car seat on the floor behind Sam.

Everyone looked for a moment as if they were going to a funeral until Sam's phone rang.

"Sam here." He said nothing for a long time as he listened. He pinched the bridge of his nose between his thumb and index finger. "Get back to me when you find out more." That was all he said before disconnecting and slipping his cell phone into his dark jacket pocket.

"Wow." Harper strode to the credenza and poured a coffee, dumping in cream and sugar. He grabbed a muffin and took a bite. "I don't know about you guys, but sitting here listening to Ryley, I was starting to wonder who this Missus Johnson is in the school and what motivation she had to be questioning Ryley the way she did. A school district employee? *Highly* inappropriate."

Sam swiveled in the high-back leather chair. "Well, we now have a starting point. My phone call just now? It appears Alison Johnson's the sister-in-law to our esteemed congressman, Fred White. But wait, it gets better. Alison was friends with Sandra in high school, and guess who Sandra introduced her to? Dan McKenzie—he was her high-school sweetheart."

CHAPTER 45

Harper's face flushed a rosy color as he threw down his pen, pressing back in his chair, then gazing up at the ceiling as if trying to figure out why he was the butt of a sick joke. He removed his glasses and rubbed his eyelids with his thick fingers.

Diane spoke when she had something to say. Otherwise, she gave everyone her undivided attention, studying everyone in the room. It was her way of getting into their heads—generally putting her one step ahead of everyone. "We need Marcie here. She knows some of Dan's friends from high school. Maybe she could shed some light on that connection. There's one thing you and I both know, Sam; there really is no such thing as coincidence. This whole thing smells, and a big old red flag is waving."

Richard sat up straight and tall, his back pressed into the soft leather of the high-back chair. He breathed deeply and quietly in a way Maggie could only describe as eerie. What was he thinking? "Dan had a lot of girlfriends. There must a hundred women ready to do something… anything for him. This shouldn't be a surprise—but it is." Richard didn't move as he spoke. He didn't look at anyone. Instead he stared at a spot on the wall above Maggie's head. "Sam, whoever your contact is, they're good. Tell me this much. Am I way off base in thinking this personal attack against Maggie is payback? How likely is it that Sandra and Alison Johnson are still friends? What is their connection to me and whoever set me up for murder?" Richard was in his protective role again. He didn't look at Maggie as he addressed Sam.

"Richard, whatever this cosmic web, Dan McKenzie's involved. With Alison Johnson, and add in Fred White too: What's their agenda?" Sam sounded even more irritated than circumstances required, if such a thing were possible.

Harper tapped his pen on the table. Lost in deep thought, he appeared to be wrestling with something. "Okay, we've got a lot to work with. First things first; we have two hours before Ryley has to be at the courthouse. As I said, I'll take him, because it's imperative the judge know you two had no influence over him. Let's hope Ryley has enough common sense, Maggie, to not bring up those times he couldn't wake you. Is it enough to take your kid away? No, not technically. This whole situation against both of you has someone's personal agenda stamped all over it. Ryley's loved—I can see that. I'll talk to him about how to talk to the judge and what to expect; but judges are unpredictable, and they don't like to be second-guessed. I'm pretty sure this judge has not been influenced by Fred White, but that's always a gray area. Judges are politicians too, and Cooper is no exception. Maggie, Richard, go home. I'm going to take Ryley for lunch and then to the courthouse. Sam, I'm going to get you to tag along. We'll bring Ryley home after he meets with the judge. Then, tomorrow morning at nine, we'll have her decision."

CHAPTER 46

"Come in, young man, and have a seat." Judge Cooper was dressed casually in a pair of tan slacks and a cream-colored sweater. She closed the door, leaving Sam and Harper outside her chambers. In her mind, Ryley was old enough to understand right from wrong with clarity.

Her chambers were far from sterile as she guided him to one of the wing-back chairs beside an electric fireplace. It had a homey feel, giving her the peace to ponder her difficult decisions undisturbed. Ryley looked around as he fidgeted in the dark green chair. His feet barely touched the ground as he slid back and then forward, perching awkwardly on the edge as if he didn't know how to sit. His face paled when he finally glanced in her direction. She leaned back and propped her elbow on the arm of her chair.

"Take a deep breath, relax. I promise I won't bite." She didn't know if she was going about this the right way. Her experience with children was, admittedly, minimal in her newly appointed position. "Ryley, do you know why you're here?"

He nodded in response and appeared to have trouble swallowing. Those wide fearful eyes on any child were never good.

"I'm not going to hurt you. I'm on your side. I want to hear from you how you're doing. You've had a rough go of it. Can you tell me about Lily?"

Tears glazed his eyes and he folded both hands together in his lap. Looking down, he spoke so low she had to lean forward to hear his words. "She was my sister, but she couldn't do anything. She screamed a lot, banged her head."

"Did you spend a lot of time with her?"

"Mom and me and Lily were pretty much always together."

"I don't know any autistic children, so I can only imagine how difficult it must have been. I was an only child. My mom and dad were never around, so I never had a brother or sister to play with. I had nannies who raised me, a new one every few years. My parents traveled a lot."

"Didn't your parents love you?"

She nearly choked and wondered for a moment what he had picked up from that small snippet of her childhood. She knew she had been a burden to her parents and wondered, growing up, why they'd had her. "Oh, they loved me in their own way. It's just that sometimes, parents can't give you what you need. Mine were too busy with their own lives. And sometimes parents get an older brother or sister to look after the younger kids. Some parents even leave their kids alone, and no child should ever be left alone. Did you look after Lily for your mom?"

Ryley shrugged his shoulders. "Sometimes."

"What did your mom do when you looked after Lily?"

"Oh, we'd be outside playing, she'd go in the house and get something or answer the phone."

"Did your mom ever go out and leave you alone with Lily?"

"No, Mom was always with us. She was so worried about Lily, both of us. When she went to the bathroom, she'd leave the door open so she could hear us. When we were outside, Mom mostly took Lily inside with her. Lily would always get into stuff. She climbed on the counter and turned the tap on, and the water ran and ran and flooded the sink and floor. After that, Mom wouldn't let Lily be in any room alone for any long time. She'd color the walls if she found a pen you left out if you didn't stay with her."

"That's a heavy burden to put on you. To watch your sister all the time. How long would you watch her for your mom? A few hours?"

He frowned, and the skin at the bridge of his nose creased. "Is that a long time?"

She smiled. "It's like watching two of your favorite TV programs."

His eyes widened in horror. "No way, my mom would never leave us *that* long! She'd get a coffee and be back. Even when she talked on the phone, she stood over us. Why would you ask that?"

She realized something wasn't quite jibing. "Can I ask you what happened the day your sister died? Do you think you could tell me how come you were outside alone with her?"

His reddened eyes filled with such pain that for a moment, she wanted to take back the question.

"It was my fault."

"What was your fault?"

"That Lily ran out onto the road. I turned my back, and she was running. I couldn't catch her. I just turned for a second. I was mad because I wanted to play with my Gameboy. I didn't want to watch Lily."

"How long were you outside, watching your sister?"

"We just went out. She ran outside after she climbed down from the table. Dad told me to watch her till they came out. Sam and Marcie were there. We'd just ate."

"Oh, I see. What happened next?"

"I couldn't catch her. She never *takes off* like that. I yelled at her, and Dad ran past me to get her, but it was too late. That car came so fast, it hit her, and she fell so hard."

Ryley cried, covering his face with his hands. What a horrible thing to witness. She leaned forward and rubbed his arm. "Did your mom and dad blame you or tell you it was your fault?"

He couldn't speak, he was sobbing so hard.

"Do you think they blamed you?"

Ryley used his sleeve to wipe his tears, his nose. "Dad talked to me about it, and Dad cried. He felt so bad. He told me it wasn't my fault, that it was his job. He should have been with Lily and none of us knew she'd take off that far up to the road. She's never done that before."

Joan Cooper got up and opened her little bar fridge behind the desk to pull out a can of soda. She cracked it open and divided it in two glasses. She was glad now she'd sent her clerk out to buy soda before Ryley came. She handed him one of the glasses. "I hope you like root beer."

He took the glass and shrugged. As he sipped, they chatted about his Gameboy—and his favorite games. They talked for over an hour. He finally relaxed and told her about moving to town with his mom and those days after Lily, how his mom had looked right through him. His mom and dad fought a lot until his dad brought his mom home.

"Did you ever see your mom take medicine?"

Ryley was slumped in the large wing chair. "She had bottles of pills the doctor gave her, but she doesn't take them anymore."

The judge stretched out long bare fingers and examined them. "How is it at home now with your mom?"

Ryley shrugged. "It's better. I love being back home. She still cries sometimes, but she sees me now, and I know she loves me. Dad's always there. He won't let me do anything alone. He takes me out with him on the ATV, in his shop, and even to the site to work sometimes. He taught me to cook! And he listens to me. I love my mom and dad. Please don't take me away."

CHAPTER 47

Dressed once again in what Richard called their "court costumes" —dark suits, ties, and Maggie with heels, a long skirt, and makeup—they perched at the defense table with Harper. Diane and Sam sat in the gallery, the first row right behind Maggie and Richard. The court clerk announced Judge Cooper. She strode in, the long black robe fluttering behind her, and took her seat. She appeared distracted, maybe even a little tired. She didn't glance at either side.

Maggie held her breath in the silent courtroom as the judge scribbled down some notes, her reading glasses balanced on the end of her nose. Then she cleared her voice.

"At times like this, I'm going to make someone really happy or very sad, but make no mistake: My job here is to ensure the safety and protection of young Ryley McCafferty. Has Children's Services proven to me that Richard and Maggie McCafferty are endangering the welfare of their child? Well, they have some compelling statements, which I believe from my chat with young Master McCafferty happened at a horrific time for the entire family." She removed her glasses, this time focusing her entire attention on Richard and Maggie.

Maggie reached for Richard's hand and leaned into him.

"To lose a child, a severely disabled child, the way you did, I can only imagine must have been pure hell. As parents, it would test your faith along with your ability to cope. I tried to imagine what I would do if it were my child, but I couldn't. What I did hear is a story of a family who has struggled over insurmountable odds to pull itself back together. At some point, Missus McCafferty, you were taking prescription medication that did make you forgetful and left you detached from reality. Whether a doctor prescribes medication or not, it's up to a parent or individual to assume responsibility. I understand you're no longer taking these pills. That you and your husband recognized a problem, took action, and are now making positive steps to rebuild your family. So no, I'll not grant the order requested by Children's Services. What I am going to do, is order periodic blood and urine screening for Maggie McCafferty to ensure she remains drug free. Also, I'm appointing Jessica Shupe as court guardian. Jessica will, for the next month, monitor the situation at home with Ryley to ensure your family continues to make positive changes. A report will be filed with me at the end of that time."

She cracked the gavel and then slipped out of the courtroom. The butterflies that butted the walls of Maggie's stomach settled into lead when she realized what had happened.

Harper stood and leaned around Richard. "Not what I expected, but this is doable."

"Are you kidding me? They're treating my wife like a drug addict. Blood and urine tests for prescription medication? And a guardian, what the hell is that about? Is someone going to be in my house, putting us under a microscope to scrutinize every detail of our life?" Richard made no attempt to keep his voice down.

"Just be grateful they didn't remove him. If there's one thing I've learned over the years, judges are unpredictable, and they're influenced. From what I've heard so far, I've got a pretty strong suspicion some pressure came down on the judge. She's smart; she played it safe for both sides. And Jessica Shupe, who I know, has integrity. Comes from money, power, but make no mistake that if she sees something she doesn't like, she'll report it. For the next month, you guys really need to pull it together. She'll pick up on a show, so keep it real. With the stress of the trial coming up, you guys need to find a way to let go of the worry and anxiety so Ryley and the guardian don't pick it up. You're going to be facing one of the greatest challenges of your life."

Sam acted as the gatekeeper in his dark pants and leather jacket, scrutinizing the court clerk, the staff of the DSHS and the sheriff who sat off to the side, monitoring the activity inside the courtroom. He directed Harper, Maggie, Richard and Diane outside.

On the courthouse steps, Harper motioned them together. "I'll call Miss Shupe when I get back to the office. I suspect she'll want to come out right away. Go home and talk to Ryley. And Maggie? This may sound harsh, but let go of the personal hurt. Get the emotion out of the drug testing. Just think of it like visiting an unwelcome relative. This will be done soon. Don't fight it. It may not be fair, but we need to work with what we've got. We'll show them you're clean and demand an apology in the end. Sam, can you and Diane follow me back to my office? We need to focus on a game plan for Richard's trial. The DA sent over all their evidence, and I need you and Diane to start taking it apart."

"Shouldn't I be there, too?" Richard stuck his hands in the pockets of his dress pants. Maggie knew it was difficult for him to allow others to have control over his problems.

"Your time will come soon enough, Richard. First, I need to get Sam and Diane to go through the evidence. We'll meet up with you either later today or tomorrow. In the meantime, you need to be home with your wife and Ryley. Also, don't forget—the monitoring station needs to be advised where you're going and when. We only alerted them to court this morning, not my office. The last thing we need is for you to end up sitting in an eight-by-ten cell for the entire trial."

"Harper's right, Richard. Go home with Maggie. Tell Marcie I'll be by later this afternoon to pick her up." Sam shoved on his dark glasses. Marcie had stayed at Richard and Maggie's with Kyla and Ryley.

The walk to Richard's truck gave Maggie a quiet moment to digest the outcome of the morning's hearing. Did she deserve to be tarnished this harshly? She couldn't help but feel like a failure to her child—an outcast. If it hadn't been for Richard, she'd still be downing those pills morning and night. How many other women out there survived year after year on pills for depression and stress to aid them in coping with the harsh realities of this world? None of them had Children's Services trying to take their kids away.

Maggie couldn't shake the feeling that this felt like some personal payback from Sandra and Dan—but that was crazy. Wasn't it? When she looked over at Richard as they drove in silence, she wondered if he thought the same thing.

"Richard, this can't be a coincidence. If Missus Johnson dated Dan, is still friends with Sandra and is related to Fred White, then add to that Fred White's daughter calling me a junkie and you a thief— there is just *far* too much here to be a coincidence."

Richard glanced at her from behind dark shades. She couldn't see his eyes but, from the look on his face, she could tell he too had his suspicions.

"That's one angle Sam's investigating. One, what is Fred White is really up to? And two, this Missus Johnson, if she's still friends with Sandra and carries a torch for Dan, is most likely neck deep in whatever shenanigans they've still got going on."

"Richard, the DSHS knows Sandra's a dealer, and they know about her illegal activity. For God's sake, a kid died on her watch. She had bags of marijuana in her house, dumped around these disabled kids, yet they gave her a contract. What the hell is Children's Services doing?" She swallowed the bile that rose just thinking of how the special needs kids' rights had been violated.

"Maggie, you and I both know the DSHS isn't about protecting the rights of the special needs. It's so deeply entrenched with predators who know how to work the system and are in it for money. They know exactly the right words to say to parents, politicians... everyone. We knew that with Lily; long before Sandra came on the scene. Anyone affiliated with the government is likely corrupt and not in the game for the true purpose of helping our kids. The government throws out money to their friends. No one ever knows what really goes on behind the scenes, because people out there just don't give a shit...." He paused as he gripped the wheel so hard she wondered if it would bend in two. "I mean, I know there are some in the system who truly do care; but you know what? They know what's going on. They know about these pedophiles, predators and abusers of the system, but they won't say anything to rock the boat. Sam already spoke with someone with the DSHS, and they told him, quote, 'We know there's something illegal going on, but we don't want to know.' Nice, huh?"

"So what now?" Maggie said. Richard turned off the truck, the screen door burst open and Daisy bounded down the stairs with Ryley tagging along. Marcie carried Kyla on her hip, her long hair fluttering in the breeze as she stood on the porch, waiting.

Richard slid his arm over the back of the seat and faced Maggie. "We need to destroy the case the DA has against me and find out who really killed Dan. My equity has dried up, and I can't sell the remaining houses. The big bad wolf—the bank—is knocking on the door. We have a lot to do.... I don't know about you, but I think it's time we start fighting back." Richard leaned over and kissed Maggie before sliding out of the truck and catching Ryley as he flew into his arms.

The powerful bond between father and son was a beautiful thing to watch. Maggie climbed out and walked around the truck, placed her hand on the hood and paused. Marcie kept her distance, standing so proud and silent. With the way she watched Maggie; for the first time, Maggie saw the hurt that had been erected like a wall between them. It had been entirely her doing. Maggie shivered. Her head was clearer and she could remember all the hateful words she'd spewed at Marcie. *You don't deserve a child! It's your fault Lily's dead. You brought this trouble into our life with your selfish lust for Dan, wanting some predator we all saw was worthless and screwed everybody. Damn you to hell!* She'd said it the day they'd buried Lily.

That emptiness in her stomach changed from a burning lump to a tight knot. Would Marcie ever forgive her?

CHAPTER 48

"What do you make of that judge's decision?" Sam asked as he and Diane joined Harper in his large, richly furnished office. Valuable oil paintings adorned the walls, and a palatial, well-organized, desk with rich black leather chairs took up a large portion of the room.

Harper loosened his blood-red tie before heaving himself into his executive black leather chair. He let out a heavy sigh and swiveled to face the floor-to-ceiling plate-glass window overlooking the ocean.

Sam was intrigued by Harper; he was a hard man to read. When he was with the DEA, he had hated him. He was a shrewd lawyer with the ability to get off any scumbag who could pay his fee.

Wasn't it funny? he thought. *When the tables are turned and you're the one on the wrong side of the law, you need this exceptional man's help.* Maybe that was why Sam was seeing a side of this man he hadn't known existed. He was a brilliant, flawed man who did his job well. Maybe he did have a conscience after all. Maybe, when this was all over, he'd sit Harper down and find out why he defended and helped guilty sons of bitches get off.

Harper continued to gaze out the window while he spoke. "I've never seen anything like it. Let's be frank: Ativan is one of the most widely prescribed medications in the US. Sleeping pills, too. I bet the judge herself has taken them a time or two. To paint Maggie as they have, as an addict, is unfair. In one breath, a doctor prescribes them to help you, but we have a congressman who appears to have used his influence to tar and feather Maggie. If something like this went to the state supreme court, they'd reverse this judge's decision. The state's trying to say she abused these prescription drugs, but they have nothing to back it up. Maggie, Richard and Ryley suffered a tragedy. For each of them to get up in the morning and keep going—I applaud them for pulling their family together after losing Lily.... They deserve a medal.

"Any fool can see how much they love Ryley. I don't get it. For the state to single out the McCaffertys the way they have makes no sense. There are children, in this area alone, left with parents who aren't fit. Parents who go out for the night and leave kids alone so they can get high, get drunk and party with friends. Kids who can't have friends over because Mom and Dad are doing something no one can find out about—growing, cooking, or drying whatever drug of choice they're doing and selling. Then there are those parents so doped up or drunk they can't look after themselves, let alone a child."

Harper swung around and, in a fraction of a second, Sam saw something reflected from this hard man that had him liking Harper in an odd, kindred way. Then it was gone, and the shrewd lawyer was back.

Harper gave his full attention to both Sam and Diane as he continued. "No, I have to say the judge was pressured. My guess is from the congressman, but no way will she ever admit it. She didn't rule for the state, so I guarantee Mister White is most likely kicking down her door as we speak. She covered herself, made it look like she was supporting the state with these ridiculous restrictions. Smart lady, knows there's no ethical way she could remove Ryley. Anyway, we've got work to do. The ruling we're going to have to live with. Ryley stays at home and Maggie will have to pee into a cup a few times this month, which I'm certain won't be an issue. Will it?"

Sam and Diane both looked at each other. "Maggie's a strong lady. She's my friend, and she has walked through hell. She'll do it, and she won't fail any drug test. I'll make sure of it." Diane spoke with such certainty that the tiny worry that flickered on Harper's face slipped away.

"What about this guardian? You said you know her?" Sam asked.

"Are you asking if she's in the judge's pocket or the state's?" Harper leaned on his forearms, his black silk jacket now draped across the back of his chair.

"Well, yes; I guess I'd like to know if she's dirty or can be bought. All of it. What exactly is she going to be doing? How much of Richard and Maggie's privacy does she get to invade? Are there lines of impropriety?" If there was one thing Sam had learned the hard way, it was to not leave things to chance, to cover his bases and to know where everyone was coming from.

"She's going to spend time with Ryley and talk to him, find out how he's feeling and get a good idea from him what's going on in the home. She'll observe Maggie and Richard when she's there, see how they respond and interact with Ryley. She'll probably speak to friends and teachers. In essence, she's going to write a report on the parenting skills of Richard and Maggie McCafferty."

For the first time since Sam had known Diane, she appeared to be thrown. As her eyes widened, she shifted her bottom in the dark leather chair. She turned to Sam, her eyebrows furrowed deeply, creating wide lines at the bridge of her nose. "Could anyone pass? Seriously?" Irritation colored Diane's tone.

Harper blinked and simply shook his head. "This is not an ideal situation, but from what I've heard in the past about Jessica Shupe, she's ethical and independent; she doesn't work for an agency. She truly does care for children. We need to hope for the best. I'm pretty sure Fred White's reach doesn't include Jessica, but let's keep an eye out for any problems."

He clapped his hands together. Then he picked up his pen and pointed at Diane. "Let's move on. We have a lot to do and very little time. Go talk to Ryley's principal at school. Hammer him on what Fred White's daughter said to Ryley about Richard being a thief and Maggie a drug addict. Find out his take on it and whether he's spoken directly with Fred White. We need to show a link. I suspect Fred White is somehow behind this agenda to discredit Maggie as a witness. So find out why."

He wielded his pen like a staff, pointing the tip straight at Sam. "You need to dig and find out everything about Fred White and what connection he has in all this."

Sam interrupted him. "And we also need to focus on finding out what Dan was involved in. He was into so many fraudulent land deals and they always had some link to drugs. He's got Richard over a barrel financially, he's one step from bankruptcy. Richard has no life insurance on Dan, so Richard has no financial motive in that regard. His only chance to get the money Dan owes him is if Dan stays alive. But on the other hand, with Dan dead, it'll be easier to get whoever Dan appointed as executor to agree to sell the property… maybe."

"Who's the executor?" Diane asked.

"Dan's mom." Sam needed to talk with Marcie to get a feel for the woman. Someone had created that monster? He could only imagine what she was like. "I'm going to poke around, find out what all Dan had his hands into, what he was really doing. I think what may happen is that we'll find out who really killed Dan."

Harper pressed back into his chair, manipulating the pen between his fingers. Then he waved at Sam to dismiss all he'd said. "That would be helpful if time was on our side. Our course of action is time sensitive. We need to focus on destroying all the state's evidence, as shaky as it is. You're going to do it my way."

Sam's cell phone interrupted what he realized was about to become a tense standoff with someone who had his own ideas of how the investigation should run. It irritated the hell out of him, so much so that it took a second to register in his brain the number displayed and who was calling. "Hey, Frank, what've you got?" He was silent for a moment as the other man spoke. His gut twisted as he gripped the chair with his other hand, glancing at Diane and then Harper. "I'm on my way," he said.

As he punched the button to end the call, his eyes remained glued with Harper's. "That was Frank Gerrard, a friend of mine, the videographer I brought in from the FBI crime lab in Seattle this morning. He found something on the tape. It's been altered."

CHAPTER 49

Frank's computer equipment had taken over Sam's office. For the past hour, Frank had shown and re-shown the piece of footage, which was just over a minute long. "There's no time code on the video, and every second of video you see contains thirty frames. I don't know how I caught it. Fluke, really, see? It's just a slight shadow in the edging." Frank pointed a long, bony finger to the laptop screen. "See? Look where you see Richard's face. That second of video was thirty frames to alter, but that one spot by his right ear doesn't meet the background. Whoever did this was good; this wasn't an amateur."

"I still don't understand," Sam said. "How did they get Richard's face on this video?"

Frank was far from a geek. His prescription dark-framed glasses were always new, the height of fashion, accentuating his striking oval face and his short, stylish brown hair. He dressed well, even when he tried to dress down in something casual. He was a good-looking single guy. Sam was sure he played it up with the ladies.

"Well, for one, Richard has to be on another tape, so there have to be other videos. Whoever did this would have copied the frames and overlaid them, altering the lighting to match this video. I can tell you this much: it took time to pull this together. Oh, and another thing:

There's no metadata or timestamp on this video, which makes it even more difficult to find out whether it's fake. If you get me the original video, I can take a look at the binary data. Everyone has a signature. It may give us an idea of who altered it." His grin told Sam that Frank was almost patting himself on the back.

Sam widened his eyes at Diane and shook his head. She too knew what a conceited, arrogant bastard Frank could be at times, but he was damn good at what he did.

"How do you know it's a copy and not the original?" Sam asked. He didn't want to tip Frank off, but he had specifically requested the original video from the DA.

"Well, duh, any second-year videographer could see it was a copy."

Sam dialed the DA's office. "This is Sam Carre. I'm working with Harper Lee on Richard McCafferty's defense."

"What can I do for you?" uttered a distracted young male.

"Well, for one thing, I asked for the original video from the surveillance of the crime scene, but our videographer has just informed me you sent a copy."

There was silence on the other end. Sam could hear papers rustling before the ADA roughly cleared his throat. "I'll have to get back to you."

Sam could feel Frank's arrogant eyes burning into him when he disconnected his phone.

"They're screwing with you," Frank said. "Welcome to the dark side."

CHAPTER 50

"I'm Jessica Shupe, the court-appointed guardian for Ryley McCafferty."

Maggie was on her knees in the winter garden with a handful of weeds no one had cleared during the fall now piled on the ground beside her. She jumped up and wiped the dirt from her hands on her torn blue jeans. Her heart sank a little more as she glanced at her stained sweatshirt, one of the comfortable, unpresentable ones she reserved for yard work, never for entertaining.

Maggie struggled to find something to ease her anxiety and calm her rattled brain—to explain to this woman that she didn't always look like this. Because this lady not only hadn't called first, which Maggie suspected was meant to rattle her, but also gazed at Maggie as if she were a nobody.

Maggie extended her trembling hand out to the other woman to shake. Jessica crossed her arms in front of herself and watched as Maggie dropped her hand. As if what she'd done had just crossed some line. She flushed, and in a moment of panic, she tripped over the bucket of weeds beside her and fell on her backside. She wanted to cry but scampered up on her knees and rose with all the dignity she could muster. The screen door rattled.

"Maggie, I was wondering if you could give me a hand… oh, I didn't know anyone was here." Marcie stepped lightly down the stairs, holding her head high, her light blue dress shimmering as she strode with confidence—confidence Maggie would have killed for right about now—toward Jessica. Her strength oozed as she invaded Jessica's space and stuck her hand out, daring the woman not to take it. For a moment, Maggie was sure the other woman was rattled. She blinked and appeared to hesitate before accepting Marcie's hand.

"I'm Marcie. Who are you?"

Jessica shot a puzzled glance at Maggie before turning back to answer this assertive woman. "I'm Jessica Shupe, the court-appointed guardian for Ryley."

"Oh, well, it's nice to meet you. We've been looking forward to it. I didn't realize you were coming over. Maggie made a fabulous salad for lunch. It would be great if you could join us."

"No, that's not necessary. I'm here to see Ryley."

Maggie could feel the air thicken between the two women, like a pissing contest. She glanced at Marcie and then Jessica, two strong, determined women, and wanted to shrink back.

"Well, unfortunately, we sit down as a family and eat together. If you check your watch, you'll see it's lunch time. You can join us at the table while we eat, and then you can spend time with Ryley after lunch. Or is it your intention to disrupt the peaceful mealtime of this family, sneaking in unannounced, maybe to catch everyone off guard?"

Maggie gasped and instantly covered her mouth with her grimy hand. Jessica re-crossed her arms and stuck out her jaw as she subtly tilted her head as if to concede to Marcie.

"I guess I'll be joining you for lunch."

"Very good," Marcie said. "I'll see to it another place is set for you. Oh, and, Miss Shupe, Richard and Maggie are good people. Whether you believe it or not, please don't play games." Marcie held her head high and raised her eyebrows at the woman.

"My interest is Ryley and I won't have my authority undermined."

Maggie felt herself shrink back even though she didn't move a step. She'd never seen this side of Marcie—in control and unwilling to cut this woman any slack.

"Well, just remember this is about a boy and his well-being, not the pocketbook of some politician or the mind games in how you usurp his parents." Marcie turned before the woman could respond.

"Maggie, honey, you should have seen what Kyla did before I put her down for her nap! She pulled herself up to the coffee table and took two steps, bouncing with her magical, toothless smile." Marcie stepped around Jessica and linked arms with Maggie, guiding her into the house. The entire way, Maggie could feel Jessica burning a hole in her back. For the life of her, she couldn't figure out what she'd done to this woman, who appeared to have already judged her as the unfit parent she prayed she wasn't. She hoped she'd have the chance to repair the damage with Ryley.

All the way inside, Marcie chatted and nudged Maggie along.

The kitchen table was set for five, and Maggie scrambled to think who else was coming. Daisy was curled up on her doggy bed by the unlit woodstove. She lifted her head and trotted over to Maggie.

"Go wash up, Maggie," Marcie whispered conspiratorially as she hugged her so Jessica couldn't hear.

Daisy growled as if she had just realized there was an intruder.

"Daisy, *enough*," Maggie said. Her loveable dog gazed up at her with those mud-brown eyes. "I'm going to get cleaned up. I'll be back." Maggie forced a smile that felt stiff and artificial as she slipped past Jessica, who now wandered the kitchen with her arms crossed. She appeared to be studying every brick and item for cleanliness. For a moment, Maggie wondered if she'd slip on a white glove and check for dust.

Maggie stood straighter and watched the intruder with fresh eyes. "Miss Shupe, there's a bathroom down the hall if you'd like to wash up." She hurried out of the kitchen before Jessica responded, and Daisy followed. Maggie stopped outside Richard's home office at the base of the stairs. Richard was engrossed in whatever he was reading. "Richard, Jessica Shupe's here. She's staying for lunch."

He dropped the papers he was holding and stood up. She knew that look, but he handled the curveballs people threw better than she. "I didn't know she was coming."

"Neither did I. Guess she decided to surprise us, catch us off guard, maybe while we're neglecting our kid. But have faith, Marcie had the first shot."

That made him smile.

"I'm going to wash up. Apparently she doesn't like dirt." Maggie held up her hands coated in garden dirt and flashed him a wicked smile.

Richard didn't seem to mind. He wrapped his arm around her waist and kissed her nose. "Don't forget that spot." He patted her bottom.

Maggie hurried up the stairs and glimpsed Ryley lying on his bed, playing with his Gameboy. She stopped outside his room. "Hey, Ryley, put it away. Lunch's ready. Before you go down, Miss Shupe's here. She's going to stay for lunch."

Ryley bolted straight up on his bed. Then he jumped up as if he had been caught doing something he shouldn't. "Mom, what do I say to her?"

She walked straight toward him and hugged him, keeping her dirty hands off his dark blue shirt. "It's okay. Just be you, relax. Remember what your dad said. Speak honestly about us and how much we love each other. Don't rehearse anything. Don't make something up. Take a deep breath. It'll be okay. Marcie's downstairs with her; so is your dad. I'm going to wash up because she doesn't like dirt." Maggie walked Ryley to the stairs and sent him down with Daisy. She offered him an encouraging smile and gestured with a sweep of her hand to keep moving. He hesitated just once at the bottom of the stairs, and then Richard must have seen him.

"Here's my champ. Come on in here, Ryley."

He hurried into the kitchen, most likely into the safety of Richard's arms, Daisy right behind him.

Maggie quickly washed up, including the dark streak of dirt across her nose and cheek. She pulled on a clean purple sweater, a newer pair of blue jeans and ran a brush through her hair. She felt the chords of the executioner's song ring as she went down the stairs into the kitchen, sitting in the empty seat between Richard and Marcie. Jessica glanced up, but her bland expression was filled with something that had Maggie leaning a little closer to Richard.

Richard broke the spell as he passed Jessica the plate of sandwiches. "Jessica, dig in. There's lots here."

Maggie whispered to Marcie just as she shoved a forkful of salad into her mouth. "Where's Sam? Isn't he joining us?"

She pressed a cloth napkin to the corner of her mouth. "No, I don't expect him till dinner."

"But I thought you set a place for him?" She didn't know why it mattered, but she couldn't let it go.

"Not for him. To welcome a stranger." Marcie smiled.

"Oh, okay."

CHAPTER 51

Harper and Diane leaned over Frank as he swiveled in Sam's cheap tan office chair and showed them the shadow again; and where Richard's face had been pasted into the video. "If we go back and look at the person who's dragging Dan, he appears the same height and weight. But it's dim, not close up, so It's hard to tell. But look here." Frank tapped a few keys on the keyboard. "When I blow this up, see the watch, that band around his wrist?"

Harper, Sam, and Diane squinted at the low-quality color video to see what he was trying to show them. The man wore black gloves and a long-sleeved dark shirt, but his left wrist was exposed and there was some type of cloth bracelet, green and white, around his wrist.

"What is that?" Harper asked.

"That is what is called a friendship bracelet, to represent a deep bond with someone. Best friends wear them to signify the powerful link they share."

Diane crossed her arms, her jean jacket pulled at the seams in back. "As far as I know, I've never seen anything like that on Richard."

"What about the original video? Have we heard back from the DA?" Harper said. He hadn't changed, still wearing the same dark Armani suit.

"Yeah, just before you got here. The DA called, said we do have the original copy the police gathered at the scene, but they're sending their copy over just to be sure there wasn't a mix-up."

"Smart, so he can show the judge how they've bent over backward to assist us." Harper pointed to the screen. "So can you testify this video is in fact a fake and show proof it's been altered?"

Frank swiveled around in the chair again, much like a bored teenager. "That's what I do best, and you've just had this piece of evidence thrown out, which throws a monkey wrench into the state's case."

There was a soft tap on the office door. A thin woman with red hair tied back in a ponytail, dressed in black casual slacks and a blazer, stood in the open doorway. "I'm Assistant District Attorney Melanie Jackson. I have our copy of the video. Did I just hear correctly that you have evidence the video's been altered?"

Harper and Sam glanced at one another. Tipping their hand to the DA was not a smart move, but neither was leaving the office door open for anyone to walk in and hear. Damn, he needed to get a bell or something on the front door.

"Yes, I'm afraid we've discovered this tape's been altered."

Frank slid his chair across the cheap industrial carpet. "Is that the only other copy of this video?" He pointed to the small cassette in her hand.

The woman appeared far from shy. She stepped up to the computer and handed the video to Frank. She stood over him and watched the screen while he loaded the video and forwarded to the last one-second frame. What Frank did next on the keyboard to bring up codes and text, Sam wasn't sure, but he leaned back, sighed and then swiveled the squeaky office chair to face the cute ADA. "Well, Miss ADA, this here's a copy, too. So where's the original?"

Her face took on a hint of pink. As Frank turned his hard pretty-boy gaze with all its charm on her, she started to stammer. "Look, the video you have was taken right from the crime scene. You're obviously confused."

Sam took a step back from the group and leaned against the side of his desk. "Well, what's clear is whoever altered this video planted a copy to be found. I'm pretty sure we just blew a big wide hole right dead center through the middle of your case. My question to you, Miss Jackson, is this: Is the DA prepared to launch a new investigation into who planted the evidence? Because I bet they're one and the same, and who really killed Dan."

Melanie was focused on the screen and the highlighted spot where Richard's face was pasted. She peered at Sam before pulling out her cell phone. She said not a word while she waited. "This tape's a copy, too. They have some tech here, and the security video was altered. He's going to testify someone pasted Richard McCafferty's face into the footage."

Whoever she spoke to on the other end was obviously in charge. She shut her eyes for a second and pressed her fingers to her forehead. "Okay, I understand, sir. I'm on my way back." She disconnected her cell. "I need my copy of the tape back."

Frank stuck the tape back in its plastic case, held it up to Melanie, and winked as he deliberately slid his finger over her hand. She frowned as she snatched it away.

"So, are you reopening the investigation?" Sam didn't move from where he leaned against the desk.

She shook her head, holding it high. "The DA wants our own people to take a look at the video. As it stands, we're still prepared to go ahead with the case. We still have enough evidence against your client to prosecute." She stepped around Frank and left as quickly as she had come.

Sam was surprised, but at the same time, he wasn't. He knew when you built a case as high profile as this, the last thing the DA wanted was to admit they had the wrong guy. Instead of doing the right thing and reopening the investigation, they were playing the same old game they always had—trying to save face.

"Sam, we need to find out who planted that tape. And I mean *we*. Diane, can you talk to whoever was at the crime scene and processed the forensics? Find out their take. Sam, Frank, great catch. We've blown a hole wide open in their case. If we can't convince the DA to look at other suspects, we have no choice but to get ready. We go to trial in less than a week. We have all their key evidence, or what they've sent over.

We need to sit down with Richard and go through his movements. They've dissected his statement line by line, they have a detailed description of his movements for the week prior and they have his cell phone records. They've talked to a lot of people. The unidentified 911 call came from an untraceable cell phone. We need to find out who she is. You find her for me. I don't care how you do it—just find her." Harper buttoned his jacket as he glanced at Sam and then Diane.

Sam rubbed his chin. He really hated not being in charge. "And then what? Find out why she lied, where the body is? It won't be that easy, Harper. But, again, I'm going to say it; maybe what we'll find is who really killed Dan."

CHAPTER 52

"You know that saying, Richard, how you can't go home again?" Maggie rested her head on Richard's bare chest. He soothed her, tracing tiny circles up and down her arm.

"I know you, Maggie, sometimes better than you know yourself. Memories are too much sometimes, but this is our home, and you want to leave."

She propped her chin on her hands where they were touching him. He was so hard sometimes. This time, he didn't shut down. "Not you, I love you. I mean us. Just leave, start over somewhere else. Let's just walk away from everything."

He smoothed back her hair and gently tucked it behind her ears. "No, we aren't going to run away. This is our home. You and I are going to get up in the morning, and we're going to keep going. We'll get through this."

She brushed her toe against his ankle bracelet. It was an ugly reminder of what they faced. "You must think I'm a coward. I don't want to lose you. I'd rather run and hide with you and Ryley than face them locking you up for the rest of your life."

He wrapped both arms around her and pulled her closer. "It won't come to that, I promise you. We'll beat this. You need to have a little more faith in Sam, Diane, and Harper. That wasn't me on the tape. They've already discovered it was altered." The way he said it, with the slight hitch in his tone, she knew those words were merely for her benefit. "I won't leave you and Ryley, whatever it comes down to."

She didn't know how long she lay there, waiting for Richard's breathing to even out. How she felt about him when he wrapped his arms around her, the way he kissed her when he was weary, every moment they were together now was bringing them closer to a place she didn't know was possible. She didn't know if he understood how he made her feel now. Coming back home, they'd both changed into different people, and she didn't know how she deserved his love.

She didn't have a restful sleep, but when she dragged herself downstairs in the morning, the entire crew was there: Sam, Diane, Harper, and Marcie with Kyla. Maggie peered at Daisy, her faithful dog, lying on her doggy bed in the corner by the woodstove. With all the stress of the last few days, she hadn't noticed how slow she was getting. Her food dish didn't appear to have been touched since yesterday, and her water dish was still full. "Richard? Did you let Daisy out?"

"No, she didn't want to go."

Maggie crouched down and smoothed the rough fur on Daisy's head. "Come on, Daisy, let's go outside." The dog struggled to get up and then shook. Her long nails clattered across the floor as they went outside, and each step appeared full of effort. Her tail hung straight down. "Come on. It's okay, girl."

Maggie encouraged her down the steps and then watched her dog as she walked around and then lifted her head to sniff the air. Maggie walked a little farther on the grass, encouraging Daisy to follow. She told herself Daisy was old. She'd perk up. Maybe she needed to change her food. Finally, Daisy found a spot and squatted, but it was so brief Maggie wondered if it was for her benefit as Daisy wandered slowly up the stairs and waited at the door. Maybe it was a virus.

"Do you want to go back and lie down?" Daisy gazed at the door, waiting for it to magically open, but then she looked up and gave Maggie a pitiful wag of her tail. That was encouraging.

Maggie followed Daisy in the house and watched her dog slump back to bed.

"She's an old dog, Maggie. She'll be okay. Just let her be for now." Richard poured her a cup of coffee. "We ate already, and Ryley's already gone to school. Do you want some eggs?"

"I'll do it."

Richard lingered for a moment until she looked up at him. She forced a tight smile. He was so strong and together. Why couldn't she be more like him? The depression and blue days had snuck up on her. She hadn't seen them coming. Maybe it was waking up with all this uncertainty; and she still carried Lily's aura, her tiny little being with her. She could see her face as clear as day. She swallowed and tried to push away the giant ache that shredded her heart in two.

Richard squeezed her shoulders in his way of letting her know he knew what she was thinking. "One day at a time, Maggie. Eat and then join us. Harper got the 911 tape. We need to listen and figure out who made the call."

He was good at distracting her, but for some reason, the pain was a giant hole right in her center. Today—this morning—it felt as wide as a crater.

She blinked hard to stop the tears that burned her eyes. She cracked an egg in the frying pan then popped two slices of bread into the toaster. Richard rubbed her back and then traipsed into the living room, where Sam was hooking up computer equipment. Maggie leaned against the counter and listened to the low chatter, rustling papers, and eagerness of this amazing group of friends, here to build a strong case, brick by brick, to save her husband.

Maggie dumped her plate in the dishwasher after she choked down breakfast and wandered into the room just as the 911 tape played.

The operator came on. "What's your emergency?"

A young woman's hysterical voice trembled on the other end. "Help, I think he's going to kill him."

"Who, ma'am? What's your address?"

"Richard's shouting at Dan. They're arguing. Please, come quick. Richard's going to kill him. Oh my God, he just pulled out a gun. He shot Dan!" the young lady screamed.

The operator came on again. "Ma'am, are you safe? Is this Richard still there, and did you say he has a gun?"

"He can't see me, but he's still there. I'm hiding, but I need to get out of here before he sees me."

"Ma'am, what's your name? What's your location?"

Maggie gazed at her husband, who frowned and held up his hand when she started to speak. Marcie stared at Sam and said not a word as they listened to the woman rattle off the address before hanging up.

"Well, that was interesting. Anyone recognize the voice?" Diane slipped off her jean jacket and tossed it over the back of the sofa.

Kyla cooed, waved her chubby little arms and kicked her legs in her pink terry sleeper. She was wrapped in a purple and white crocheted blanket and rested on her mother's hip. Marcie swayed the way a mother does to keep her baby content.

"Marcie?" Something passed between Sam and Marcie before she shrugged, frowned, and patted Kyla's back.

"I don't know. It's familiar, but…"

"There was a lot of noise in the background, kind of hard to hear, to make out who it is." Richard sounded irritated.

"That's traffic you're hearing, Richard. A lot of traffic." Diane never turned around while she adjusted something on the computer.

"Traffic? How? The property's off the highway. It's isolated. No way you can hear that kind of noise. Play it again, Diane." Richard hovered closer to the computer.

They played the recording about a dozen times. As Maggie listened, she hoped there was something about the voice that would be familiar, but there wasn't. Marcie watched her and said nothing.

"There's no way that call was made from the Gardiner property. It's off the highway and still too isolated for that kind of traffic. We know the number came from a disposable cell. We need to find the young woman who made that call." Sam appeared to be strategizing something as he eyed both Diane and Richard.

Someone pounded on the back door.

"I'll get it." Sam hurried to the back door and, a minute later, reappeared with a good-looking, trendy, guy oozing so much confidence that Maggie had to take a step back.

"Maggie, Richard, this is Frank, my techy FBI guy."

Frank reached for Maggie's hand and grinned. "Charmed."

Maggie yanked her hand away and Richard stiffened beside her.

"Hey, Diane, heard you need some help." Frank fairly swatted Diane away from the computer and took over the tape. Whatever he was doing on the computer, his fingers were flying over the keyboard. Diane stood behind him and frowned the way a big sister does at her irritating younger brother.

"Frank, can you filter out the background noise so we can hear the woman's voice clearly?" Harper leaned against the table and looked down at the computer.

"No problem. Why don't you all take a break and give me a minute to clean it up?"

"Marcie, we're going to rely a lot on you here. You knew Dan's friends, the ones he hung around with, some from his past. Do you remember an Alison Johnson from high school? She was Sandra's friend and apparently dated Dan back then."

Maggie saw Marcie glance at Sam and sensed something odd pass between them. One thing Maggie had noticed recently was how unusually quiet and distant Marcie had become. Kyla started fussing as she rubbed her eyes.

"I'll take her and put her down for a nap," Sam said. He touched Marcie's cheek, hesitating only a second before taking his daughter.

"Maggie, is that playpen still set up in Richard's office?"

"Yeah, Sam. No sense moving it."

Sam hurried away as Kyla started to fuss. Marcie wandered into the kitchen.

Maggie followed. "Is this coming between you and Sam?" she asked. How would she even begin to make up for all the hurtful things she'd said to Marcie? She wanted to say she was sorry, to take everything back, but she didn't know how.

"No. This is hard, though. No matter where Sam and I are, talking about Dan and his friends still hurts him. It hurts me to talk about when we were together. It's a part of my life that's over. Sam's determined to bring him down. I guess that's his right. I've passed it over and off me." She raised her hand up. "You ever heard that phrase, let go and let God? Well, that's where I am. At some point after you've done all you can, you have to step back. That's where I am with bringing Dan down. I mean, for God's sake, the man's dead." Marcie walked over to the sink with such an odd look on her face.

"Marcie, I never apologized for what I said to you that awful day we buried Lily…. I never meant one of those hateful words or—"

Marcie touched her arm so kindly. "I know, Maggie. I never believed you did. It's okay." Marcie leaned against the sink and looked away. "Alison Johnson was Dan's high-school girlfriend. I didn't know her. She was a friend of Sandra's. Dan's type back then—big boobs, hourglass figure; a body I would have given my right arm for at the time. Sandra introduced her and Dan. They dated for a few years, I think. Why would you want to know about her?"

"She works at Ryley's school," Richard interjected. "Wow, she's really changed. Overweight troublemaker now. She's been questioning Ryley for some time about Maggie." Richard rested his hands on Maggie's shoulders. "She's related to Fred White," he continued. "White's daughter painted a really ugly picture to Ryley of me and Maggie. Alison's affidavit in court, the fact she was friends with Sandra and that Sandra still has a contract for respite care, doesn't all of this sound too coincidental? Like someone put together a plan to nail me, maybe get back at me and Maggie."

Marcie leaned against the sink and narrowed her eyes. "Yes, it does, Richard, but let me ask you this: Why has the focus been put on just you and Maggie? I'm the one who betrayed Dan and Sandra, yet they've done nothing to me."

"That's because, my sweet thing, they're smart enough to know right now you're untouchable," Sam interrupted as he handed Kyla to Marcie. "She's hungry, and I can't help her in that department." Sam kissed Marcie as she wandered off to Maggie's sunroom with her daughter to nurse.

"What do you mean she's untouchable?" Maggie asked.

It was Sam who answered. "Haven't you watched her? It's as if she's walking in and creating miracles around her. I mean that higher power stuff she's always talking about. Surrounding herself in light, her angels. I see the miracles every day just being around her. Nothing bad touches her. She sends love out to everyone around her and when she does something, it's out of love. Don't create bad karma, that's what she says all the time. It's as if she's doing her part to clean up all the bad and darkness that's been created here. Whether you believe or not—nothing can touch her."

Maggie and Richard stared at each other. This mystical new-age weirdness was something neither expected from Sam.

Before anyone could say anything further, Frank hollered from the living room, "Break's over, let's rock and roll! I've reworked this tape and cleared off enough of the background noise to get a better listen to who this chick is."

Diane and Harper wandered away from the dining room table, where they'd hunkered down, organizing and prioritizing a list, shuffling papers and devising some strategy to poke holes in the state's case against Richard. They were detail people and good at it, but it was Diane who added, "I spoke with forensics. Apparently that videotape at the crime scene was pulled right from the security camera."

"Someone's sure doing a bang-up job trying to frame me, Diane, and they've gone to a lot of trouble," Richard said.

Everyone stood around the computer when the clear voice played on the 911 call again. And it was clearer, easy now to pick up the slight twang in the way she lingered on Richard and Dan's names. But even then, Maggie couldn't place the voice. Richard shook his head and Maggie knew he was frustrated to near a snapping point.

Sam must have realized the stress this put on Richard, as he slapped his shoulder. "Don't push too hard. We'll figure it out," he said.

Harper crossed his arms. He'd been pretty quiet while they listened to the tape. "We have very little time left; since no one recognizes that voice, let's pack it in. Sam and Diane, we need to sit down with Richard and go through the other evidence the state's prepared."

"Her name is Jane. She's Sandra's little sister," Marcie suddenly said. She spoke over Harper as she carried Kyla and walked straight into the circle. "I'd know her voice anywhere. She's your 911 caller."

"Well, hello." Frank grinned from his seat on the sidelines. "So, Harper, guess you have a place to start, now."

CHAPTER 53

"Marcie, are you sure the voice you hear on the tape is this woman, Jane?" Harper stepped in front of Marcie.

"Yes, I am."

"Would you testify in court?"

Sam stepped in front of Marcie. "No, she won't."

Maggie knew why Sam had said it. So did Richard. Harper had no knowledge of Marcie's past with Dan. The last thing Sam wanted was the DA poking around in Marcie's past relationship with Dan, or into the marijuana plants she'd helped cultivate with him. In the end, it could backfire and hurt Richard even more.

"Let's talk to Jane. Sam, you and me. We'll take the tape to get her to confess. Marcie's name doesn't need to come into this," Diane suggested. She was on her feet, but Harper's eyes remained glued on Marcie.

"Harper," added Richard, "you're the expert here. Wouldn't it be better to confront Jane, to let Sam and Diane lean on her?"

"Frank," Sam chimed in, "any chance you can figure out from the background noise where she's calling from?"

"If *anyone* can," Frank said with a grin.

Maggie knew she had missed something. "What is it? Is there something about the background noise that's important?"

Sam answered, "All the traffic noise *can't* be around their property —the property where Dan was killed. That property's isolated off the highway, and it's quiet. That was city noise."

Excitement filled every part of Maggie. She wanted to jump up and down in victory. "This will clear Richard, won't it? The DA will have to drop the charges." The way everyone looked at her made her realize there must be a problem. "Won't they?"

"I can isolate the background noise. I'll be able to pick up something that stands out. But that's slim." Frank wasn't smiling now; he was all business.

"Everyone come over here." Sam hurried to the dining room table, where notes and papers were spread out. He grabbed a pen, blank paper, and scribbled notes on several sheets, lining up each page side by side in some kind of order.

Everyone crowded around him. "Let's deal with what we know and believe to be true. Richard and Dan are partners. They bought land together for a development project three years ago. They start building houses. Dan sweet-talks some woman at the county into helping him rezone the land so he can sell the houses, legally, as mobile homes and have a steady revenue from pad rent year after year. A really gray area… possible fraud. Over here." Sam tapped the next sheet of paper with marijuana written at the top. "Last year, Dan coerces Maggie and Marcie to bring in and deliver his marijuana. Maggie delivers to Sandra, the middleman, who handles the distribution of illegal narcotics. Sandra Carter has care of several, severely disabled, kids while in possession of illegal narcotics—one kid dies on her watch. Marcie and I work with the DEA and attempt to catch Dan with the marijuana and a suspected cocaine exchange. Richard did help in the background. We also know—"

"Take a breath, Sam," said Harper. "I like to think I'm brighter than the average bulb, but this is a lot to chew on at once. Sandra is this Jane's older sister, and she—Sandra—was in with Dan McKenzie's drug-dealing?"

Sam nodded. "Uh-huh. And someone from the team was tipping

Dan off. We also know Marcie's granny's cabin was bugged, so we're pretty sure Dan knew Richard and Maggie were helping us nail him on narcotics charges. This would be an absolute betrayal in Dan's eyes from you, Richard. And Sandra, well, she knows Marcie and Maggie talked about the marijuana and broke the cardinal rules in the dark underworld: *Keep your head down and your mouth shut.* Let's just say, with Sandra's apparent connections pretty high up in the drug scene, she's pissed and looking for payback. And with Dan's connection to Lance Silver, it's possible that the hit-and-run driver may have had another agenda, but hitting Lily—she may have been an unplanned casualty." Sam stopped and glanced at the puzzled expression on Harper's face. "How much of this do you really want to know?"

Harper shook his head as he shut his eyes. "Just answer one question. Is anyone in this room involved in illegal activities now, such as growing, cultivating, and/or transporting marijuana or drugs?"

"No." Sam spoke for everyone.

"At this point, I don't need to know any more. Sam, we'll talk later." Harper let out a heavy sigh.

"Let's go over here to the next one." Sam scribbled notes on a third page and wrote "Lily" at the top. He didn't face Maggie when he continued, but she could feel a powerful ache, like none she'd experienced, building inside. "We need to talk about this. I'm sorry if it hurts you, Maggie and Richard. I know it does. When Lily was killed, the car that hit her was never found. We can chalk it up to coincidence, but something about it never sat right with me."

Maggie's ears were ringing, and she wondered if the room was swaying.

"Sam? Are you telling me Dan and Sandra… you think they were behind the killing of my daughter, that it wasn't some random hit and run?" The venom that spewed from Richard rattled Maggie even further. She didn't even realize she'd cried out until Diane wrapped her arm around her shoulders.

"I'm sorry, Maggie," Diane said, "but Sam and I always wondered. We have no proof, we checked. It's an angle we've never looked at or talked about."

Richard paced. He wouldn't come near Maggie. She recognized his self-preservation—the evasiveness when he pulled into himself. How many times had he done that after Lily died? She hated that guy and never wanted to see that part of Richard again.

Sam ripped off another sheet of paper and began scribbling. Richard leaned over Sam's shoulder, reading every word. "Richard and Maggie, your life fell apart. You split up and spent over a year pulling it together. During that time, Dan disappeared. He left you holding the bag. Payments were due on the houses. You kept building to sell each house; to get your money so you could pay off the mortgage on this property. You physically buried yourself in building those houses as a way to cope. You weren't thinking of the consequences for your actions.

"The lawyer who handled the sale of each house divided the amount equally. Your half in one account, the other half in an account for Dan. Yet you ended up having to pay for all the subcontractors and materials because Dan couldn't be found. You didn't have the money to hire another lawyer to find and sue him, so you were buried deeper in a financial nightmare while Dan was building his empire from some hideaway. Then, a month ago, he suddenly reappears and offers you his truck. Help him make it disappear, and he'll give you the insurance money. If you don't, he won't pay you. You have the bank pounding on the back door. Loans are due. You can't wait to drag him through court, but you'll be bankrupt and will have lost this house by then, so you agree. But Dan, being Dan, screws you. You help him dump the truck into the lake. He files a stolen vehicle report with Seattle PD, saying it was stolen on the mainland, but the insurance company won't pay out for ninety days in case it's recovered. Then, as luck would have it, Search and Rescue discovers the truck when they fly over. Divers go down and get the serial number and match it up to the stolen truck. Dan suddenly signs over the truck registration, gives it to you and changes his story to the sheriff. But then you, Richard, help Dan drag the truck deeper into the lake, where the depth will safely hide the truck. The divers can't find it now."

Sam wrote a big question mark at the top of the next page. "So, Richard, where did you get the money to pay your loans?"

Everyone looked at Richard. And this time, Maggie said nothing.

CHAPTER 54

"We've got no more time. Find out where Sam and Diane are." Harper spoke to Maggie in a low voice.

Maggie stood in the gallery behind her husband, once again in their "court costumes." This time, the courtroom was bigger, packed with people, and had an ominous feel to it. She was alone because Marcie, for some reason, had taken Kyla and returned to Las Seta the night before.

Maggie raced out of the courtroom to use Richard's cell phone. These few days had taken on a spin where nothing went as planned. They'd been unable to track down Jane. Sam and Diane had beaten every bush, calling in favors from every lowlife trying to find the broad. When Diane called her social worker friend about Sandra, apparently she'd put in for two weeks vacation, and no one knew where she'd gone.

She hurried outside the building and shivered in her thin black blazer and knee-length skirt, teetering on her three-inch heels. She glanced down and saw her stocking had a run from her ankle to mid-calf. *Dammit!* "Shit, voicemail. Sam, where are you? It's Maggie. Harper sent me out to find you. Court's about to start. What do I tell Harper?" She hurried back in, turning the phone to vibrate.

Even yesterday, when Jean had phoned, she'd been short, half expecting her to ask for help with Angie. But Maggie couldn't help her, not now, so she was happy, to hear Angie had found a place and was moving. With Dan now dead, she no longer had a way to sue him. Everything he owned was now in probate, and unfortunately, Dan's mother was upholding the eviction. It was unlikely Angie would see a dime of her money anyway. Even in death, Dan was still screwing people.

The clerk outside the courtroom shook his head when she tried to get back in. "Court's about to start."

"My husband's the one on trial. I was sent out by our lawyer, Harper Lee, to make a call. Please let me in. He needs me," she pleaded.

Her sincerity must have seemed genuine, because the tall, stocky guy in uniform opened the door a crack and peeked in. "Okay, go ahead."

She hurried to the front bench seat, this time having to climb over a few spectators and ask one, who'd taken her spot, to make room.

The clerk announced the arrival of the judge, an overweight gray-haired man. Everyone rose. Maggie reached forward, tapped Harper and shrugged to him. Richard met her gaze and squeezed her hand. She knew he was worried. Hell, she was worried even though they had the best damn lawyer on the West Coast.

The gavel cracked, and Maggie sat. The same good-looking DA who'd been at the arraignment stood up and approached the jury, questioning juror one in the jury selection process. The entire time, Maggie kept glancing at the door as the knots twisted tighter. Her pocket vibrated. She shoved her hand inside and glanced at the screen and text. *Found her. On our way now.*

Maggie leaned forward and tapped Harper's shoulder, showing him the text.

Harper stood. "Excuse me, Your Honor, we must respectfully interrupt. We must request a brief recess, as my investigator—"

The courtroom doors flung open, and Sam hurried in alone. Glancing at Maggie, he nodded in a way that had her releasing a relieved sigh.

The judge frowned. "Mister Lee, are we *interrupting* you?"

The DA glared at Harper as if he'd been wronged in some way. "Your Honor, this is highly inappropriate! We've just started."

"My apologies to District Attorney Hamilton, and I beg the court's indulgence. I'm sure the DA is going to want to hear that my investigators have just uncovered a witness and evidence that will clear my client of these charges and save the state the expense of taking an innocent man to trial. If I could request a brief recess and—"

The judge smacked his gavel. "No, Mister Lee. I'll give you ten minutes. Then you and the DA will meet in my chambers with your investigators and this so-called witness."

Maggie was so caught up in the theatrics that she had to push her way to the aisle to catch up with Harper and Richard as both followed Sam out of the courtroom.

Diane stood off to the side with a very attractive blonde who was wearing a denim skirt, black boots and a tan jacket; she was in her early twenties, if that.

"Harper, this is Jane, the young lady who made the mysterious 911 call." Sam stood in front of Richard, except it wasn't Richard's wrath this blonde bombshell needed to fear—it was Maggie's.

"I only did what he told me," the girl said.

Maggie pushed past Sam and slapped Jane hard across the face. "You lying bitch! You set my husband up for that prick!"

Richard grabbed Maggie and lifted her while taking two steps away from Sam before putting her down. "Maggie, stop; but thank you." He smirked.

He held her shoulders, and she felt sheltered, protected and treasured. When her brain caught up to her heart, Maggie realized in that moment what she'd done. She covered her mouth with her hand and laughed so hard that tears fell.

CHAPTER 55

Jane, Sam and Diane sat across from the judge at the sterling mahogany desk. The DA and Harper stood just behind them in the cozy chambers decorated in reds and browns.

"Okay, everyone have a seat," said the judge.

Harper effected the introduction. "Your Honor, this is Jane Carter. She is the young lady who made the mysterious 911 call that identified my client, Richard McCafferty, as the man shooting Dan McKenzie."

The blue-eyed DA stood beside Harper, and for once, he didn't object. Jane sat up straight in her chair, not slouching, nor did any remorse appear on any part of her.

Sam and Diane both stared at her as if they'd rehearsed some part. "Jane, will you please tell the judge what you told us?" Diane said.

She breathed deeply through her nose, but not in a scared way. "It was a joke, really. Dan told me to call 911 and say that I saw Richard with a gun; to say I saw him shoot Dan. I just did what Dan asked."

The DA strode briskly to the judge's desk and faced Jane, his face reddening. "Dan McKenzie told you to call 911 and make a false statement?" he yelled, slamming his fist on the side of the judge's desk.

"Yes."

"So you didn't see Richard McCafferty and Dan McKenzie arguing, or see Richard pull out a gun and shoot Dan McKenzie?"

"I've seen them argue many times. But not that night."

"Jane," Diane said, "please tell the judge and the DA what you told us about the night you called 911, and where you called from." Diane gently motioned with her hand as she spoke slowly and clearly.

"I called from Sequim, outside the downtown sports bar. I'd had a few drinks… and, well, my sister Sandra was there. I used her cell phone. I'd talked to Dan earlier in the day. He called me and told me how Richard had jammed him up. Richard owed him money. After everything he'd done to help Richard and Maggie after their daughter was killed, well, it just didn't seem right. He said Richard put their housing project in jeopardy with his erratic behavior. Dan was putting out all the money to the tradespeople for materials; having to constantly play peacekeeper and repair all the bridges Richard burned with them. Dan's my friend—and he asked me for help. He just wanted to scare Richard to get him to back off. Give him a reality check. Dan tried to buy Richard out, but Richard refused to sell to him. The man just wasn't being reasonable. What else was Dan to do?"

At this point the judge finally spoke. "Do you understand you can go to jail for what you did? For God's sake, woman, the man was charged with murder."

For the first time, Jane flushed and fidgeted with her fingers. "I didn't know it had gone that far. I didn't know Dan had really been killed. I've been in Portland with my sister since I made the call." Tears streamed down her face. "I loved him. You know he wanted to marry me?"

Sam stared at Jane as if she'd suddenly changed the script—as if she'd lost her mind.

"Well, this doesn't change the state's case, Your Honor," the DA said. "There's still the matter of the video that shows Richard McCafferty dragging Dan McKenzie's body from the crime scene, so we're still prepared to proceed."

Sam cleared his throat. "Your Honor, the tape has been altered. My FBI crime lab technician will swear to this and can show the court how Richard McCafferty's face was pasted into the frame. The DA is aware of this already, and they've been unable to provide the original copy of the tape. The DA was supposed to have their own technicians look at the video."

"Is this true, Mister Hamilton?"

"Your Honor, our technicians are backlogged at the moment and haven't had a chance to confirm or deny the defense's theory."

Harper strode back and forth at the back of the room. "Your Honor, the state has no case. I'm requesting the state drop charges against my client. Their so-called evidence, the 911 tape, well, here's your 911 caller, and you've just heard her. And the video—come on, I've heard flimsier excuses from a high school student as to why he didn't get his homework done. What other evidence do they have? There's no murder weapon. My client was home with his wife and child all evening."

Hamilton squared both shoulders and shook his head. "Your Honor, there is motive."

"But no body," said Harper.

"The lab matched the blood type to Dan McKenzie's medical records."

Lee turned to address Hamilton directly. "You're seriously going to waste the taxpayers' money on a witch hunt when you know my client didn't kill Dan McKenzie? We just produced the 911 caller who admitted she lied, that the whole dramatic call was orchestrated by Dan McKenzie. The video is also not genuine. What's your agenda here? Or should I say, Fred White's agenda? Something personal, send an innocent man to prison? What other false evidence is suddenly going to appear that we'll once again prove to be false?"

"Okay, okay, Mister Lee." The judge raised his fat, wrinkled hand. "I must agree, Mister Hamilton. The 911 tape's out. What else do you have?"

Rick Hamilton crossed his arms and rocked on the balls of his feet.

"Drop the charges, Mister Hamilton," the judge said. "I would think twice about wasting taxpayer money and my time on a trial until you can produce some real evidence. Once you do, re-file. But I can tell you now, I'll be declaring a mistrial if you insist on proceeding."

DA Hamilton appeared to consider what the judge was saying. "A mistrial will not work for us, Your Honor," he finally said.

CHAPTER 56

Jessica Shupe was waiting in her white Lexus when Richard and Maggie parked in front of their house. She'd shown up during the chaos of the last few days, when they were at their worst. Through it all, Maggie had managed to keep a civil tongue. Though, each time the woman invaded her space and Ryley's, she'd wanted to yank out every strand of Ms. Shupe's hair. Now, after this morning's drama, she didn't know if she had a diplomatic bone left in her body. Richard must have known this, because he came around the front of the truck and took Maggie's hand, holding her beside and behind him as if he thought she'd repeat what she'd done to Jane earlier.

"Miss Shupe, Ryley's not here. We had court this morning, which I'm sure you know. Ryley's grandma's in town and he's with her right now." Richard was all business when he wanted to be.

"Yes, I know you were in court. I also heard the state dropped the charges. I was directed to close my investigation. I just wanted to stop by and let you know my findings will not be filed."

Richard and Maggie stared at each other just as Richard's cell phone buzzed in Maggie's jacket pocket, where she'd left it. She reached for it and glanced at Harper's number on the screen before passing the phone to Richard.

"Hi, Harper." Richard stared at Jessica Shupe while he listened to what Harper had to say. "Well, Miss Shupe is here. She was waiting in her car when we drove in, and she just advised me of that very same thing. I find it interesting that she knew before I did." Richard nodded, turning his back to Jessica and watching Maggie. "I'll put her on." Richard strode straight to Jessica, the power in each step showing Maggie how pissed off he really was. "Miss Shupe, my lawyer would like a word with you."

Jessica appeared startled, but to her credit, she accepted the phone and reluctantly put it to her ear. "Hello, this is Jessica Shupe." She lowered her gaze to the ground. "No, sir, I'm not aware of any impropriety. I came here after I received word from Judge Cooper. I thought they knew." When she glanced up at Maggie, she blushed. "Mister Lee, I am not here to harass your clients and I am done. Yes, yes, I understand." She handed the phone back to Richard and strode straight to Maggie. Richard walked farther away as he spoke to his lawyer.

"I just wanted to say, Missus McCafferty, this wasn't personal. Off the record, you're a good mother. I've seen some things… well, parents who have no interest in their children and expose them to all kinds of unethical behavior, drugs, alcohol and parties. But not you." Jessica extended her hand to Maggie, and even though Maggie wanted to slap it away out of spite, she recognized a woman trying to make amends. So Maggie accepted her hand. For a second, Maggie wondered if the woman really knew the game she'd just been part of and whether she really was no more than a pawn. Jessica walked away, climbed into her fancy car, and drove away.

Richard watched Maggie and then glanced at the trail of dust in the driveway as Jessica turned onto the road. Richard hurried over to Maggie, and he lifted her in his arms and pressed his lips to hers as he walked her toward the house. He lowered her onto the step. "Well, she was right. The charges against me were dropped. Harper—I've never heard him so mad. He said he'd just found out from the DA, and Judge Cooper apparently called Jessica and told her. They both knew before Harper."

She rested her palms on Richard's shoulders as his hands lowered to her waist and held her in a way he hadn't in a long time. "You don't care, do you?" she said.

He shook his head and smiled, and a hint of light touched his eyes. "I'm free, and this damn ankle bracelet will be gone this afternoon. I don't give a shit who told who first and what politician leaned on who. I have the bank beating on the back door and we could very well lose this place and everything. But for the first time, in I don't know how long, I know what's really important: you and Ryley."

"What about the property you own with Dan? What if we lose this house?"

"I'll call Dan's mom and meet with her about what Dan owes me. I'm pretty sure she can be reasoned with. At least Dan's not around, trying to find new ways to screw me. But if we lose everything … we'll start over."

Daisy barked and scratched at the door. Richard's hand fell away as he went around Maggie and opened the door. The dog wandered out and rubbed against her, demanding a good pat. Maggie scratched her dog behind the ears. Daisy went down the stairs slowly but with a little more energy. She wandered over to the grass and squatted.

"Richard, what about what Sam and Diane said? I mean, about Dan and Sandra being responsible for Lily's death? Just the thought, Richard…" Her heart twisted as she struggled to not think about it, but that very thought had been in the back of her mind for the past few days.

"Don't go there, Maggie. She's gone. No one planned for her to run out on the road, and there's no way they waited for that exact moment to hit her. Whoever that person was, we'll never know what they really wanted. And Dan's dead, anyway. We need to let it go and get on with our life. Ryley can't afford for either of us to go there."

She watched the dark shadow on his face and the hardness in his tone as he spoke, and wondered if he truly believed what he said or if it was for her benefit.

"Come on," he said. "Let's get changed and go get Ryley."

CHAPTER 57

"Your housekeeper's okay with Kyla, Mister Silver?" Marcie sat in one of the leather wing chairs in front of the plate-glass window. She crossed her jean-clad legs and felt overdressed in the bulky blue sweater in this warm, dark-paneled study.

"Oh, she's fine. What a little *angel* you have. Nellie loves kids, and she'll enjoy spoiling your baby."

Marcie accepted the coffee Lance Silver poured for her. "Thank you."

Lance Silver was a handsome, distinguished man wearing dark blue jeans, cowboy boots and a tailored white shirt. In his late fifties, average height and still in good physical shape, he could've almost passed for a man in his thirties. He sat across from her in the other wing-back chair and set his coffee on the marble end table.

"It was such a surprise to get your call last night. To ask for my help, you must truly care for your friends. And for you to come here! I don't believe you've ever been to my humble dwelling." He flicked his hand to the side.

She sipped her coffee and watched the man she'd feared for most of her life. The man who controlled the highway of drugs flowing down the West Coast and across the country, with deep ties into South

America. No one on Las Seta grew any marijuana or did anything sketchy without Lance Silver's okay. As she sipped her coffee and glanced at Lance, she wondered for a moment what she'd opened the door to.

"Granny and Sally would never allow you anywhere near me," he said. "I've seen your closed gates and have walked by here when I knew you were gone. But no, I've never been past the gates. Heard about it, though. It's lovely."

She glanced around the warm and expensive room, staring at the rich oil paintings on the wall that surely cost more than she'd see in a lifetime. This grand mansion had turned the reclusive, off-the-grid, island of Las Seta upside down when Lance built it. She smiled warmly at the man, who appeared genuine, honorable. But then, so could a snake just before it struck. "Thank you for… helping me," she said.

Lance held up the flat of his hand to stop her. "No, Marcie, no need for thanks. I'm happy to help you. Any time you need anything, you call me."

She set her hot mug down on the oval table beside her. For the life of her, she couldn't decide whether she'd just sold her soul to the devil. "So what about the threat to Richard? Will you be able to help him? I mean, Sam and Diane haven't been able to find Jane Carter, Sandra's sister… and we know she made the fake call to set Richard up. It's as if she dropped off the face of the Earth."

Lance smiled and folded his hands in his lap. "Jane was found. What you may not know, since you've been patiently waiting here for a few hours, is that the charges against Richard were dropped, and your Maggie will no longer be bothered by any further investigation by Children's Services into her suitability as a mother. What a horrible, horrible thing to have been done to her after losing her daughter the way she did." Lance shook his head.

She nodded as a lump tightened in her throat. She couldn't imagine the power this man before her had with politicians, state officials and, of course, the drug underworld. He knew what everyone was up to; where they hid, what they were doing. One call from him could make or break a man. Or so she thought.

"Your Sam doesn't know you're here?" he said.

She glanced at her hands, afraid of what showed in her eyes. "No, he doesn't. I should be going. Sam will be wondering where I am." Marcie stood up. So did Lance, and he gazed at her in a way that appeared caring in some odd, familiar way. She held out her hand. He took it and kissed the back of her hand before holding it between both of his own.

"Stay for lunch."

She pulled her hand away. "I can't." She hurried out of the study and found her way to the kitchen, where Lance's housekeeper, Nellie, was cuddling Kyla.

"Thank you for watching her." Marcie reached for Kyla and cradled her in her arms.

"Oh, she's such a good baby." The small, overweight housekeeper touched Kyla on the arm. "Goodbye, Miss Kyla. You come back and see me."

Marcie turned to leave, and Lance Silver stood in the large archway, watching her.

"Yes, Marcie, please come back again. I'll walk you out," he said, and he did, right behind her, holding the front door open for her. Standing on the wide stone porch, he watched as she drove away.

"Sir, shall I have one of my guys keep an eye on her and Mister Carre?"

Lance Silver never turned his head to the large balding man who handled all his business affairs. "No, keep the men away from her," he instructed. "Did Mister White pose a problem?"

"No, sir, he did just as you ordered."

Lance Silver watched the trail of dust that disappeared with Marcie outside the gate. "I'll be seeing you again soon, Marcie," he said.

CHAPTER 58

"Push harder!"

The two men on the large wooden raft pushed toward shore as the sun peeked over the horizon. "You know, man, there are easier ways to get to South America," one said.

"Just keep moving. Is that the village up ahead?"

"We must be careful coming into Colombia this way. Keep your papers with you, Señor." The shorter Mexican used his oars to move the raft to shore.

The tall American jumped into the shallow water, wearing his dark shorts and sandals, and pulled the raft the rest of the way to the rocky shore. In the early morning dawn, the orange and yellow colors flashed as the sun peeked over the horizon. The red-haired man with the light beard from several unshaven days grabbed his knapsack and tossed it over his shoulder. "This village have any women?"

"Sí, Señor Dan, lots of pretty single girls. They'll love a tall, good-looking American like you."

Turn the page for a sneak peek of
BOUNTY
Available in eBook, paperback & audio

Most cops have a past.
A past, they can speak of.
A past, they can share.
But not Diane....

That is until one night a body is discovered on the highway close to her home. But Diane Larsen, a tough cop chick who has had to prove herself over and over to the cops she works with is ordered by her new boss to investigate the one case that could be her undoing.

When she meets Zac the mysterious and sexy new forensics guy, and former military surgeon with secrets of his own, he somehow discovers through her bizarre behavior all she's been hiding. Instead of outing her, he steps in and helps her investigate this case that has hit way too close to home. And Diane finds herself face to face with the one man, who can find a way into her heart.

BOUNTY CHAPTER 1

She slid out from behind the wheel and checked her holster, flicking her finger over her Glock and the smooth shiny badge she had clipped to the waistband of her jeans. She balled her hands into a fist once, twice, yanked on the edge of her jean jacket, and stepped forward, putting all her attention into first one step, then another, on the pavement that was glistening under the half moon. Her breath misted in the damp night air, picking up the scent she had always associated with a fresh kill. She shivered as goose bumps pricked her skin, not from the cold, and she fought the instinct to cross her arms.

Flashing red lights cast an eerie shadow over the thick trees that lined both sides of the dark highway; headlights from a dozen vehicles spotlighting the scene. It was unnerving, and every sound of the night —the shouting, the whisper of the wind through the treetops, voices over the police radio, footsteps, and car doors opening and closing— became more defined, drawing her attention to each minute detail. Diane nodded to a uniformed deputy who was holding a bright red flare and turning away the few cars that travelled the highway this late at night back toward Port Townsend. The state police and deputies lingered around the scene.

"Diane." Baby-faced Green, now a lieutenant for the Sequim detachment, strutted over to Diane, holding his hand out as if to stop her. He wore a ratty tweed jacket and faded blue jeans. The skin on his bald head shone like a smoothly polished billiard ball from the backdrop of the headlights. "Hey, Stan." Green waved to another uniformed officer Diane didn't recognize and pasted on one of his phony good ol' boy smiles.

She hated the prick, so she decided to ignore him and tried to step around him, but he matched her strides step for step as if trying to cut her off. On any other night, she would have cut him down with one of her hard, unforgiving glares and then finished him off with a sharp remark, telling him to get lost, but not tonight. The prick could say or do anything, and even though Diane itched to slam her fist in his face, it would be unlike her and would stand out as a red flag to everyone. For the life of her, she still couldn't figure out how Green had ended up as a lieutenant, but he could pull rank and she'd likely find herself written up. She reminded herself again, *Keep your cool. Calm down.*

Her entire focus was riveted on the scene in front of her as she strode straight toward the five crime scene technicians hunched down over a young woman who lay on her back across the yellow line in the center of the highway. It would have been a bone-chilling sight to anyone, but Diane's attention wasn't drawn by the fact that the woman was lying spread-eagle across the center line, her legs and arms set perfectly straight, nor by the fact that the young woman's once beautiful face was marked with fresh bruising, nor by the black mark around her neck from where she'd been strangled as her sightless eyes stared heavenward. Even her long plain dress, a tired blue, was neatly pulled to her ankles, smoothed down as if the woman had simply lain down on the road and straightened it. Her long dark hair hung in one thick braid across her breast. She wore only one tennis shoe on her left foot and a thick white sock on her right.

It was none of that which filled every part of Diane with a terror so icy that she wanted to shut her eyes, get in her car, and drive and drive until she was a dozen counties away. She couldn't run—not again—not from this. She stared at the one thing that could unleash the deep-seated fear she'd safely tucked away. She broke out in a cold sweat. A note was pinned to that serviceable dress, written in uniform black letters: *Keep sweet.*

ABOUT THE AUTHOR

"Lorhainne Eckhart is one of my go to authors when I want a guaranteed good book. So many twists and turns, but also so much love and such a strong sense of family."

(LORA W., REVIEWER)

New York Times & USA Today bestseller Lorhainne Eckhart is best known for writing Raw Relatable Real Romance where "Morals and family are running themes." As one fan calls her, she is the "Queen of the family saga." (aherman) writing "the ups and downs of what goes on within a family but also with some suspense, angst and of course a bit of romance thrown in for good measure." Follow Lorhainne on Bookbub to receive alerts on New Releases and Sales and join her mailing list at LorhainneEckhart.com for her Monday Blog, all book news, giveaways and FREE reads. With over 120 books, audiobooks, and multiple series published and available at all, retailers now translated into six languages. She is a multiple recipient of the Readers' Favorite Award for Suspense and Romance, and lives in the Pacific Northwest on an island, is the mother of three, her oldest has autism and she is an advocate for never giving up on your dreams.

"Lorhainne Eckhart has this uncanny way of just hitting the spot every time with her books."

(CAROLINE L., REVIEWER)

> *The O'Connells: The O'Connells of Livingston, Montana are not your typical family. A riveting collection of stories surrounding the ups and downs of what goes on within a family but also with some suspense, angst and of course a bit of romance thrown in for good measure. "I thought I loved the Friessens, but I absolutely adore the O'Connell's. Each and every book has different genres of stories, but the one thing in common is how she is able to wrap it around the family, which is the heart of each story." (C. Logue)*

> *The Friessens: An emotional big family romance series, the Friessen family siblings find their relationships tested, lay their hearts on the line, and discover lasting love! "Lorhainne Eckhart is one of my go to authors when I want a guaranteed good book. So many twists and turns, but also so much love and such a strong sense of family." (Lora W., Reviewer)*

> *The Parker Sisters: The Parker Sisters are a close-knit family, and like any other family they have their ups and downs. Eckhart has crafted another intense family drama… "The*

character development is outstanding, and the emotional investment is high…" (Aherman, Reviewer)

The McCabe Brothers: *Join the five McCabe siblings on their journeys to the dark and dangerous side of love! An intense, exhilarating collection of romantic thrillers you won't want to miss. — "Eckhart has a new series that is definitely worth the read. The queen of the family saga started this series with a spin-off of her wildly successful Friessen series." From a Readers' Favorite award—winning author and "queen of the family saga" (Aherman)*

Lorhainne loves to hear from her readers! You can connect with me at:
www.LorhainneEckhart.com
lorhainneeckhart.le@gmail.com

ALSO BY LORHAINNE ECKHART

The Outsider Series
The Forgotten Child (Brad and Emily)
A Baby and a Wedding *(An Outsider Series Short)*
Fallen Hero (Andy, Jed, and Diana)
The Awakening (Andy and Laura)
Secrets (Jed and Diana)
Runaway (Andy and Laura)
Overdue *(An Outsider Series Short)*
The Unexpected Storm (Neil and Candy)
The Wedding (Neil and Candy)

The Friessens: A New Beginning
The Deadline (Andy and Laura)
The Price to Love (Neil and Candy)
A Different Kind of Love (Brad and Emily)
A Vow of Love, A Friessen Family Christmas

The Friessens
The Reunion
The Bloodline (Andy & Laura)
The Promise (Diana & Jed)
The Business Plan (Neil & Candy)
The Decision (Brad & Emily)
First Love (Katy)
Family First
Leave the Light On
In the Moment
In the Family
In the Silence
In the Charm
Unexpected Consequences

The Gatekeeper
The Hunted

The McCabe Brothers
Don't Stop Me (Vic)
Don't Catch Me (Chase)
Don't Run From Me (Aaron)
Don't Hide From Me (Luc)
Don't Leave Me (Claudia)
Out of Time

A Billy Jo McCabe Mystery
Nothing As it Seems
Hiding in Plain Sight
The Cold Case
The Trap
Above the Law
The Stranger at the Door
The Children
The Last Stand
The Charity
The Sacrifice

The Wilde Brothers
The One (Joe and Margaret)
The Honeymoon, A Wilde Brothers Short
Friendly Fire (Logan and Julia)
Not Quite Married, A Wilde Brothers Short
A Matter of Trust (Ben and Carrie)
The Reckoning, A Wilde Brothers Christmas
Traded (Jake)
Unforgiven (Samuel)
The Holiday Bride

Married in Montana
His Promise

Love's Promise
A Promise of Forever

The Parker Sisters
Thrill of the Chase
The Dating Game
Play Hard to Get
What We Can't Have
Go Your Own Way
A June Wedding

Kate & Walker
One Night
Edge of Night
Last Night

Walk the Right Road Series
The Choice
Lost and Found
Merkaba
Bounty
Blown Away: The Final Chapter
He Came Back

The Saved Series
Saved
Vanished
Captured

Single Titles
Loving Christine